THE LIBERATORS

Books by Brien A. Roche

The Prohibition Series
The Last Stand
The Liberators

Stuff We All Should Know
Law 101
Objections: Interrogatories, Depositions and Trial
Virginia Torts Case Finder
Virginia Domestic Relations Case Finder
Baseball Coaches' Handbook, Co-authored by Brien Roche

Coming Soon!
The Prohibition Series
The Counterattack

THE LIBERATORS

Brien A. Roche

SPEAKING VOLUMES, LLC
NAPLES, FLORIDA
2023

The Liberators

ISBN 978-1-64540-951-9

.

Dedication

Doc Adams, the counterweight to the devil.

Acknowledgments

Sometimes life is lived between the devil and the deep blue sea.

Prologue

WWI is over. The three Custer brothers are still at war. Bos (short for Boston), Thomas, and Nevin have spent nearly 18 months in Northern France. They fought the Germans with the Harlem Hellfighters. Their 369th Infantry Regiment was not "good enough" to fight with white American infantry units. They were assigned to the French army. Not satisfied with being mere ground pounders, the Custer brothers volunteered as storm troopers to emulate and counteract German storm troopers that raided Allied lines. They created fear, havoc, and confusion with spellbinding success. Their reputation followed them back to the states.

Now, hoping to rebuild their father's pork distribution business, they have branched out into distributing liquor, precipitated by the approach of Prohibition.

Bos Custer calculated he could avoid the enforcement of the Volstead Act implementing the 19th Amendment by "donating" his alcohol to Black churches up and down the East Coast. The Prohibition enforcers will not prohibit alcohol consumption for "religious" reasons. The Custers expected a 2% to 3% return on their investment and further that the income stream would be used to promote other businesses within the Black religious community.

Race riots in Washington, D.C. beginning July 19, 1919 taught the Custer brothers that Black soldiers will not be honored for their service in WWI. If they want any doors to a good life opened for them in white America, they will have to kick the door down.

Their battles on land spill over to the waterways. To facilitate the delivery of their liquor, the Custers buy 10 high-powered Liberator boats built for naval combat operations in Northern Europe. They are for sale to the public. The Custers put the boats to good use. They discover that the soon-to-be liquor distribution king, Al Capone, is not allowing these "coloreds" to have free run of America's waterways or highways.

For the Custer brothers, it's time to take up arms in a brand-new battle.

Al Capone moves from Brooklyn to Chicago. He prepares to take over the operation of Johnny Torrio's Southside gang. The Custer brothers prove to be more than just an annoyance to him. Capone convinces Torrio that the Custers need to be dealt with harshly. But the battle-hardened Custer brothers and the women and men loyal to them are not about to do a lay-down.

They are loaded for bear.

Chapter One

The Navy Yard
October 1, 1919
Portsmouth, Virginia, Navy Yard

During WWI, the Navy Yard, located on the Elizabeth River, expanded and now accommodated 11,000 employees and their families.

Bos Custer and his two brothers, Thomas and Nevin, had shipped out to Europe from there just a few years earlier. Now, the three of them drove a Tin Lizzy to the northeast corner of the yard where the Liberators sit in the dry dock, just a short distance from what's called Hampton Roads.

Bos could see rows of the boats. There were nearly 100 of them. Each 45 feet long and 15 feet wide, with three props and three 500-horsepower Packard engines.

Bos stopped the car and got out. He looked at the boat closest to him.

"These things need a lot of work," he said.

"They look okay by me," Nevin Custer said.

"No," said Bos. "We need open cockpits and a center console. All the storage space is going to be on deck. There's no reason why each of them couldn't carry 100 10-gallon barrels. They could be stored side by side. Each barrel weighs a little under 100 pounds. That makes loading and unloading fairly manageable."

The three brothers looked alike but varied in size. Bos was six feet two, 230 pounds. Thomas was five feet eleven and 210 pounds and was the only one of the three that might be described as being mediumcomplected. Nevin was the youngest at 28, lean and mean at six feet two, 170 pounds.

"You the boys lookin' at buyin' these?"

The three Custer brothers turned and saw a chief petty officer approaching.

"Good morning, chief," Bos said.

"Nothin' good about it," said the chief.

"Well, it ain't rainin', and it ain't humid," Thomas Custer said.

"That's true but it's still mosquito infested. They've got hundreds of deepwater ports north of here that don't have the mosquito problem, but they built their Navy Yard right in the center of mosquito heaven."

"Mosquitoes don't like Black people," Nevin said.

"I doubt that," said the chief. "The blood in your veins is just like mine. That's all they want."

"You mean they don't discriminate?" Nevin said.

The chief didn't respond.

"The front gate called me and said you were here," said the chief. "What are you lookin' to do with ten of these boats?"

"We're settin' up a little business enterprise. We need quick, reliable transport."

"Well, I don't even know if they're for sale," the chief said.

"Oh, they're for sale," said Bos. "I checked with the War Department, and they're happy to get rid of 'em."

Emmett Jay Scott served as special advisor of Black affairs to Newton Baker, the secretary of war. Scott confirmed that the boats no longer served any military purpose. They had been constructed in anticipation of America's entry into the European war. The navy planned to use them on European rivers for combat and transport. They served neither purpose. The Europeans wanted "ground pounders" that would move in cadence to unforgiving machine gunfire.

Bos knew he could finalize a deal with Scott. It would be much better than what any white noncommissioned or commissioned officer would ever give him.

"I'm in the building near the gatehouse," said the chief. "If you have any questions, stop by and give me a holler."

Bos waited until the man was out of earshot before addressing his brothers.

"We can't change the length or width of these boats. We can't change the hull construction. What we can change is the deck construction. I also want the props protected so that we can beach these boats almost anywhere."

"Give me more specifics," said Thomas.

"What I'm seein' is two metal blades toward the back of the hull in front of each prop to protect them from any damage. I want two powerful winches fixed to the stern. When we get into shallow water, we drop anchor, and the winches extract the boat back into deep water."

"That should be easy to do," Thomas said.

"I want Lewis guns set at the front, sides, and rear. A total of six. They need to be set low so the gunner can shoot from a kneeling position. I want a raised console that's about 10 feet higher than the deck. The helmsman can stand there. We're gonna need two holsters up there for Thompsons. The helmsman's position needs to be surrounded by a bubble for protection from any incoming gunfire. What I would suggest is a bubble or a wall of half-inch steel plates curved to conform to the console. They need sight slits about six feet off the base. The helmsman gets some protection but still has visibility."

"Keep it simple," Nevin said. "Sounds good to me."

"Thomas, I want you to take charge of this. I'll head back to Washington and purchase 10 of these. We'll station three in Washington and one at each of the major cities up and down the East Coast. Many of these cities were slave import areas. I'm thinkin' Annapolis, Baltimore, Cape Charles, Wilmington, Charleston, Jacksonville, and maybe Miami. That makes seven. I'd prefer to limit our number to seven. We'll see how that goes."

"Man, you're a dreamer," Thomas said.

"Nope," said Bos. "I'm a doer. We've only got two months before Prohibition starts. We've got a lot to do."

During the war in France, some of the men had come to First Sergeant Boston Custer and complained that they were running out of beer. That was the only thing that got some of the men through the bloody massacre they witnessed each day. Bos said he would do what he could. In fact, he did more.

During one midnight raid behind German lines, he and his brothers discovered a stash of beer in the German compound near the route they had planned on taking back to their base. Bos figured they could only handle three barrels. The Germans had rigged an all-purpose horse-drawn cart to transport beer barrels and other things. Bos and Nevin were able to load nearly 30 barrels on the bed of the cart. Bos gave the order for the cart to pull out. He guided the horse while Nevin and Thomas stayed behind the cart with 20 German contact grenades. They threw them into the German camp. The Germans were shellshocked. They had no idea that the Custers were stealing their beer.

It was a five-mile trip back to their base. When the three Custers arrived and word spread about what they brought back, the troops demanded a speech from Bos.

"We have struck the enemy at his core," he said. "They have bled profusely. We will drink their beer and savor our triumph. Victory will be ours because the beer is ours. Hail to German beer!"

Lieutenant Colonel Bardot, commander of the French battalion, made note of Bos Custer.

"If that man wasn't Black, he would make a damn fine officer."

The executive officer standing next to the lieutenant colonel thought that Custer would've made a damn fine officer regardless of color.

Chapter Two

Brotherly Love
October 3, 1919
LeDroit Park, Washington, D.C.

"Down and to the left," Bos said.

Bos held the ball as if he had just taken a snap from center and moved on the balls of his feet. As soon as his brother began to move left, he threw the football and hit him right on the numbers.

"Where'd you even get this football?" Thomas shouted at him.

"Don't you remember? It's the ball that Pops gave me after that year we all played on the same team. We won most of our games that year through forfeits. The white teams refused to even show up and play."

"Remember the coach telling us they were just afraid of us? Thought we might hurt 'em," Thomas said.

"That's not the way I remember it," Nevin said. "They weren't about to play with a bunch of coloreds."

T Street was a two-lane roadway. The asphalt surface had not been treated in many years. As was true with many of the streets in the Black section of the city, streets were poorly maintained. This street was passable by both horse-drawn and motor-driven vehicles. It also was highly walkable. Down the middle of the street came Cookie Custer. Bos looked over his shoulder. LeDroit Park was a mix of single-family homes, town houses and small unit apartment buildings.

"Well look who's here! The footballer himself," Bos said.

"I taught you three everything you know about football," Cookie said.

The smile on his face was as bright as the sunshine overhead. Trees in Washington, D.C. were beginning to change colors on this crisp fall day. At six foot five, 280 pounds, this 72-year-old hulk moved with some agility. Each foot landed flat on the roadway and simultaneously rotated upward from the heel. He had learned early in life as an enslaved man in Alabama that running from the cat o' nine tails of the master sometimes meant knowing how to grab the ground in front of you with the front of your foot and pushing off from the ground underneath with the back of the foot.

"The only thing you knew about football was the clothesline. In fact, it shouldn't have been called 'the clothesline.' It should have been called 'the pendulum,'" Thomas joked.

"Let me see that football. Let's see who can throw it the farthest," Cookie said.

Cookie motioned to Thomas to run down the street. He threw a pass over Thomas's left shoulder that was probably 40 or 50 yards. Thomas caught it.

Bos's first pass was long enough, but it was wide of the receiver. Thomas's pass overshot his receiver. Nevin's pass was on the target, but Bos couldn't handle it because it was right at his head.

Several more rounds of passes resulted in several catches and an equal number of dropped balls.

After a half hour, Cookie owned up. "If I throw another pass, my arm is going to fall off."

"You've done okay for an old man," Nevin smiled.

"This old man's gonna sit down." Cookie had a seat on the stone curb at the edge of T Street near the intersection with 5th Street. The three boys sat down on either side of their father.

Cookie looked at his oldest son. "Tell me more about this operation you're about to engage in," the family elder said.

"I've given you all of the details, Pop. You know what my goal is. You know how I'm gonna implement it."

"When I talk about an operation, I don't mean just a business operation. I mean, how is this going to impact your personal life? How is this going to affect Lee Ann? How is this going to affect any children you might have?"

"You know Bos hasn't thought about that," Thomas quipped.

"He ain't givin' that a minute's thought," Nevin said. "You know that. He just acts and thinks later. That's what he does with everything."

"So far that's worked out well," Bos said. "I like being spontaneous. I like flyin' low. It gives me a lot more maneuverability."

"You need to start flyin' high. You need to start looking at the big picture. You're gettin' ready to marry a woman who knows what she wants, and she knows how to get there. You've known her all your life. You'd better not disappoint her."

"You sound like you wanna marry her," Bos said.

"If I was 40 years younger and didn't have a wife, I might consider it. I had a wife. There's no replacing her. You could have the same kind of wife. But you've gotta include her. You gotta tell her what you're thinkin'. You gotta tell her what you're doin'. If you do, she'll help you. She'll support you. She'll be your ally. But if you shut her out, you will have hell to pay. You can't treat her the way you treat your brothers. They know you. They tolerate you. They allow you to lead them around by the nose. But you can't do that with this woman. Do you hear what I'm sayin'?"

Bos didn't answer.

"I need to have you look at me and give me an answer," Cookie said.

"I hear you, Pops."

"That's not an answer. You're just dodging my question."

"I hear you, and I understand you."

"That's better. You damn well better understand me. Now go get my football and give it back to me."

Bos got up and walked across the street to where the football had fallen. He threw it back to his father who caught it with one hand and walked away.

Chapter Three

Wilson Disabled
October 4, 1919
The White House

The private residence inside 1600 Pennsylvania Avenue was now more private than ever. The president was confined to the master bedroom. He and the first Mrs. Wilson had always shared the same bed. The same was true with the second Mrs. Wilson. Edith Wilson had now become her husband's caregiver, gatekeeper, and mouthpiece.

Aides were lined up outside the bedroom door, waiting to talk to the president and hoping to get his signature on numerous documents. None of them were allowed entry.

Inside the bedroom, Edith looked at her husband. He stared blankly back at her. He was conscious and heard what she was saying. He responded in clipped sentences of two or three words.

Woodrow Wilson never had a chief of staff. Since his first wife passed, Edith served that function. She maintained his calendar and shielded him from people who she thought were not prepared to promote his best interests.

A banging on the door startled her. She instructed the Secret Service that no one was to knock on the door.

Someone is going to pay for this.

She strode to the door. She was not about to open it. Anyone standing in the doorway could see the president. She placed her hand on the doorknob and gripped it tightly.

"Who is it?"

"Robert Lansing."

"Where is the Secret Service?" said Edith.

"They're standing right next to me, acting like they want to arrest me," Lansing said. "Mrs. Wilson, I need to see the president. It's been at least two days since anybody's seen him. What is going on?"

"Nothing is going on. My husband is resting peacefully."

"That's all fine and dandy, but he's got a country to run. With all due respect, if he's not coming out, I'm coming in."

"No, you're not."

Mrs. Wilson could hear Lansing pacing outside the door. She opened it a crack.

"I need to see the Secret Service," she said.

Two young men responded from around the corner.

"I told you that no one knocks on this door."

"Yes, Ma'am, but the gentleman is the secretary of state."

The two agents were apologetic as they responded softly to their boss.

"I don't care who he is. No one means no one. Do you understand my order?"

"Yes, Ma'am."

She closed the door and locked it. The vigil continued. Edith Wilson knew that she could maintain this isolation for a few more days. She was hoping that by October 6th her husband would at least be mobile and able to communicate in complete sentences.

Up to this point, the only people who had seen the president were medical staff, who were sworn to total confidentiality. Even the domestic staff had not been allowed into the president's bedroom. The public was clueless about their president being near catatonic.

Edith walked to the window that overlooked the South Lawn. The sheep were still out there grazing. People had said she was crazy to allow sheep to graze on the grounds of the White House. She didn't care. She was not concerned in the least with what any of them thought.

This is my house, and I am in charge.

She stepped back from the window and looked around the bedroom. She had decorated it exactly as she pleased, with her personal mementos, including pictures of her family home in Wytheville, Virginia. She had wanted to hang pictures of her first husband on the wall, but she knew it would not go over well. However, she did include pictures of her eight surviving siblings, many of whom still lived in the Wytheville area, where her father had served as a circuit judge.

Edith had spent many years taking care of her grandmother while she was confined to bed. Her grandmother had overseen Edith's education and had taught her to make quick judgments and to hold strong opinions. There were pictures of her wedding to Woodrow on December 15, 1915, with 40 invited guests. There were pictures of their two trips to Europe. In 1918, she had accompanied her husband there to visit the troops and to observe him signing the Treaty of Versailles. Their second trip to Europe was to visit remaining US troops. She loved the pictures of Woodrow and herself among European royalty.

She walked back to the window and smiled as she looked at the sheep. She marveled for a moment at her great success. This widow and daughter of a plantation owner was at the pinnacle of power. She resolved to maintain the facade of her husband ruling the country. She had been accused of being the éminence grise. Now she would fulfill that role.

Edith heard more knocking, only this time she knew who it was. Whenever Lee Ann knocked, she did it with three short taps and one bang. Edith didn't hesitate to let her in. She was Mrs. Wilson's one and only trusted advisor and the only person working in the White House who was allowed to enter the private bedroom of the president.

Lee Ann hurried inside and sat at the desk in the sitting room where she and Mrs. Wilson reviewed papers and prepared presidential directives. President Wilson was not able to sign his name, so Mrs. Wilson forged it. Over time, she had become quite adept at doing so.

"How do we handle this?" Mrs. Wilson said.

"One day, one event, one hour at a time," said Lee Ann. "Women can't yet vote, but between the two of us, we can run this country. I need to know whether or not your heart is in this. If it is not, we need to quit now. If it is, I will do everything in my power to make it work."

Chapter Four

Visit with Alvin
October 4, 1919
Washington, D.C.

Bos approached his brothers and several neighbors who had gathered at the family home in LeDroit Park. "Anyone know Alvin's last name or where he lives?"

"I don't know the exact address, but I can take you to his home," said one of the men.

"Great. Let's go," Bos said.

"I'm Joe Taylor."

"Bos."

Bos carried one .45 on his right hip in a holster and a second one in the small of his back in a holster with a keeper. The holster on his right hip had no keeper, as he needed quick access to the sidearm.

He slung a full-length shirt on his back and put his arms through the arm holes. He wanted the .45 on his hip accessible, but he also wanted it concealed.

He exited the house onto T Street with the man who volunteered to take him to Alvin's house.

The front portico at 520 T Street, N.W. Washington, D.C., was shallow. It led to three steps and down to a brick path. The path was no more than 20 feet long. At the end was a metal gate that opened outward as it swung on its hinge to the right of Bos. Two steps led down to a brick sidewalk on T Street. They turned right and headed west.

"Were you in France?" Bos said.

"I was," said Joe Taylor. "I served with an American infantry unit. I had the usual basic training and infantry training and then, guess what?"

"They made you a cook."

Bos laughed.

"You got it," Taylor said. "Not good enough to fight but good enough to cook."

"You would have thought they'd keep you away from the food for fear you'd poison it."

"If they'd had any sense, they would have. A lot of us wanted to poison the food, but we didn't."

"Good thing. They would've lynched you."

"It wasn't until the summer of 1918 that they actually let us fight. During the second battle of the Marne, the Germans overran us. Our white officers wouldn't even give us weapons. There were 10 of us who were cooks. All we had were meat cleavers, carving knives, and broomsticks. Between the 10 of us, we probably killed 100 Germans. Our white officer was nowhere to be seen. When the battle was over, nobody said a word. They just wanted to know where the meat cleavers and carving knives were. They thought we'd stolen 'em. I tried to tell the new CO that they were all stuck in German bellies. He didn't believe us."

"Sounds familiar."

"There was one guy from Kansas who stood up, and he told the new white officer how we'd fought. He said he'd be proud to fight with us. He was the only white guy who stood up for us. There were a lot of them who saw us fightin'. Five of us died. But as soon as the battle ended, we were back in the kitchen."

They both hopped in the car owned by Taylor. Every car on the road looked almost the same. Taylor's car was no different. He had a small statue in front of the gearshift. Bos looked at it and asked what it was.

"It got me through France. It's a small cross with the letter J, which stands for Joseph, patron saint of the Josephites who cater to the needs of Black Catholics. It means a lot to me."

Taylor made a left on 3rd Street and drove up toward U Street. Half-way down the block, he stopped by a house to his left.

"That's where he lives."

"Thanks, Joe. Can you introduce me?"

"Sure. Alvin's a little cranky though, so be prepared."

Taylor approached the front door and knocked. He could hear movement inside. Nobody came to the door. Taylor and Bos waited for several minutes.

"Alvin, you in there?"

"Who wants to know?"

"Bos Custer. You helped us over on Florida Avenue a few months ago."

The man stuck his head out a second-floor window.

"I remember you. You were that do-gooder who didn't want to kill any of those white boys," Morrison said.

"Well, I'm no do-gooder but I don't believe in killin' if I don't have to."

"What can I do for you?"

"I'd like to talk to you."

"I'm busy right now entertaining a lady."

"If I could have five minutes of your time, I'd appreciate it."

"Well, okay. I'll be down in a minute."

Bos and Taylor stepped away from the front door, not knowing what to expect. Within a couple of minutes, Alvin Morrison came to the front door. He was wearing a pair of pants that he'd just put on. No shirt. He stepped out the front door and closed it behind him like there was a hoard of cats inside trying to escape.

"Sorry to interrupt," Bos said.

"Not as sorry as I am," said Morrison.

"I need some men to help me with a business proposition."

"Well, I'm not in business at the moment. I'm in school. Howard University. I'm hoping to sit for the bar one day."

"I guess you know Prohibition is comin'. My hope is to put together a liquor production operation and a fleet of boats to distribute it to Black churches up and down the East Coast. I'm lookin' for good men who want to join me."

"I'm busy during the week with school, but my weekends are free. I could use some cash."

"Everybody gets a salary. They get paid based on collections. I'll front some money at the start, but once we start delivering and collecting receipts, I'll expect the boat runner to collect the cash and deliver it all back to me. Everybody gets paid outta receipts."

"How do you know the distribution network can work?" Morrison said.

"You may remember my pop has a pork business. The biggest one on the East Coast. We've got our own distribution chain. All our delivery people have their own trucks and customers."

"And suppose I get caught runnin' liquor? Isn't that the end of my legal career?"

"I like to focus on the 'if,'" said Bos.

"So, what would be my area of distribution?"

"I'd probably have you runnin' down to Cape Charles. That's a good run. Over 100 miles from D.C. down the Potomac."

"I hope you don't think I'm gonna be sailin' that distance."

"Nope. I bought ten Liberators. Each one has three Packard 500-horse-power engines. Those babies can hum at 100 miles per hour," Bos said.

"You're expecting me to drive that boat?"

"Drive it, navigate it, load and unload it, and protect its precious cargo."

"Liquor?"

"Nope. Ethyl alcohol. Two hundred proof in 100 oak barrels, each with a 10-gallon capacity. Each weigh about 100 pounds. You and your first mate need to load 'em, transport 'em, unload 'em, and then get your butt back home."

"So, if I left on a Friday night, I'd be back by Saturday morning?"

"Probably should count on Saturday afternoon."

"Do you have the boats ready to go?"

"I hope to take delivery of the first one's next week."

"How 'bout if we do a test run next Friday?" said Morrison. "Friday, October 10th."

"Sounds good," Bos said. "I'll meet you at the Georgetown harbor at 10:00 p.m. I'll be the Black guy driving the big boat."

"What color is the boat?"

"It's as black as you are."

Morrison smiled. He shook his head and walked back into his house.

Bos liked him. Morrison was a big man. Six feet three, 220 pounds. Almost the same size as Bos. He knew how to use an axe handle. Bos had seen him take down at least half a dozen raging white men coming at him from all directions. He'd been an inspiration to the other men. Many of them were not accustomed to fighting a white man. They knew from their days as sharecroppers that this kind of encounter didn't end well.

Bos walked back toward the street and smiled at Joe Taylor.

"I need 10 more men like him," said Bos.

"You can count on me, Bos," Taylor said.

"I know, and I will," Bos said.

Chapter Five

Second Visit to the Yard

October 5, 1919

Norfolk Navy Yard

On Sunday night they'd normally be at home on T Street. When their mom was alive, she'd cook dinner. The main course was pork. Bos used to joke that it would be sometimes pulled, sometimes beaten, sometimes juicy, sometimes barbequed. But it was always pork on Sunday night.

Bos had picked a Sunday night for picking up three of the boats, thinking that the base would be deserted, and the entry of several Black men would go unnoticed.

They arrived at 10:00 p.m. The sentry at the front gate was asleep in the guard shed.

Bos thought back to his days in Northern France. Sleeping on a post was a capital offense. A man might be shot on the spot by an officer.

Bos was happy to bypass him. He pulled his car down the road over to a shed and got out. The chief petty officer came to the front door.

"A good day for a test run," he said.

"Yep," said Bos. "I'll follow you down to where the boats are located."

"Okay. I'm parked over here. I'll wait for you to turn around."

Bos noticed that rather than waiting, the petty officer hopped in his navy vehicle and sped off. Bos smelled a setup. He looked toward the front gate of the Navy Yard 100 yards away and saw four vehicles approaching with their headlights blazing. The sentry at the front gate was no longer in the guard house.

Bos shouted to his brothers.

"It's a setup!"

"Get the Thompsons out," said Nevin. "Each backpack has four drums in it."

Each brother strapped a knapsack on their back and slung a Thompson over their shoulder with the sling strap.

"I'll get on the roof of the building where the chief was. Let's flip this vehicle and rip off the gas tank so it doesn't explode on us," Nevin said.

The three of them stood on one side of the Ford Model T and flipped it on its side. Thomas disconnected the gas tank and threw it off to the side. He stayed by the overturned Tin Lizzy while Bos ran into the shed and turned out the lights. As soon as the four approaching vehicles passed by the guard shed, the gunfire erupted.

The Thompsons weren't known for their range. Bos had always said that their effective range was no more than half a football field. That was an overstatement.

Thomas was the first of the Custers to open fire. He stood behind the overturned Model T, using the engine block for protection. He poked the muzzle of the Thompson in between the bumper and the front fender and opened fire on the first vehicle that approached, loaded with at least six men. One of them was firing a Thompson wildly. The .45 rounds were spraying everywhere, except where the shooter intended them to go.

Knowing that they might be using these weapons at night, Nevin had dipped every tenth round in a magnesium powder that would illuminate in flight. With that, he could better gauge his aim.

The second burst from Thomas's Tommy gun contained a tracer. It told him he was firing too low. He adjusted his aim and hit the lead vehicle with what was probably a nine-round burst. The vehicle pulled to the left and turned over.

Nevin had reached the peak of the roof of the nearby shed. He took aim at the third vehicle, and after two or three bursts, some with tracers, the vehicle came to a stop. He couldn't tell whether any of the occupants were still alive.

Bos, on the first floor of the nearby shed, broke out the glass in one of the windows. He had his Springfield rifle. He could hear men coming toward him. Bos had received word from Johnny Torrio in Chicago that if he was thinking about putting together a liquor distribution business, he should give up those thoughts. Al Capone had become Torrio's enforcer. Torrio had informers up and down the East Coast. Bos had calculated that the Chicago mob and the New York mob would make a run at him at some point. He had not figured that it would come before Prohibition was on the books.

Bos took aim with his Springfield. He hit several men who were approaching the shed. He could hear his brother overhead and Thomas alongside the Model T using their Thompsons.

A window to his left burst open. A small man came barreling through holding a .45 handgun. Bos hit the floor and low crawled toward the man. He put down the Springfield. The Thompson was still strapped to his back. Still crawling, he brought it around and struck the man with the butt of the gun. Holding the muzzle, he turned it around and fired off a short burst just as the man fired his .45 at him. The round nicked Bos's right shoulder by the scapula. It felt like the bullet had actually glanced off the bone. He could feel blood oozing into his shirt and down his back.

Bos kept low crawling toward the man he had shot. When he got close to him, he felt for a pulse. None.

Bos removed the backpack containing the drums of .45 caliber Thompson rounds. If the .45 round had hit one of those, more than one of them would have exploded. Instead, it was simply Bos who had caught the round. He laid on his back for a few minutes, trying to apply direct pressure to the wound. The pain was stinging. It felt like the bleeding was slowing down.

"Bos, you okay?"

Thomas ran toward the shed and opened the front door.

"I'm in here," Bos said.

"I know where ya are. I'm surprised I didn't see more gunfire comin' from your window."

"This crazy man jumped through the other window. He came in shootin'."

"Remember that used to be us. When we went into a town and had to clear it of Germans, that's just what we did."

"I can't forget it. How many times did we use that same tactic?"

"Nevin, you up there?" said Bos.

"Yep," said Nevin.

"What's the score?" Thomas said.

Everyone was shouting in the chaos.

"I can't really tell. It looks like the fourth vehicle turned around and left town."

"Stay up there another 10 minutes. You've got the best vantage point. Make sure there's no movement," Bos said.

"Should I use my wristwatch to count that 10 minutes or should I count it on my fingers?"

"I don't think you can count that high."

Ten minutes later, Thomas and Bos could hear Nevin walking on the roof. There was no easy way down, so he jumped. He landed on the ground, tucked and rolled, and came up on his feet in firing position.

Thomas was looking out the window.

"Damn, you're good!" he said.

"I can't afford to lose my edge," said Nevin.

He came into the shed and saw Bos lying on the floor.

"I hope it's not a gut wound," Nevin said.

"Nope. Just a glancing wound to the back."

"Let's go into the next room and let me take a look at it," Thomas said.

They low crawled into the next room. Thomas lit a lamp. It gave them enough light to look at the wound.

"Doesn't look like there's that much blood loss," Thomas said.

"Let me go out to the car and see if we can get the bandages we had in the front seat. Hopefully, they haven't all been shot to hell," Nevin said.

Five minutes later, he returned with a small package of bandages. Thomas unsealed them and began to wrap the cloth around Bos's chest to cover the wound site on his back. Within a few minutes, he had his entire upper body crisscrossed in bandages.

"I should've washed the site before I bandaged it."

"No worry. I'll wash it when I get home."

"We ain't goin' home right away. We're gonna find that chief petty officer. This was a setup."

"I agree."

"I think a kneecapping might be appropriate," Thomas said.

"Kneecapping?" said Nevin.

"Yeah. That's what the Irish Republican Army uses on turncoats. You put a pistol behind the knee, and you blow the kneecap off."

"Sounds appropriate for the circumstances," Bos said.

"You're gettin' tough in your old age," Thomas said.

"Not really, but there is some logic in sending messages. These boys can't play with us with impunity."

"I love those big words," Nevin said.

He smiled.

"Makes me think of Mom."

Without saying a word, all three men shared thoughts about their mother, Calpurnia. How she had drilled them on vocabulary, spelling, elocution. Three Black men who spoke better English than the king himself.

Chapter Six

The Chief
October 5, 1919
Norfolk Navy Yard

Bos was a bit suspicious of the chief. He had checked the man out. Chief Petty Officer Wilson had been in the US Navy for 18 years. As a noncommissioned officer, Bos could relate to him. But his suspicions remained. He was much too cooperative.

Wilson had been a quartermaster for most of his navy career. He dealt with supplies and logistics. Bos and his brothers had been combatants. They appreciated what the supply and logistics people did, but he knew they were a different breed than the grunts he had known, fought with, and held in his arms when they died.

Wilson wasn't expecting to see these three Black men approach him. They didn't. Bos had stopped about 100 yards from where he knew the Liberators were stored.

"Let's spread out. He's probably not expecting us."

"How do you know he's alone?" Nevin said.

"I don't. My sense is he's a lone wolf. He has no idea that we just killed 15 of Johnny Torrio's men."

"Okay," Thomas said.

"I'm walkin' straight at 'im. You take my Thompson. I doubt he's armed."

The two brothers spread out. One went right. One went left.

This part of the boatyard was loaded with vessels in dry dock. It was more than a mile from where the shootout had just occurred. Bos approached where he believed the Liberators were stored, walking between rows of boats perched on dry dock frames. When he was 50 yards from the Liberators, he saw Wilson standing next to his Ford.

Bos waved. Wilson did not wave back. Instead, he jumped into his vehicle and took off. Nevin fired from the right. Thomas fired from the left and two tires were blown out in seconds.

Wilson got out of the car untouched. Bos figured he was probably unarmed, which he was. He withdrew the 18-inch Ka-Bar from a scabbard he carried on his left hip. It flashed in the moonlight. Bos had never really cleaned it, other than to remove blood and tissue. The weapon was every bit as intimidating as it had ever been.

When he got within earshot of Wilson, Bos didn't mince words.

"Get on your knees."

Wilson complied. Nevin and Thomas approached from each side.

"Bos, I had no idea what they had in mind. They just told me they wanted to meet with you boys."

"All 20 of them?" said Bos.

"I didn't see 20 of them," Wilson said.

"You must have coordinated things with the gate guard," Thomas said.

"Of course, of course," Wilson said. "I didn't know anything about any gunfire."

"I see," Thomas said.

"So, you just figured these thugs from Chicago were coming down here to have a little chat with these three Black boys?" said Nevin.

"I think we need to skin this man alive," Thomas said.

"For once I agree with you," Bos said.

He held the Ka-Bar up at eye level.

"I got you your three Liberators."

"You didn't get us nothing," Bos said. "I got 'em myself."

The three Liberators sat on the dry dock skids, ready to be eased into the water for the trip north.

Bos approached the kneeling Wilson.

"Don't you move."

The three Custer brothers approached the Liberators and began to ease one into the water. Nevin jumped on board and fired up the engine. All of the gas tanks were topped off. Thomas checked out the other boat, and Bos examined the third one. All three appeared to be in order and fully gassed up for the trip north.

Bos came back to where Wilson was kneeling.

"I ought to kill you on the spot. I ought to just slit your throat with this Ka-Bar."

"But . . ."

"I don't want to hear your excuses. I'm not gonna kill you, but I am gonna leave you some reminders."

Bos proceeded to cut a two-inch path on the man's right cheek, a two-inch path on his left cheek, and a two-inch slit under his nose. His face bled profusely.

"Somethin' to remember us by," Bos said.

The brothers slid the other two Liberators into the water, put the engines into reverse, and backed out of the harbor. As they began the trip home to Washington, D.C., they could hear howls of pain coming from Chief Wilson.

Chapter Seven

Second Battle of the Marne

July 15, 1918

East of Reims, France

General Ludendorff drew the battle plans. His intentions were to draw Allied troops away from Belgium through a diversionary attack along the Marne. The real attack was coming through Belgium. Its target was the British Expeditionary Force.

On the opening day of the offensive, the Allied troops on the south bank of the Marne were charged with holding the riverbank. The Germans unleashed a large number of gas shells. German Storm troopers came across the river in 30-man canvas boats and rafts.

What the storm troopers had not known is that the American forces fighting with the French had their own storm troopers. The three Custer brothers, armed with Springfield rifles and .45 handguns, followed the German storm troopers across the river in a single canoe.

Bos Custer was in the front of the canoe. His brother Thomas was in the rear of the canoe. Nevin was in the center of the canoe with the paddle.

As the last 30-man canvas boat of German storm troopers landed, the Custer brothers opened up.

The Germans had no sense that they had been followed. Their commander, acting under cover of darkness, had expected that the Allied defenders would be surprised. Instead, the Allied defenders had anticipated the nighttime raid. The Custers began their small unit attack. Shooting German soldiers in the back was not what the Custers were accustomed to. But their orders were specific. *Disrupt the German storm troopers and stay out of the line of Allied fire.* What the Custers didn't know is that the Allied commander had not been told of their presence.

When the Custers hit the riverbank, they positioned themselves at a 90-degree angle to the German storm trooper assault.

The Allied machine gunners, unaware of the presence of the Custers and seeing small arms fire coming from their direction, also fired at the Custers.

"That heavy machine gun fire has gotta be from Allied forces," Bos shouted out to his two brothers.

"You're right. Let's move upstream to see if we can avoid that," Thomas said.

The run alongside the river was not easy. The ground was muddy. In stretches, the water grass was more than a foot high. In 20 minutes, they had positioned themselves directly behind the German storm troopers. A slight knoll less than 20 feet from the water's edge gave them protective cover from both the Allied fire and the German storm trooper fire. They began picking off the German troops one by one. Of the nearly 100 storm troopers who had landed, Bos estimated that he and his brothers had killed 40 of them.

From 20 yards away, Nevin could see 10 figures moving toward him.

"They're comin' at us!" Nevin shouted.

The German troops were all dressed in black. Their helmets were black. Their faces were covered with black coal markings. At 1:00 a.m., they were well-disguised by the lack of contrast with the darkness in the background.

The first of the men attacked Bos's position. Bos saw him coming. He stood up and charged the German. He had left his Springfield rifle strapped to his back. He emptied the rest of the clip in his .45 as the

German approached. Bos held on to the .45 and attacked the man, tackling him at thigh-level. The two dropped and together they rolled down the hill. At the bottom of the hill, Bos was able to unloose his Ka-Bar from his left hip. He drove the tip under the German's breastbone.

Nevin and Thomas continued firing at the other storm troopers running up the hill. Two of them managed to break the crest. Nevin shot the man who was closest to him in the center of his gut. The man groaned and kept coming at Nevin. Two more rounds stopped him for good.

Thomas's attacker had gotten the drop on him. The man leaped on top of Thomas and rolled with him back down toward the river. By the time they got to the riverbank, both men had lost their sidearms.

Thomas stood up and charged the man, attempting to ram his helmet straight into his face. Both men went down. The German grabbed ahold of Thomas and hit him several times in the kidney. Thomas rolled over with the attacker and attempted to push him deeper into the muddy riverbank to suffocate him. The German broke free and pushed Thomas into the river. Both men grabbed each other as if the other was a life preserver. Both men were weighted down with heavy combat boots and gear. Thomas could feel the current carrying both of them. He knew he had to end this quickly if he was going to survive. Thomas pushed the German underwater and attempted to hold him there. The German sprung up as if pushing himself off the bottom and rammed his helmet into Thomas's jaw. Thomas grabbed for the man's helmet, pushed it toward the back of his head, and attempted to use the helmet with the strap that was now around the man's neck as a means of pulling the man further into the deep.

Thomas knew that his swimming skills were strong. He could hear the man gurgling as Thomas was pulling him further and further into the channel. The German was being pulled on his back.

After a minute of this, the German storm trooper was still. Thomas was careful not to let the man get close to him to pull him down. He let go of the helmet and watched the body float downstream.

"Hail, mighty warrior," Thomas said to the combatant as he floated away. Thomas looked to the shore and noticed that he was at least 50 feet from the bank and was in a rapid current. He knew that with the heavy combat boots on, he would have trouble making it to shore. While treading water, he tried to unlace the boots and kick them off. The thought of trying to preserve the boots had not occurred to him. No longer weighted down by the footwear, Thomas was able to make it to shore.

He slogged upstream. After a 100-yard trek, he could see what appeared to be the figures of Bos and Nevin nestled behind the small knoll where the hand-to-hand combat had begun.

He began whistling "Dixie." At the beginning of the war, the three Custer brothers had agreed that was their identifier. That was their code. They had agreed no one would expect to hear that tune from three Black soldiers.

Bos reciprocated.

When Thomas appeared with no boots and soaking wet, Bos smiled.

"Well, I wish the cat was here. I could say this is what the cat dragged in."

"Just barely," Thomas said. "That damn German wouldn't let go. I had to take him out to the middle of the river and drown him. For all I know, he might be comin' back."

"You disappeared so quickly, neither one of us had any idea where you'd gone to."

"Well, the Black face don't help," Thomas smiled.

Bos rolled over and hugged him. "I thought we'd lost ya," Bos said.

Thomas thought he'd detected some tears in Bos's eyes. This was a first.

Chapter Eight

The Ride Home
October 5, 1919
The Potomac River

At its mouth, the Potomac River is more than a mile wide. It narrows as you head north.

Neither Bos nor his brothers were experienced navigators. They had decided collectively that they would head north, traveling in formation. They were used to that. The lead boat and two following boats would all stay in the center of the river, hoping that kept them in the channel. They had no maps of the river or markings, showing where the channel might be. Each boat would take an hour in the lead position, serving as navigator while keeping a close eye on depth and any obstructions in the river.

The river was known to be full of debris, including logs and large wood pieces from trees overhanging the river along with mountains of sewage and trash from Washington, D.C. They could deal with the sewage and the trash, but the logs posed a potential danger to their wooden-hull ships.

As he took the lead, Bos fell into a reverie. The thoughts of his experiences in Northern France with his brothers were never far from his mind. Now, he had more pressing matters to handle. He was about to become a married man. Lee Ann, his soon-to-be wife, still worked for President Wilson in the White House. While she was little known outside those grounds, the Wilsons had come to rely on her more and more. Because of the president's recent health setback, Lee Ann and Edith Wilson were running the country.

Mrs. Wilson knew that she could trust Lee Ann to keep the condition of the president a secret. Lee Ann could tell from looking at Woodrow Wilson that there was no way he could ever run for a third term. He was finished. He was stubborn, though, and refused to admit his condition, but it was the truth. His term would end with his wife holding the reins of power.

Bos worried about his two brothers. He knew Thomas would fare well. He was cut from the same cloth as Bos. Nevin, on the other hand, was unpredictable. He was talking about marrying a girl from Murfreesboro, North Carolina. Bos had only met her once. She had a fiery temperament. She was quite adamant that a Black man had to fit a certain mold. Nevin had his own fire in his belly. Bos was skeptical as to whether two fiery, hot-blooded individuals could make it together. He figured that it could be a rough ride.

He knew his father, Cookie, was failing. At 75 years of age, his war-ravaged body was showing signs of failing. He'd wrestled thousands of hogs to the ground and suffered the loss of his wife, Calpurnia. Several gunshot wounds had also taken their toll. Cookie Custer was a mountain of a man, but Bos knew the mountain was beginning to shrink. He questioned how much longer his father could live alone in the house in LeDroit Park in the heart of Washington, D.C.

Bos's upcoming wedding was just a formality, but it was still a major event. The consummation had been effected months earlier. Bos smiled, thinking of his wife-to-be. They had known each other since childhood. They hunted together, played together, killed hogs together, and then butchered them together. They knew each other as well as any two people could.

But marriage and living together would be much more loaded than anything they had ever done together. They knew an interracial marriage would not be easy, but together they could make it work. In particular, they could make it succeed if they migrated to West Virginia. Four thousand acres of land owned by the Custer family could produce a lot of isolation. Bos wondered whether or not his wife-to-be could handle that.

He had been reluctant to open up the throttle on his Liberator. He knew they could reach speeds of well over 60 miles per hour, but he figured that traveling at 30 miles an hour, on an unfamiliar river, was more than enough.

Around the bend ahead, he saw a steamboat approaching. It was traveling in the middle of the river, much as he was. He would give it a wide berth, but he still wanted to maintain a steady course as close to the center of the river as he could. As they approached the steamboat, the captain blew his horn, signaling the sighting. Bos had no way to reciprocate. From his center console at the helm, he waved at the boat captain as they passed. There was no wave back. As a Black man, he was used to being ignored. He made nothing of it.

Bos increased the speed of his boat by 10 miles an hour. He figured he was moving at about 40 miles an hour at this point. With the exception of the waves created by the passing steamboat, the water was like glass. The riverbanks were uninhabited. The brown, muddy water of the Potomac parted gently as his boat cut through it.

Bos calculated they would be home before sunrise. He had three landing spots on the shore of Camp Humphreys at Pohick Bay off the Potomac River where he planned to store the boats. They would stay there until he hired the men he needed to run them. The other boats he had bought would stay at the Norfolk Navy Yard until he was ready to use them.

He was ready for married life. Ready to begin his new business distributing spirits to Black churches up and down the East Coast. If the pastors did what Bos said, they could generate substantial donations, pay Bos's two to three percent margin, and have substantial funds left over to help Black businesses in the area. His hope was to promote business.

Chapter Nine

Construction Begins

October 20, 1919

Harpers Ferry, West Virginia

Bos had hired three capable carpenters from Washington, D.C., to handle the construction of their house. He, Nevin, and Thomas chipped in as much as time permitted.

The 16 metal plates Bos had ordered from Carnegie Steel had arrived. The trick was going to be raising them up to the second floor to serve as defensive structures. His plan had been to build a second-floor fort on each end of the house. Each fort would be surrounded by metal plates, each one seven feet tall when standing up. He had ordered that each plate be no more than 100 pounds so that one or two men could carry them up to the second-floor level. He was happy to see that his specifications had been met. The gun holes and sight holes had all been drilled in the metal plates just as Bos had ordered. The hard part was going to be getting them up in place so they were secured.

His construction plan was simple. Each metal plate would stand on three two-by-eight beams stacked on top of each other. The metal plates would be secured by two-by-eight braces. There would be similar bracing at the top to make sure that the metal plates could not be dislodged. Each fort would have an open-air roof constructed to keep the rain and weather out. The only means of entry or exit would be through a trap door in the floor of each fort. The floor otherwise would consist of solid two-by-eights laid side to side. The two-by-eights were already in place.

Bos recognized that the home construction might be the easy part. The more difficult construction item was the still.

The Custer family had been dry. Calpurnia had been ahead of her time. She was not only a temperance advocate but a suffragette and an advocate for equal rights. She believed in beginning at home. If her husband drank anything, it might be a glass of wine with dinner. Nothing else. Her boys had grown up never tasting alcohol. She had grown up enslaved in northern Alabama. After the Civil War, she had seen the ravages of alcohol on Black men. When she left Alabama with Cookie Custer, she resolved that alcohol would not ravage this man.

Now, Bos was getting into the alcohol production and distribution business. He knew it would be dangerous. He also knew how to avoid the dangers.

He had assembled the basics. He had a 100-gallon copper cooker, 100 feet of copper flexible tubing, and a large bucket. He fitted the cooker with copper tubing and a thermometer. The liquid that ended up in the copper bucket had to be over 173 degrees. The distilled fermented fluid would acquire some taste from the copper, but the real taste was going to come from the oak barrels.

There were plenty of oak trees in West Virginia. So far they had made over 1,000 barrels. They were producing 100 barrels per day.

Cookie had set up the barrel-making operation. That required some skill. The barrels were held together by metal straps. Each piece of the barrel had to be bowed and fitted with the adjoining pieces so they would swell when they got wet. The metal straps held the pieces together. The barrels held the contents inside and prevented leakage due to the swelling of the pieces. They swelled to the point where they would not allow any liquid to escape.

Bos calculated an aging time of 12 months.

He sat on a tree stump nearby, which was slated for removal. For the time being, it made a good seat. He thought back to when he was 15 and Lee Ann was 12. They were hunting with his brothers. Each had their own .22 rifle. Lee Ann had demonstrated that she was the superior shooter. Her problem was that she was too deliberate. The boys could get off three or four shots to her one shot.

She had an uncanny ability to hear a deer in the forest. She spotted the deer before anyone else. Bos had joked more than once that she must have friends who slept in the woods and communicated to Lee Ann the location of the prey they were after. It used to infuriate her.

They had been hunting for more than two hours. They were operating in their usual triangle formation. Lee Ann was in the lead position. She knelt down and fired off one round into the distance at what turned out to be a deer. The .22 round hit the deer in the back of the skull. It was an immediate kill shot. She could have and should have taken credit. Instead, she insisted on Nevin getting half of the credit since he was the one who had seen the deer and signaled to Lee Ann. That was just the way she was.

Chapter Ten

Yanqui
November 10, 1917, 2:00 a.m.
Small Village in Northern France

None of the Custer brothers thought the mission was of great significance. They had been sent out by the French commander to identify a German encampment that was three miles away in a straight northerly direction from their own encampment.

They stayed off all roadways. They knew from prior experience these were ambushes waiting to happen. As they peaked the slight knoll in front of them, they could see a fire burning in a series of houses. Even at this distance, Bos felt that he could hear the sounds of people screaming. The fire was a mile away.

"Man, you must have the hearing of a dog," Thomas laughed.

"I swear I can hear people screaming," Bos said.

"You've been around too many artillery shells," Nevin said.

"I follow my instincts," Bos said. "Let's get closer and see what's goin' on."

They were carrying no pack. The heaviest object they were carrying was their Springfields that weighed 12 pounds. The three of them spread out and began jogging toward the fire.

Within 10 minutes, they were close enough to see the details. All three now heard the screaming. Part of the town was on fire. People were carrying buckets to the burning buildings.

"We gotta help," Bos said. All three of them ran to the fire.

Twenty townspeople were gathered around the three burning buildings. A nearby pump was the only source of water. That was not working well.

Bos could see two children in a third-floor window. They were terrified.

"I know what you're thinkin'," Nevin said. "Ain't no way you're goin' up there."

"Ain't no way I'm stayin' here," Bos said. He handed his rifle to Thomas. He removed the .45 from his hip and all of the ammunition clips from his web belt.

"It looks like the fire has not consumed the back part of the building. You two stay here and get that pump workin' so we can get more water on this fire," Bos said.

He ran to the back of the building and could see the back door. He ran back to the front of the building, removed his shirt, and stuck it into a pail of water. With that, he ran back to the back door with his shirt now over his head covering his mouth and nose. The stairway to the second level was to the right of the door. The paint on the wall going up the stairway was beginning to burn. Bos rushed up the stairway to the second level. To the right, he could see what appeared to be a fireman's pole with a circular hole above that led up to the third level. He tied his water-drenched shirt loosely around his neck and over his head. He pulled himself up the pole to the third level. He crawled to the front of the building where he'd seen the two children. The room they were in was engulfed in flames. The bed was burning. The drapes surrounding the windows were totally consumed. The two children were lying on the floor hugging each other. The girl's long hair was singed.

Bos scooped up both of them. They each weighed about 50 pounds.

He low-crawled back to the area where he thought the fireman's pole was. The circular hole around the fireman's pole was licking flames. The pole was made of metal. It had been hot when he climbed up to the third level. He touched it now with the back of his hand and it was hotter. He lowered his two feet into the hole and grasped the pole with both feet and thrust himself with the children onto the pole using his feet and the pressure of the two children to slow his descent. He fell onto the second floor. The nearby rug was engulfed in flames. He kicked it away.

He tightened the shirt around his neck. Whatever water had been in the shirt had now evaporated. He scooped up both children and ran for the stairs. Each stair was now on fire. The fire itself appeared to be a surface fire, as if it was the paint on the stairs that was burning. It gave off an acrid smell. As he descended, he could feel the fire penetrating his pant legs.

When he got to the first-floor level, he could feel a rush of air. It was like the fire was sucking the air into the building from the outside. The air startled him. It startled the children. Both began to wiggle. He ran out through the doorway, fell to his knees, and covered the children with his body. He was satisfied that they were not on fire. He looked up and could see two buckets full of water coming at him. What a relief. It further startled the children to consciousness. Both began to cry.

Nevin and Thomas smiled. "I've been waiting to do that for a long time," they both said.

Several townspeople surrounded Bos, Nevin, and Thomas. Two adults, no doubt the parents, stepped forward to pick up their children. The tears were plenty. Both parents hugged the children.

"I guess we've done our good deed for the day. How about the mission?" Thomas asked.

"You're right. Where's my rifle?" Bos asked.

He stood up and walked toward the front of the building. The fire at this point was out of control, and the entire building was in flames.

The townspeople began to surround the three men. They were chanting, "Yanquis, yanquis, yanquis."

One member of the townspeople stepped forward. "How can we help you? We must repay you," the man said.

"You could tell us where we are."

"You are 10 miles east of Mons."

"Is there a German encampment nearby?" Thomas asked.

"Yes. I can lead you to it."

"Well that would be very nice. We're hoping to give them a little welcome," Nevin smiled.

"I can help you," the man said. "We have no food to offer you. The German troops came through here an hour ago and took all of the food. One of them stayed behind and then set the fire."

"Which way did he go?" Bos asked.

The man pointed due north.

Bos strapped the rifle over his right shoulder. "I guess we know where we're goin'."

The three of them began moving in that direction. They got about 10 yards away when they heard "Yanquis, yanquis."

They turned around and saw two children running at them. These were the same two children who Bos had removed from the burning house. Both children hugged Bos and said, "Merci beaucoup, Yanqui."

Chapter Eleven

The Circle
October 24, 1919
Harpers Ferry, West Virginia

"Sylvester, is your forge still burnin'?" Bos asked Sylvester Scott.

Scott had become the informal gunsmith. All of the men employed in Harpers Ferry were given instruction on firing a .45, a Springfield and also a Thompson. Bos had set aside an isolated area about a mile away with a steep cliff as a backdrop as their firing range. All of the employees were taken there once a week by Sylvester for instruction on gun safety and marksmanship. Scott also maintained a small forge alongside the workers' cabin to repair weapons that needed any re-forging.

"I'm sure the fire's still smolderin'," Scott replied.

"I'd like to have you do me a favor. An unusual one."

"You name it."

"Let's go outside."

When they got outside, Bos walked over towards the forge. "You know I'm gettin' married tomorrow. I've been lookin' forward to this for years. I've known Lee Ann all my life. I want you to put a brand on my right shoulder."

"You want what?"

"A brand. A simple circle about three inches in diameter. Right here on my upper arm by the shoulder."

"You must be nuts."

"I probably am but that's what I want. Will you do it or not?"

"I'll do whatever you want, Bos but this ain't gonna be pretty."

"I know and I know it's gonna be painful. I brought a little bit of liquor with me to deaden the pain."

"That ain't gonna deaden the pain. And the pain ain't gonna go away for a couple of days."

"That's okay."

"Exactly what kind of brand do you want?"

"A simple circle about three inches in diameter."

"Well I guess what I can do is I've got a poker that has a curl on the end. I could close that curl. That would make the circle about three inches in diameter. Is that what you want me to do?"

"Yep. Sounds just right."

Scott set about heating up the poker. It was made out of steel. Bending it was not easy. After about 15 minutes, he had a red-hot poker that had a three-inch circle on the end.

"If I stick you with this red-hot poker, you're gonna squeal like a pig. As tough a man as you may be, you're still gonna squeal."

"I don't disagree. Is there a way we could cool it a bit?"

"Sure. I could put some water on it or just dip it in the water."

"What I want is a scar. A scar that's visible. Visible to me and to others."

"And what is this scar supposed to mean?"

I'll tell 'ya about that later."

Scott went ahead and dipped it in a nearby bucket of water. The poker sizzled but was still hot.

"You might want to take your shirt off and brace yourself."

Bos complied. He sat down on a nearby stool and let his right arm drop to his side. "Right here," he pointed to his upper right arm.

Scott applied the poker to the skin. He had never smelled burning flesh. It was not a pleasant smell.

Bos sat upright on the stool when the hot poker came in contact with his right shoulder.

Scott held it in place for several seconds and then removed it. The imprint was noticeable. It was circular. It was about three inches in diameter.

"I delivered," Scott said.

Bos couldn't speak for several minutes. "You delivered alright." He looked at Scott, "Nobody knows about this except the two of us."

"I don't think anybody would believe me, Bos, even if I tried to tell 'em."

Bos took a sip of the liquor he had brought with him. Scott was right. It didn't deaden the pain.

Chapter Twelve

The Wedding
October 25, 1919
Harpers Ferry, West Virginia

Bos and Lee Ann knew there would only be three white people at the wedding: Joe and Mary Harper and Lee Ann.

Bos had sometimes wondered why Lee Ann had not taken on the Harper last name. Joe and Mary had raised Lee Ann. She had been born with the last name Custer. Her father was the son of Thomas Custer, two-time Medal of Honor winner in the Civil War and brother of General George Armstrong Custer. When Lee Ann's father died, Bos's father went out to Wyoming to get the girl and bring her back East. It hadn't been Lee Ann's choice to keep the Custer name. She was proud of it. No one suggested a change. Changing her name never became an issue.

Bos and Lee Ann had laughed over the fact that they both had the same last name even though they were unrelated. One was the grandniece of a Union Army general. The other was the son of two enslaved people from Alabama.

Bos and Lee Ann had gotten their marriage license the day before in Harpers Ferry. The license application had inquired about race. Bos and Lee Ann reported it all correctly. The clerk of the court had issued the license without any questions.

As they exited the courthouse, Bos smiled at Lee Ann and asked her if she knew that on the other side of the Potomac River, they could get locked up for what they were doing. The miscegenation laws in Virginia were still enforced.

Their home on top of the knoll was still under construction. Bos had made significant progress in terms of the construction of the still. He had hired 25 men, all Black, to work on the construction of the house and the 10-gallon barrels. Their first day on the job they had built a small barracks that would house 30 men. The building wasn't much, but at least it protected them from the elements. It was located a quarter mile from the main house at the same elevation and enjoyed the same constant breeze. Bos had invited all 25 of these men to the wedding. They showed up as clean as they could wearing their work clothes. They were happy to be invited to a wedding, knowing they'd have a grand meal.

Bos and Lee Ann wanted to show their gratitude to these men.

The Baptist minister from Loudoun County, Virginia, on the other side of the river, arrived at 11:00 a.m., an hour early for the ceremony. Pastor Wilson reminded Bos of his father. At six foot five and 240 pounds, he wasn't as big as Cookie, but he had a smile just like his father. The pastor was a jovial man who worked with his hands, which were huge. As is true with many men who do manual labor, his hands were rippling with muscles.

Bos had purposely looked for a pastor from outside the Harpers Ferry area. He knew the wedding would be the subject of gossip, and he wanted as little of that as possible. Although Leesburg, Virginia, was not far away, it was a different community. The pastor had agreed to perform the ceremony but told Bos up front that he would have to get paid. The pastor had to get a court order entered in Harpers Ferry authorizing him to perform the ceremony since he was only licensed as a minister in the state of Virginia.

Bos met the minister as he entered through the front gate at the base of the hill. As soon as the preacher saw Bos, he started waving a piece of paper.

"I got it, I got it," the preacher said.

"You got what?" said Bos.

"I got the court order that says I can marry you."

"I didn't know it took a court order."

"It does in your case because I'm from outta state."

"Do they know that my wife is a white woman?"

"Nobody asked."

Bos knew that Lee Ann would be radiant. They had not slept in the same bed the night before. He had actually slept out in the barracks with his workers. Some of them were men he had served with in Northern France. Some of them were roustabouts he had picked up in Washington, D.C., and offered employment. He knew they were all working men. He also knew they were men who needed to be kept in line. They would have good food after the wedding ceremony, but no liquor would be served. Bos wanted to set a tone. Even though they were about to start producing alcohol, there would be no consumption by the producers.

Their house was fully under roof, but the second floor was not finished. Lee Ann came out the front door onto the front porch. The waiting crowd applauded when she emerged. She was on the arm of her adoptive father, Joe Harper.

Nevin and Thomas stood on either side of Bos as Lee Ann emerged from the front door of the house. Bos took Lee Ann's hand. The preacher stood in front of them and began his work in a loud and clear voice.

"Are you ready?"

Bos and Lee Ann both smiled.

"We are."

They proceeded down the stairs.

The wedding ceremony began at 12:00 noon with close to 50 people in attendance. The ceremony took place in front of the porch. Lee Ann had set up a small arch that she had covered with a mix of roses, hydrangea, and sunflowers. She wore a white dress she had purchased in Washington, D.C. Bos had not seen her in it until that afternoon. He was awestruck. Her blonde hair was done up in curls on top of her head. She wore a white veil over her hair. He had never seen her hair up as it was. It made her look more mature. Every bit as beautiful.

It occurred to Bos that people off the compound might be able to hear the preacher's booming voice. He wasn't going to worry about that. For the moment, he was happy with everything: the way construction was progressing, how the liquor distribution was developing, and the way his personal life was changing.

The pastor looked at Bos.

"Do you take this woman to be your wife?"

Bos smiled. He couldn't believe the question was even being posed. The hesitation might have made some who didn't know him think he was hesitant.

"You bet I do."

The pastor smiled.

"You're supposed to say, 'I do.'"

"I did you one better," said Bos.

Pastor Wilson looked at Lee Ann and smiled.

"Let's see if you can get it right."

Chapter Thirteen

Wedding Night
October 25, 1919
Harpers Ferry, West Virginia

The celebration went on until 10:00 p.m. Bos had offered the pastor overnight accommodations. He told Bos that he had some obligations the following day and had to get back home. He mentioned that his wife was expecting him. Bos knew that his day job was a laboring job. Being a pastor was a part-time calling but a full-time commitment.

Bos walked the pastor down to the driveway where his car had been parked. He helped him back it up and begin to exit.

"Thanks again for all of your help. We couldn't have done it without you," Bos said.

"Oh I think you could have," the pastor smiled. "I think you could have indeed." He waved to Bos as he pulled away.

As he walked back to the house, he thought about how many wonderful people he had in his life. People who supported him. People who made him strong. People who made him happy. People who made him laugh. People who sometimes made him cry.

Lee Ann was waiting at the front porch as he returned.

"Did you remember to pay him?" she said.

"I paid him up front. For a country minister, he drives a hard bargain, but he was worth it," he smiled.

"He sure was. You're worth it too." She came close to him and kissed him.

She still only weighed 120 pounds. He picked her up in both arms and carried her up the steps.

"I wasn't sure we'd have a threshold. But we do, so I guess this is where I carry you over the threshold," he smiled.

"Your work's not done yet. There's a second threshold upstairs. I want to be carried over that one too."

Bos carried Lee Ann upstairs. They crossed the threshold. He laid her on the marital bed and bent over and kissed her. She touched his right shoulder. He winced.

"What's wrong?" Lee Ann asked.

"Nothin'. Nothin' that some lovin' won't cure."

Chapter Fourteen

Kentucky Barrels

October 27, 1919

Harpers Ferry, West Virginia

Bos's cat, UA, was having trouble adjusting. He was used to the environs of Washington, D.C., West Virginia was different. He had never seen a fox or a coyote. They were predators for whom he was no match. He had also learned the hard way that there were certain types of trees he couldn't climb very well. He needed to stay away from them. Other trees were more cat-friendly. The oaks and maples that had bark close to the hardwood were easier to get his claws into. The pines with their loose bark, which pulled away, were dangerous when a fox or coyote was in pursuit.

UA's safe haven was a small area under the front porch that Bos built for him. The entry was through a four-inch crawlspace with three metal bars inside that only a 12-pound cat could maneuver under and then over.

On Bos and Lee Ann's wedding night, UA had insisted on sleeping with them. Lee Ann finally consented as long as the cat remained at the foot of the bed on Bos's side.

The next morning, Nevin and Thomas were talking about returning to LeDroit Park.

"I've heard that there are Kentucky barrels available for sale that are cured and will speed up the aging process of our alcohol," said Bos. "We could use a steady supply of those."

"And you're saying this to us for what reason?" said Thomas.

"It'd be helpful if the two of you could go to Kentucky and price these barrels and maybe bring back two or three truckloads."

"What's so special about these barrels?" Thomas said.

"They've been cured. The interior of the barrel has been sealed from the inside and the barrel has its own aroma and flavor, which will seep into the alcohol. Plus they have more white oak in Kentucky than we have here."

"I thought that all we've been using here is white oak?" Nevin said.

"We have, but look at how many trees we've cut down so far to get those white oak. We don't have that large a supply of 'em," Bos said.

Bos knew what he wanted. He couldn't cure the scotch for five to ten years. One year would do. But if the curing took place in barrels that gave the spirit more flavor, he figured it would be doing the Lord's work with vengeance. Good scotch. Distinctive taste. Short turnaround time on production. More wealth created for all involved.

"So how long a trip is this to Kentucky?" said Thomas.

"You're lookin' at three days."

"I guess I can spare that," Nevin said.

"Me too," Thomas said.

"Great. Why don't you take four men with you, and I can tell you where this place is that sells the barrels. I'll give you $1,000, and just load up as many barrels as you can."

"If we're just picking up barrels, why do we need four men with us?" said Thomas.

"I suspect Torrio's gang is still around, and they may well be monitoring what we're doing," Bos said.

"We better load up our Thompsons and take with us four shooters," Nevin said.

"Two trucks," Thomas said.

"Good idea," said Bos.

They loaded four mattresses in each truck. Two men would sleep while the other drove.

Bos had arranged holsters in the back of each truck for several Thompsons. Each truck was also loaded with a chest full of Thompson drums, each with 100 .45 rounds. All six of the men carried two .45s. This wasn't supposed to be a hunting trip. The Custers had learned that they could easily become the prey.

The first 100 miles of the trip was uneventful. Two trucks traveling on back roads, each driven by a Black man. They no sooner passed into Kentucky when things started getting weird. About 100 miles from Pikeville, their destination, the right front tire of the lead vehicle was shot out. Thomas was driving. He was able to control the vehicle and bring it to a stop. He had heard the gunshot. The second truck pulled up behind the first. Each truck had a canvas over the bed area of the truck. The sideboards were made of metal. They rolled up the canvas cover about six inches. Four of the men were in one of the trucks and two in the other. All six were armed with their Thompsons.

The firing continued. It seemed to be two gunmen, one on each side of the highway. Nevin identified one of the gunmen at about four o'clock in relation to the side of the second truck. The other gunman was at about eight o'clock in relation to the second truck. Nevin directed that Thomas and two of his men attack the four o'clock location. Nevin and a third man would take the eight o'clock. The sixth man stayed in the truck.

It was noon. The highway ahead was fully visible. The wooded areas were dark and shadowy. In Northern France, the Custer brothers had been used to attacking a well-fortified location. Now, they were dealing with what appeared to be two gunmen, at ground level.

Nevin took the point in approaching the eight o'clock position. He had brought the Thompson with him, but at close range he felt more comfortable with the .45. The shooter had an advantage with a rifle.

Thomas had managed to get behind the position of his shooter. Thomas and his employee, a man named Willie McCants, now had the shooter in a 45-degree crossfire. The shooter was silent. Thomas shouted.

"We can see your position, whoever you are."

"I can see your position too."

The shooter fired at McCants and hit the large maple he was hiding behind. The wood splintered. Thomas figured it was probably a .30-caliber round that had penetrated the side of the tree. Thomas looked at McCants to make sure he was okay. McCants signaled to Thomas to begin firing. As soon as the firing began, McCants approached the shooter and ran from tree to tree for cover. When he was within 10 yards of him, he fired off three rounds from his .45. The shooter threw out his rifle and came out with his hands up.

"What the hell are you doin'?" McCants said.

"We were paid by some guys to ambush your trucks. They gave us each $50 to shoot as many tires out as we could."

Thomas picked up the rifle the shooter had thrown out. He approached the man and butt-stroked him in the face with the rifle. The man fell to the ground unconscious.

"We need to get out of here," Thomas said.

"Sounds like Torrio's gang is coming for us," McCants said.

"Yep," said Thomas.

They ran back to where they'd left the two trucks. Nevin was back with his two men and a prisoner in tow.

"We can't afford to take prisoners," Thomas said.

He took hold of the rifle the man had been using and butt-stroked him in the face.

"Let's get the tire changed and get out of here."

"When did you adopt the policy of taking no prisoners?"

"Look around. We can't take prisoners. We can't leave these guys to possibly take another shot at us. They want to rent themselves out for hire, they take the consequences."

"I don't disagree. We are leaving a trail of bodies wherever we go. But that's what we did in France," Nevin said.

It took about 20 minutes to get the axle supported and change the tire. Nevin and Thomas tied the two prisoners to nearby trees. One of the men had regained consciousness.

"You're not gonna just leave us here, are you?" he said. "The coyotes and other critters will pick us apart."

"You should've thought of that before you went to work for these Chicago boys," Thomas said. "We'll be back by this way in about two days. See you then."

They hopped in their trucks and continued heading in a southwesterly direction. Kentucky called.

Cooperstown and Pikesville were barrel heaven. They were selling barrels as quick as they could put a price tag on them. The two brothers and the others loaded up 100 10-gallon barrels in the back of the trucks and arranged them on their sides so that the mattresses were protected by barrels on two sides.

Thomas hoped that the trip back to Harpers Ferry would be less eventful than the trip down. When they got back to where they had left the two prisoners, they could see that both of them were gone. The ropes were left behind. Nevin observed that both had been cut. "It looks like we've had visitors."

"Good. Maybe the word will get around," Nevin said.

"What word?" said Thomas.

"Well, not that we don't take prisoners, but just that we don't take prisoners with us to where we're going."

"You're such a charmer."

Chapter Fifteen

Cookie is Failing

November 1, 1919

LeDroit Park, Washington, D.C.

"Cookie, I haven't seen you sittin' on the front porch in years," said Lester.

Cookie's neighbor had stopped as he walked by on the sidewalk.

"Lester, I haven't been here in years," said Cookie. "I'm not feelin' well."

"Tell me what I can do to help," Lester said. "You know I'd do anything for you."

"I know you would, Lester. See, I miss Calpurnia. I miss my boys. I miss the active life I used to have. That bullet wound from a few months ago sure has slowed me down. The pain is just incredible."

"Have you tried scotch?"

"I've tried everything. Scotch is good, but you can only do so much of that."

"I hope you let me know if I can help you at all." Lester smiled as he continued on his way.

Cookie sat there for another 10 minutes until he looked up.

"Well, what a ray of sunshine I see comin' down the road," he said.

He could see Lee Ann driving his old Ford converted truck. She was back working at the White House. Cookie figured she was probably running the country. He stood up from the step on the porch where he was sitting and waved as she approached the driveway. He walked slowly down to the front gate, opened it, and stepped onto the public sidewalk.

"Man, what are you doin' here?" Cookie said.

He reached out to her with a big smile.

"I told you I'd be stoppin' by every couple of days. I've got my orders from Bos," Lee Ann said.

"Oh, I see. Duty calls."

Cookie smiled.

"It ain't duty at all. You know that."

Lee Ann stopped the vehicle in the alley, jumped out, and ran toward Cookie. "I just love seeing you."

"I know. I'm one of the last warriors. The general and his brothers are gone. Jack Sanders is no longer. Who needs me?"

"We all need you. You're our inspiration. The boys need you. They may need you now more than ever, Cookie."

"Yeah I know. I just question how much they want me."

"The three of them are strikin' out on their own. They need your guidance. They need your wisdom. They need your hand." She hit him in the chest with her fist. "They need you."

"You know how to motivate a man, don't you?"

"I know how to whip a man into action."

"Okay, so what do I do today?"

"I need to have you find me as much barley as you can. We're going to start transporting it every weekend to West Virginia. This Friday, you and I are leaving for West Virginia. I want to leave around 3:30 p.m. so we have a chance of getting there before dark. I'm gonna be carryin' as many rounds as I can. These are for the Thompsons."

"Where are you gettin' .45 rounds?"

"You forget I work at the White House." Lee Ann smiled.

"Can't you get the barley from the White House too?"

"The White House is dry," Lee Ann said. "In fact, it's more than dry. It's arid."

"Okay. I understand. So, do you know how to make this alcoholic brew that Bos is concocting?"

"Mr. Custer, it's called scotch. We're only making a single malt. We make the malt from the barley by soakin' it, then we dry it over a peat flame, then we grind it up and add the water and the yeast and let it ferment. We're not goin' to be able to age our scotch for three years. One year will be enough. The boys were able to get more than 100 barrels from Kentucky, which have been used for sherry or bourbon. All of that is going to give our scotch a distinctive taste."

"You have done your homework."

"You know me, Cookie. I like homework. I'll be back Friday afternoon at 3:00. Be ready to go. I've been meaning to ask you, do you have any idea as to what that brand is on Bos' right shoulder? It's new."

"I haven't seen it. What is it?"

"Okay. I thought maybe you had seen it. If not, I'll ask his brothers."

Lee Ann kissed him on the cheek and was on her way back to the White House.

Cookie was not in control anymore. He knew Lee Ann would guide her husband. Would stay at the helm while Bos barked some orders. But was the enterprise about to swallow them up? She'd make sure that did not happen.

Chapter Sixteen

Sailor's Creek
April 6, 1865
Farmville, Virginia

A 280-pound man riding a draft horse was something to behold. The front legs of the horse were massive. They were covered with long hair that disguised the true girth. The man on top of the horse looked like he could have weighed as much as the horse. He didn't. The cavalryman's hat was pulled down over the eyes and made the Black man look intimidating. The blue hat and the Black face created a lack of contrast. No one could see where the cavalryman was looking. That was exactly what he wanted.

When he saw his commander break for a barricade and leap over it, Cookie Custer knew that there was no way his horse could do that. Even absent the rider, this horse could not do that. Cookie followed Captain Custer toward the barricade and urged the horse straight through it. The barricade gave way. Enemy fire was coming from both sides. Cookie Custer had caught up with his captain, and riding in single file, both men fired their pistols to both sides.

Captain Custer saw the Confederates attempting to make a new battle line. He also saw the color bearer rally the Confederate troops. Captain Custer charged. Cookie stayed close behind.

Captain Custer's commander, Colonel Charles Capehart, later wrote to Thomas Custer's wife and reported that the captain wrested the colors singlehanded. Captain Custer took a shot in the face, which knocked him back on his horse, but he regained control. He then reached out and grasped the flag from the color bearer and shot the color bearer in the center of his chest. The bullet to Captain Custer's face only caused minor damage to his lower jaw, extending up to just below the right ear.

Captain Custer and Cookie Custer returned to George Armstrong Custer's command position waving the Confederate flag. The captain planted the flag and then returned to rejoin the battle. George Armstrong Custer ordered his brother to report to the surgeon. The captain refused. At that point, George Custer ordered his brother to be placed under arrest and taken to the rear by a Black cavalryman wearing the three stripes of a sergeant.

No mention was made of the gallantry of the Black slave on the draft horse wearing the three hard stripes of the sergeant.

Chapter Seventeen

Preachers Try to Undermine Bos

November 4, 1919

Baltimore, Maryland

Bos hadn't been inside a church in 15 years; 1300 Druid Hill Avenue was a foreboding address. The large gothic church didn't fit in with what Bos had known as a typical Black church. It had been there for nearly 40 years and had a thriving congregation. AME churches were a mix of Methodist and Episcopal, similar to Baptist but different.

AME churches were less focused on baptism, but Bos knew that his pitch might still be a hard sell for these Bible-thumping religious people. He figured he could appeal to their taste buds and pocketbooks. That's what he hoped to do today, if he could get past the Bible thumpers. Pastor Wilson, who had married Bos and Lee Ann, had introduced Bos to the pastor of this church, who he claimed was a friend. Wilson got Bos an opportunity to make his pitch.

Bos had thought about bringing Cookie with him. He related better to these older men. The long car ride and the stress of meeting new people was too much. He opted not to bring him. As he walked down the center aisle of the church, he thought he might have made a mistake. Cookie was not a religious man, but he knew how to appear to be religious. He knew the Negro spirituals that were sung in plantations throughout the South. Now, they were sung in churches up and down the East Coast and in the Midwest. They hadn't changed much. But the emotion had become stronger.

Pastor Johnson was the oldest man of the four. He was tall and stood erect. He had a close-cropped white beard. His large head and round face almost were out of place with his rail-thin body. Johnson broke away from the crowd and extended his hand to Bos.

"Welcome, Mr. Custer."

"Thank you, pastor," said Bos.

The other men gathered around. Bos was introduced to two of them. A fourth man stood off to the side, listening but not looking at Bos.

The church was run by four elders, none of whom were actually old. They were all men in their 40s. The pastor was the leader of the flock. The board of trustees broke into two camps. One sought to take a strident role in promoting Black economic interests and the rights of Black people. The other camp, which included the pastor, preferred a more "wait your turn" approach. Bos wanted to ask those folks exactly how long they wanted to wait.

Bos had heard the four-member board was equally divided. Two were in favor of Bos's proposal and two were opposed. Bos talked for a minute with the three men who had joined around him. He stepped aside and introduced himself to the fourth member of the board of trustees.

"Hello. I'm Bos Custer."

He extended his hand, but the man didn't take it.

"I know who you are. I've known your kind all my life," Bertram Davis said. "You always got some fancy phrase or fancy idea to help Black folk, but all you're trying to do is help yourself."

"You're right. I *am* tryin' to help myself. I am tryin' to make some money. I am tryin' to sell some alcohol. I know that may soon become a risky endeavor, but as a byproduct of helpin' myself, I hope I can help some other folks. In particular the Black people of this church."

"Suppose we all get locked up?" Davis said.

"I don't think that's gonna happen. The Prohibition enforcement team is going to be focused on the distribution of potable alcohol to businesses that can sell it. The alcohol I'm gonna deliver to your church is not for sale. It's not drinkable unless you choose to dilute it to make it drinkable. I'm not sellin' it to you. I'm givin' it to you. I know what my cost of production and delivery are. I expect to get that money back plus about two or three percent. What you do with the alcohol is up to you. You can use that as a base for donations. I believe you're gonna make a lot more than two percent over my cost. With that profit, you can help the people of Baltimore."

"How do you know so much about the people of Baltimore?" said Pastor Johnson.

"I don't know much of anything about Baltimore. I have a friend who lives in this neighborhood that I fought with in Northern France. He told me something about this church. He also told me about Baltimore."

"Have you ever lived in Baltimore?" Davis said.

"Nope. This is the second time I've ever been. What I do see is you got a lot of people here livin' in close quarters who probably don't know where their next meal is comin' from. With some money, you can help those folks out, get 'em on their feet and maybe they can start workin' and pay you back for what you've done for 'em."

"I like your approach," the third man said. "I'm Hiram Walker."

"I know that you know alcohol," Bos said.

He smiled.

"You're right. I do," Walker said. "My family's copper still produces some of the best alcohol around."

"I hope you're not going to be my competition," Bos said.

"Nope. We're small potatoes." Walker smiled.

"Let me try to explain how I see this operation workin'," Bos said.

The three men nodded. Bos stepped up on the bottom step leading to the raised altar. The three men took a seat in the pews in front of him.

Bos proceeded to explain how he envisioned his production and distribution working. When he finished, he felt happy with his presentation and the questions and answers that followed. He had learned the mindset of these people and had a deeper sense of what they wanted and needed.

They were concerned about enforcement. Bos tried to allay those fears by telling them that he knew from reliable sources inside the government that the people enforcing Prohibition would leave the churches alone.

"If we water down this undrinkable liquid, aren't we going to destroy the flavor?" one of them asked.

"It will lose some flavor. But my plan is to stockpile thousands of barrels for the curin' time. That will give this one-year-old scotch plenty of flavor."

After one hour of Bos talking and the board of trustees asking questions, he could see that he was beginning to lose some of them. These were all men who worked with their hands. They were used to being on the move and not sitting in a church pew.

He approached all four of them, extended his hand, and thanked them for their courtesy. They told him that they would think about his proposal and get back to him. If they supported it, then there were several other Black churches in the Baltimore area that would get on board.

As Bos approached the front door of the church, he hesitated. He didn't think he had been followed to Baltimore. But he didn't know for sure. He knew there was now a price on his head. It was best if he went out a side door.

Once outdoors, he looked for an area providing some cover. At the edge of the building, he stood behind a column that allowed him to survey the area across the street without being fully exposed. He could see the glint of metal in the distance. The shooter was not an experienced hunter. He had attempted to hide himself about 90 feet from the far side of Druid Hill Road. But he had ignored the fact that the sun was behind him.

Bos retreated alongside the church. He proceeded to the nearest public street and circled around to get behind the shooter. The circumferential route took him 10 minutes.

As he would tell his brothers, if asked, the shooter might know how to fire a true shot, but he didn't know how to hide himself. Bos didn't want to make the same mistake. All of the buildings in that neighborhood were three stories with fire escapes on the side. Bos looked for a building with a pull-down fire escape. He got onto the roof, trying to avoid puddles of water, and walked toward the front of the building where he could keep an eye on the shooter and the surrounding area.

He waited 20 minutes. He could see Hiram Walker come out the front door of the church. The meeting must have broken up. A decision had been made.

Bos saw no other movements suggesting a second shooter. He got down from the roof and approached a small knoll across from the church where the shooter was laying. He got within 10 feet when the shooter looked over his shoulder.

"Not a move or I shoot," Bos said. "Put the rifle down flat."

The man followed instructions.

"Turn around and sit up," Bos said. "Who sent you?"

No response. Bos took the butt of his .45 and snapped it against the man's right clavicle. He could hear the bone snap. There was a cry of pain.

"You know I can't give you any information. If I do, they'll kill me," the shooter said.

"How much are they payin' ya?"

"They said a colored was only worth 100 bucks."

Brien A. Roche

"Thanks for the compliment."

Bos took the butt of his .45 and broke the man's other clavicle.

"I want to make sure I don't ever forget you. Two broken clavicles almost guarantee one of them won't heal straight. If I see you again, I'll kill you on the spot."

Bos took the butt of the .45 and jammed it into the man's nose. Then, he patted the man down to see if he had any sidearms. He picked up the .30 caliber rifle and walked back to his car. He stopped when he was a block away and asked himself what Cookie would have done. He had seen his father act with brutality and also with compassion. Overall, he had little sympathy for those who were trying to kill him.

General Custer had always taken the position of no mercy. He knew that was what Grant expected of him, and he delivered. Cookie had always said that the general was a simple man. Kill or be killed. That was simple. Bos couldn't argue with that.

He looked around to see if there were any other shooters. He knew that Torrio's men were not lone rangers. They liked company.

Bos didn't see any other shooters. He waited another 15 minutes to see if there was any movement. He walked to his vehicle and cranked it up.

Chapter Nineteen

The Movement West
November 6, 1919
Washington, D.C.

Friday afternoon came around as expected. Lee Ann pulled into the alley next to the Custer house. Cookie was sitting on the front steps. His truck was parked in front of the house, loaded with 25 to 30 bags.

As Lee Ann approached the front porch, Cookie hollered. "I got it!"

"You got what?"

"I got the barley."

"I knew you would. I understand they're runnin' low, so hopefully this will keep the operation goin'."

"Did you get the ammo?"

"Of course I did. It's loaded in the metal boxes. Hopefully it doesn't explode."

"That's unlikely."

Bos pulled up in a third vehicle. The flatbed area of his converted truck was also loaded with bags of barley.

"I guess you two went shoppin' at the same store," Lee Ann said.

"Of course we did. The old man needed me to load his truck for him." Bos scoffed but then he smiled at his father.

"The devil I did. If I can't load my own truck, I'm not gonna show up."

"Too bad we can't load all this stuff in one vehicle. That way, we could travel together and talk," Lee Ann said.

"That won't interfere with Pops. We can hear him 100 yards away."

"You're right, son. I still got my voice. I can still wake the dead."

"We all know the way. I'm just headin' west on Leesburg Turn-pike," Bos said.

"I brought some sandwiches. Maybe after about an hour we can stop alongside the road and have a little picnic."

"We'll have to put a blanket over you, Lee Ann, so nobody sees you," said Cookie.

"I think that's what we did last time. I think it's your turn now," Lee Ann said.

Lee Ann took the lead in the caravan. When they got north of Leesburg, she pulled over to the side of the road to a clearing. All three vehicles came to a stop.

Lee Ann went back and kissed her husband.

"Hungry?"

"You bet I am," Cookie said.

"She wasn't talkin' to you, Pops."

"Makes no difference. I'm hungry, and she brought food for all of us."

Within seconds, two vehicles pulled up alongside them. Each one was loaded with four men. They all had axe handles except one. He carried a shotgun.

Lee Ann ran back to her vehicle. Bos and Cookie spread out. Bos was uncertain if Cookie still carried a .45 or another handgun. He slipped his .45 out from the small of his back and tossed it to Cookie. He also tossed him a clip loaded with .45 rounds.

The white men hadn't seen the gun change hands as they got out of the two trucks. One of them addressed Bos and Cookie.

"What are you two doing here with this white woman?"

"Why don't you ask the white woman?" Bos said.

"This is none of your business as to what we're doing here," said Lee Ann.

She had a .32 pistol in her right hand hidden behind her skirt. Cookie held the .45 on his right hip. He positioned himself so the men couldn't see the handgun.

"I think we need to teach you boys a lesson," one of the white men said.

"We're pretty well schooled already," Bos said.

"A real smartass," one of the men said.

"You need to reconsider what you're doin' here," said Bos.

He unholstered his .45 and pointed it at one of the men. Cookie brought his .45 from behind his right hip and pointed it at one of the other men. Then they looked at Lee Ann. She had her .32 pistol pointing at them, too.

"I suggest you get back in your cars and turn around. Don't come back. If we see ya again, we open fire."

The white men began to retreat toward their vehicles. One of the drivers had a shotgun and was standing on the roof of the car.

"I might not get all three of you with this shotgun, but I'll get at least one of you."

"That depends on what it's loaded with," Bos said. "I doubt you'll do any damage to even one of us. Meanwhile, we'll kill all eight of you."

"Uppity."

The next word was muffled but Bos was pretty sure he knew what it was.

"I don't much care for that word. You need to get movin' and you need to get movin' now," Bos said.

The man with the shotgun came down from the roof and hopped back in his car. The others followed suit. They did a U-turn and disappeared.

"Well, that was the appetizer. Now, it's time for the main course."

Bos smiled. Cookie handed the .45 back to Bos, butt first.

"What happened to your sidearm, Pops?"

"I can't be carryin' a sidearm in D.C. Bad enough bein' a Black man in that city. A Black man with a weapon is definitely guilty of something."

He laughed. Lee Ann spread out a blanket alongside Bos's vehicle.

"Should we say grace before the meal?" Lee Ann smiled.

"You know me," said Bos. "I'm not the religious type. I worship my .45." He smiled.

"I've been meaning to talk to you about that. Your mother was religious. Your father pretends to be religious. At least he used to. You need to do one or the other. But you can't be contrarian. There's no room for debate on this," Lee Ann said.

"I guess the law has been laid down for you, son," said Cookie. "I don't see any wiggle room on this one." Cookie laughed.

"You're right, Pops. No more negative talk about religion. From now on, I'll fake it. People will think I am a religious man even though I'm not. It's against my nature to do that, but I'll do it for you." Bos looked at Lee Ann and smiled.

"Enough of that talkin'. Let's get down to business and eat this good food your wife brought for us."

Chapter Twenty

South Side
November 7, 1919
Chicago, Illinois

"Boss, we didn't get him," the speaker said.

"What do you mean, you didn't get him?" said Johnny Torrio. "I thought we hired the right guy this time."

As the leader of the South Side outfit, Torrio had learned that the only way to succeed was to stay focused. All he cared about were results. That's what you got paid for and that's what people respected.

"I thought we did, too. The guy came back with two broken clavicles and a broken nose," Al Capone said.

Capone, a newcomer to the Chicago scene, hadn't fully adjusted to Torrio's ways. He viewed the older man as being too conservative. He had grown up in New York City, where everything was challenged—sometimes even the boss.

"Did you pay the guy?" Torrio said.

"I did. I gave him a kick in the ass and told him to go home," Capone said.

"You shouldn't have paid him. Guys need to know they do the job or they don't get paid."

"I think this guy got the message. He's got at least three broken bones in his body, and he can't move. The guy suffered."

"Yeah. I get it, but next time don't pay these guys if they don't get the results we want. They need to understand that's all we care about."

Capone thought about what Torrio was saying. He had three scars on the left side of his face because he didn't get the desired result. He called them war wounds even though he'd never seen a minute of combat.

"If I could spare you, I'd send you to kill this guy," Torrio said. "I need you to stay in New York for at least another month to keep track of things."

"You know the cops are constantly on me, Boss. Every time I turn a corner, one of them is there."

"Maybe it's time for you to come out here."

"That sounds like a good idea. Christmas in Chicago."

"Yeah. Just remember there's no Santa Clauses in our outfit. The only red we wear is the blood of the guys we've killed. Think about what I've said. I want two or three of our men following this guy day and night. They need to report back to us every day."

"I got it. If you really want, I could slip down to D.C. and kill him myself."

"No, you've got enough heat on you now, Al. The New York cops will know right away that something's up if they find out you're in D.C. They'll probably think you're trying to kill the president."

"We probably should. I understand he don't like I-talians. I don't much care about that. People think I'm from Sicily, you know. I'm not, but I don't mind people thinking that, if you know what I mean."

"Think about what I said, Al. I'd like to have you out here by the middle of December. Pick someone to fill your shoes," Torrio said.

"That's a tall order," Capone said. "I'm joking."

"Not in your case it's not. Just get 'em filled. Get out here by the 15th, and I want two guys on this colored guy around the clock and daily reports about what he's doing. We can't have this guy settin' up his own operation."

"You're right, Boss. After all, we're the outfit."

Torrio had never liked the name "Outfit." He was territorial and proud of where he lived in South Chicago. He thought the crime family should be called the South Side Gang. That was what he called it. His wife was from South Side. She liked being associated with that neighborhood. She liked images. South Side Gang conveyed an image. The Outfit didn't convey an image. She told Johnny that images were important. They told the story of the organization. They said more than anything Johnny could say. Johnny believed her.

"No, we're not the Outfit. We're the South Side Gang. Don't forget that."

Chapter Twenty-One

Construction Ends

December 10, 1919

Harpers Ferry, West Virginia

"Did you ever study Isaac Newton?" said Bos.

"Of course we did. We just didn't get much out of it," Nevin said.

"We also studied Archimedes," said Thomas.

"I think Newton might have an idea or two about how to make this job a little bit simpler."

At this point, all of the steel plates had been put in place. They had managed to construct a tetrahedron structure of four tree trunks. The trunks were leaning against each other at the top. There was a line and a pulley at the top of the pyramid that allowed several men to pull each steel piece up to the second-floor level.

Getting each piece in place had been torture. There was a total of 16 pieces for each "fort." Each fort was fully surrounded by steel, except for the side closest to the house and the top. Most important to Bos, the work had been done without injuries to any of the men.

"We'll finish the second fort tomorrow. Now that we've got the knack of it, things should move a bit more quickly," Bos said.

"These guys are exhausted, Bos. They deserve some refreshment."

Bos and Nevin had been making several barrels of beer. They didn't know exactly what they'd do with it, but they figured that with 25 working men on site, it would get consumed.

Bos rang the bell. This was the signal for all the workers to congregate in front of the house.

"I want to thank all of you for your hard work. My wife has been cooking for two days. We're plannin' a big meal for all of you tonight, and there will be plenty of beer."

He had decided to relax his "no alcohol" policy. There were some oompahs of satisfaction.

"We'll start a little late tomorrow. Startin' time will be 9:00 a.m. I'm hopin' we can finish up the other fort tomorrow. Any men who want to go home after that can go home. I'd like to have you all stay on. I've got more work for you, but it's not construction work. We can talk about that tomorrow if you want," Bos said.

"I've set up two long tables inside our house," said Lee Ann. "You men are all welcome to come in and join us. There are several large wash buckets over by the porch. Feel free to wash up before you come in."

Lee Ann smiled at the men. Bos went over and gave her a hug and kept his arm around her as they walked up the stairs together.

By early evening the beer was starting to have some effect. Inhibitions were easing. The talk was getting louder. Bos, Nevin, and Thomas were as loud as any of them. Lee Ann decided to go upstairs and leave the men to themselves.

An hour later, she heard Bos talking to the group, explaining what he had in mind. He invited all 25 of the men to stay on board. They would not be doing construction work. They would be doing defense work. Defending the Last Stand from what Bos said would be an eventual attack by the Chicago outfit. He knew it was just a matter of time. He knew that Torrio would not allow this interference to stand.

What he didn't know was the extent of Torrio's wealth and manpower. The whorehouses he ran in Chicago had provided a constant stream of cash. Torrio now had an endless supply of alcohol from Canada. In addition, there were a number of suppliers in Europe willing to deliver scotch and other liquors to the East Coast. The thirst for alcohol was unquenchable. It was getting stronger with the advent of Prohibition.

Bos understood human appetites. There was no reason why he couldn't make it work to his advantage.

Chapter Twenty-Two

Capone Moves West
December 15, 1919
Chicago, Illinois

"Mae and I celebrate our first anniversary in about two weeks," Capone said.

"You need to bring her by. I understand she's a very sweet girl," Johnny Torrio said.

"Indeed she is."

"Irish?" said Torrio.

"Yep."

"Catholic?"

"Yep again."

"Let's the four of us get together sometime."

Capone thought about that. They now had a toddler at home. He didn't have the same flexibility anymore. Mae was accustomed to the odd hours that Capone kept. She kept her complaints to herself.

"You understand Big Jim is the boss here?" Torrio said.

"I do," said Capone, "but I think someday you're going to be the boss."

"And then someday you're going to be the boss."

"That's my plan."

"How do we get there?"

"A step at a time. One step at a time."

"I like that. Slow but easy. Right now, what I need is some help with the brothels. I know they're busy, but I'm not seeing all the cash.

Here are 10 addresses. Take three of the boys with you and make sure that all of these operators understand that all of the cash comes to me."

"Speak softly but carry a big stick?"

"Definitely speak softly. These are mostly women you're gonna be dealing with."

"That's good. I like women, and they like me."

"That's great but keep your hands off 'em. Business and pleasure don't mix. What I need is head counts. Customers in and customers out. I can tell ya what each of these houses ought to be generating. Some of them were only producing about half of what I think they should. The money's goin' somewhere."

"If you got 10 houses and they're averaging two to three thousand per night, that's $20,000 to $30,000 per night. Over $100,000 per week."

"Sounds like you're good at math."

"I am. The nuns always said that." Capone laughed.

"I think that cash flow ought to double. See what you can do to make our operation more efficient."

"Efficiency is my middle name."

"That's why the cops in New York were all over your ass for those murders."

"They never got me on anything. Yeah, I was guilty, but they couldn't prove nothin'."

"Let's keep it that way. No notes, no letters, no writings, nothin'. Everything is oral only. The cops have a tougher time proving anything if you keep it off the printed page."

"No paper. Nothing in writing. That should be easy for me since I don't know how to write."

"That's part of the reason why I hired you. I figured you couldn't read my stuff, so how could you betray me?" Torrio laughed and slapped his knee.

Chapter Twenty-Three

The Plan is Hatched
December 24, 1919
Chicago, Illinois

"We need to hit the ground runnin' on January 16th," Capone said.

The assembled group of men controlled much of the criminal enterprise in Chicago and throughout the Midwest.

"Where do we stand as far as the importation from Canada?" Capone said.

"The trucks start rollin' in three days, boss."

"What's the volume?"

"Each truck can carry 50 20-gallon barrels."

"Our colored friend from Washington, D.C., is buying 10-gallon barrels," said Capone. "I like that. One man can carry a barrel. Hell, when it comes to a 20-gallon barrel, I'm not even sure I could carry that," Capone laughed.

"Oh, sure you could, Al," one of the men said.

As Capone faced the crowd, he kept the right side of his face showing as much as he could. He was conscious of the scars on the left side of his face and tried to hide them.

He looked at the man. "You mean that?"

"You bet I do."

"How old are you, kid?" said Capone.

"Nineteen."

"You can't even vote yet."

"Al, you can't vote either for a couple of weeks."

"I like you, kid. What's your name?"

"Frankie. Frankie LaPorte."

"What do we know about the quality of the booze coming in?" said Capone.

"We know it's top quality. Seagram's has been making all types of distilled liquors for years. They know how to do it. They can just drop it at the border, and we pick it up."

"What's going to be the margin?" Capone said.

No one responded.

"What's the profit?" he paused.

"If we're doing 20-gallon barrels of whiskey, there's no reason why the profit shouldn't be at least a thousand bucks per barrel." Capone paused again.

"I want 10-gallon barrels and I want a thousand bucks per barrel," Capone said.

"There's no reason why we can't do that, boss."

"Now these coloreds in West Virginia and D.C. What are we going to do about them?"

"These guys are hard cases, Al. They're all veterans. They fought in Northern France."

"I don't care where they fought. I fought, too. They're not going to cut into our distribution," Capone said.

He had directed two of his men from New York to go south to D.C. and keep an eye on the Custers. The information flow coming back was slow but useful.

"We know they've got a big spread out in West Virginia near Harpers Ferry," one of the men said.

"Is that where they're makin' the stuff?" said Capone.

"It looks like it, boss."

"We need to figure out exactly what their operation is there in West Virginia, how big it is, and how many men they've got."

"Al, you need to understand. These guys are all combat veterans. They could shoot a fly off your shoulder at 100 yards."

"Nobody can shoot a fly off my shoulder at 100 yards. I'm movin' too quick." Capone laughed.

At five feet ten and more than 200 pounds, he moved athletically for a man his size. He finally got in close to the man he was shadow-boxing with and threw two inside punches to the abdomen. The man doubled over and fell to the floor.

"We need guys who can fight. We need guys to keep the Canadians in line. We can't have them Canucks raising their prices. The prices need to be stable. We need to control these coloreds. How many of you are with me?"

They all raised their hands.

Frankie Laporte was the loudest. He raised his fist.

"We're with you, Al. All the way."

"You'll all make a lot of money. I'll make most of it, but I'll share it with you. Think of me as Robin Hood."

"We like the Hood. Does this mean we get to go hunting?"

"No hunting," said Capone. "We need information. Just information. No scalps yet."

"Am I going alone?" said LaPorte.

"No. The other guys who have been there will be with you. You'll be in charge. We need more details about their operation. Details, details, details. You understand?" Capone looked around at his men.

"We're with you, Robin," Frankie La Porte said.

"You'd better be. If you're not with me, you're against me. We need to figure out what their operation consists of and how we attack it. If they have an operation in D.C., then we need a plan to attack that. Do I have some more volunteers to get that information?"

Frankie LaPorte approached Capone. Both men had similar builds. Capone was slightly taller. The two men stood face to face. Capone was accustomed to hiding the scars on his face. Now, they were fully visible to LaPorte. Capone could see him looking at his face.

"Do you know where they came from?"

"I guess you're going to tell me," LaPorte said.

Capone was about to tell yet his third version of how he got the scars.

"I killed two guys. Both of them were bigger than me. I had a hunting knife. One of the guys had a four-inch blade. The other one had a .32 pistol. I killed the guy with the .32 by slicing his throat and then used him as a shield to attack the guy with the knife. He was a good shield. He took two more knife wounds that were meant for me. Then, I stuck the other guy in the shoulder and then in the gut. He cried like a baby." Capone smiled.

"Al, we know you're a fighter," said LaPorte. "We know you got Torrio's ear. We are all fighters. We all want in. But we all want our fair share."

"Stick with me. You'll see some fighting. You'll see some cash. Maybe we'll have a few laughs."

Chapter Twenty-Four

Scouting
December 27, 1919
Harpers Ferry, West Virginia

"I was born in Sicily. I know the jungle," LaPorte said.

"Well, I was born in Brooklyn. I came out to Chicago with Capone, and I don't know the jungle at all," Joey LaDuca said.

"I don't either," said a third man.

The three of them were about a mile from what the Custers called "The Last Stand."

LaPorte had told the other two men to come prepared. They needed boots, an outdoor jacket that was dark in color, and layered clothing that would keep them warm.

"I told you clowns to wear the right clothing. We're goin' into the jungle. We're not goin' on a picnic," LaPorte said.

The two other men looked at each other. Each of them was wearing street clothes with a tie and a felt hat. One of the men had a knee-length topcoat.

LaPorte looked at them. "Are you going to crawl in the mud in that topcoat?"

"Frankie, we're city boys."

"Yesterday, you may have been city boys. Today, you're country boys. I told you to adapt."

LaPorte walked around the car once and then shouted at them. "You're no good to me. You're not gonna be able to go anywhere in those clothes with those shoes on. Just head back to where you came from."

"We can stay here, Frankie and start a fire. You'll be nice and warm when you get back," the third man said.

"I don't want no fire. A fire is gonna tell them that we're comin' for 'em."

LaDuca was no older than LaPorte. He might have been 20. At six feet four, he was several inches taller than LaPorte. He also had 50 pounds on him. Both were tough looking men. LaPorte's nose had been broken more than once and never straightened. LaDuca's nose looked like it had been broken and someone had attempted to straighten it. The thickness between the eyes showed that the cartilage had been compressed and never reshaped. Whatever had impacted the nose had been flat and powerful. He used to joke that he could take a hit with a two-by-four. He was right.

All three men were Sicilians. They had come to this country as young boys. They had vague memories of Sicily from their childhood. Those memories had been reinforced as runners for Italian bosses. It was an unforgiving childhood. One slipup and they would get cuffed in the face by one of the older men, many of whom themselves were boys. They had learned early on that the culture was one of violence and allegiance. Those allegiances were temporary. All anyone cared about was what you brought in and how well you could fight.

LaPorte looked at his two companions. He knew that neither of the two would last long in the Capone outfit.

"I'll go out alone," LaPorte said. "You two clowns stay here. Keep the car lights off. No fires. No noise. I'll be back in two hours. Don't leave without me."

He trudged off alone. He knew that the complex was being built somewhere to the east. He had talked with one of the clerks at a nearby general store. She told him there was some construction on a nearby hilltop. LaPorte moved in that direction.

He had been very precise in his preparations. He had told LaDuca and the other man what to wear, what to bring with them, and where to meet him. The only thing they had gotten right was the meeting place.

How do I run an outfit when the guys who work for me can't follow instructions?

He would figure that out later.

Meanwhile, LaPorte had proceeded a half mile when he noticed that the thick brush and bushes that were waist high had started to recede. He could see in the distance the rooftop of a large structure.

It was only 7:00 p.m.

He figured the guys he was searching for might be smart enough to have spotters. Any sort of movement, even at this distance, might alert someone at the Custer compound. Even the birds could be easily rustled, which would send a warning. LaPorte decided to lie down behind a fallen tree trunk to get a better look.

He had a pair of old prism binoculars he had stolen from an optical shop five years earlier. The optician had been Italian. LaPorte figured that they at least had the right lineage.

He took his position behind the fallen tree trunk and focused on the structure about a half mile away. He could see men all around the house. He could see the one "fort" closest to him and puzzled over why it was constructed differently than the rest of the house. He didn't notice the fort on the other end or the gun portholes in the fort he could see.

What he did notice was that all the men working around the compound were Black. Seated on the porch at a table with one man was a young woman with long blonde hair. No one had told him that Bos Custer was married . . . to a white woman . . . with blonde hair. He could tell by their movements that there was some intimacy between the two. He didn't know what to make of that.

The only contact LaPorte had previously had with a Black man was a two-round fight on the south side of Chicago. He had heard about the chance to earn $100 in a boxing match. He figured he'd be fighting another Italian. Instead, he was put into the ring with a Black man who was 20 pounds lighter than him.

Their fists had been taped. No gloves were provided. He fought in a pair of swim trunks, bare-chested, and was wearing an old pair of army boots. The Black man fought in a pair of coveralls with no shirt on top. What LaPorte lacked in speed, he made up for in toughness. The Black man, however, was twice as fast. LaPorte stayed focused and came straight at the man. Every punch was right down the middle. After a pair of two-minute rounds, they were both a bloody mess. The umpire declared a draw, and the purse was split. LaPorte got his $100.

After the fight out on the street, LaPorte had run into the Black man. They acknowledged each other. Each admired the other for his skills.

"Whatcha make?" LaPorte said.

"Nothing near what you made," the Black man said.

"That ain't fair. You fought good," LaPorte said.

"Good ain't enough around here," the Black man said. "Maybe we'll see each other again."

LaPorte rolled over on his back, still hidden behind the fallen tree trunk. He didn't know what to make of what he'd seen. It was clearly a well-built structure. Two levels tall. A Black man and a white woman sitting on the front porch. He'd like to get closer, but he knew that was too dangerous.

He rolled back onto his stomach and took another look at the land-scape. He tried to memorize what was there. A large house sitting on a knoll. Two gravel roads led up to the house. The grade up to the house was about 10 degrees. The clearing on the front side of the house was at least a 200-foot setback. Open field all the way, which had been cleaned bare. There was nothing to hide behind. The back of the house was set against a cliff, but LaPorte could not determine how high it was.

He saw large nets along the tree line, but he had no idea why they were there or what they were for. He figured if there was going to be any assault on the house, it would have to come under the cover of darkness.

LaPorte rolled over onto his back and raised up. As he did, he twirled the binoculars onto his back. The strap around the binoculars held them up, hanging around his neck. As they moved, they gave off a slight reflection of moonlight. Bos could see it in the distance from his front porch. He knew the watchers were back.

Chapter Twenty-Five

Back to Chicago
December 28, 1919
Harpers Ferry, West Virginia

"Do you really think it's wise to go out there?" Lee Ann said.

"I don't think I have any choice," said Bos. "They've been here. They've been keepin' eyes on us. There's no doubt in my mind that they're comin' for us. We need to strike first, otherwise we may not be able to strike at all."

"How many men are you takin' with you?"

"Ten. Alvin Morrison said he would join us. I'm gonna leave Thomas and Nevin here. They've been through enough. Nevin's already told me he wants to go down to North Carolina to see his girl."

"That's good of you," Lee Ann said. "They both need some time off. I can see it in their faces."

"What do you see in my face?"

"I see a man who would like peace. I see a man who recognizes there's never gonna be peace. I see a man who's ready to take the battle to the enemy as long as the enemy is out there. I think that's the man I married. The same man your mother married."

"You're right, Lee Ann, but once we have children, I'm takin' a back seat."

Lee Ann smiled at her husband.

"I'd like to see that, but I'll believe it when I do."

Bos left the front porch and walked toward the barracks building where most of the men slept. As he entered the hall, he heard a lot of noise. Some of the men were playing cards. Some were playing musical instruments. Some were writing letters.

"I'm sorry to bother you on your free time. Some of you know we've been under surveillance. The mob from Chicago and New York is concerned about us," Bos said.

"They oughta be," one of the men said.

"You're right. They oughta be, but you know that I'm not one to sit still in the face of a threat."

"Who's crazy enough to threaten you, Bos?"

"Johnny Torrio from Chicago and one of his young upstarts who tells people he fought in France."

"What's his name?"

"He calls himself Capone."

"And let me guess. You want us to go after him?"

"You got it," said Bos. "I need some volunteers."

All 25 men stood up.

"I appreciate your loyalty. I can't take 25. All I need is 10. In fact, I don't even need that many. What I really need is 9. Some of you may know Alvin Morrison. He's agreed to join us."

"We're happy to draw straws, Bos. I think I speak for all the men that we'll follow you anywhere."

"I don't want you to follow me anywhere," said Bos. "I want you to follow me to those places that make sense, and if you don't think they do, then you say so. What I really need are men with some experience with a Thompson and probably four long-distance marksmen, and I need a cook. Joe Taylor, you out there?"

Joe Taylor stood up. "I'm here, Bos. I'm with ya."

"Some of you may know that Joe was a cook at the Marne when the Germans overran the forces in the back. He went at 'em with a meat cleaver. After that, we called him 'knockwurst.' He could knock a man worse than anybody I'd ever seen."

Bos laughed.

"I guess you're down to eight now," one man said.

"Who are my four best marksmen?" said Bos.

"There's no question about that. The best is Sylvester Scott. Tied for a close second are Tommy Johnson, Jack Jackson, and Hiram Washington."

"You've seen them out there in the fields, Bos, shootin' away."

"I know."

"We're all with you, Bos," the four men said.

"I'll let you pick the other four. I don't need to tell you how much I appreciate your loyalty. Some of us may not come back from Chicago. My plan is to go out there and teach Johnny Torrio a lesson."

"A good lesson I hope," Sylvester Scott said.

"We're leaving tomorrow at 9:00 a.m. We'll take two trucks. I'm leavin' my brothers behind. We can alternate the driving."

Bos looked around the barracks. He was searching for alcohol, but there was none. These men were used to drinking, but they had followed his orders. He knew what damage alcohol could do, especially among men who worked hard all day and had little to look forward to when it was over. He smiled. These were the same type of men he had fought with in France. He turned around and walked back to his house.

Chapter Twenty-Six

Fireworks
December 31, 1919
Chicago, Illinois

The trip west was cold and rainy. Six mattresses had been placed in the back of each truck. Aside from the driver and a man riding shotgun, one man sat in the back with a Thompson. Since the truck covers would provide little protection from the wind and the cold, all of the men had dressed warmly. They were prepared for the much colder weather in Chicago, especially in South Side, which was close to the water.

Bos had spent hours planning the route. He knew the location of Torrio's warehouse. His plan was to set up an overnight encampment on the rooftop of an empty building that was two blocks away. They would pitch tents and sleep in sleeping bags on the roof. He had brought 12 simple cots. Each cot was seven feet long. Many of his men were over six feet tall. Bos and Lee Ann had made the cots. They were simple stretches of canvas wrapped around one-by-four pieces of wood that were supported by three sets of two-by-fours held together with a bolt, a washer, and a wing nut. Each would easily support a man of at least 250 pounds. Bos had more than one of those in his command.

They arrived at the location on New Year's Eve. Bos had heard that Torrio and Capone would be at the warehouse that night with their wives and 20 close companions and friends.

Bos had decided ahead of time that the families were off limits. He just wanted to know where each of these men lived so that if he needed to visit their homes, he could.

He had bought three Tin Lizzies through one of his friends in Chicago and had them stored at a warehouse two blocks away from Torrio's. He would use these to follow Torrio, Capone, and LaPorte to their homes that evening when they left the warehouse party.

The following morning, the fireworks would begin. At midnight, Bos called all of the men together on the rooftop.

"From right here we can see the front door of Torrio's warehouse," Bos said. "We know that Torrio, Capone, and LaPorte went in that front door. Torrio and Capone are with their wives. LaPorte is not married. They should be leavin' soon through that same door. I want Sylvester, Tony, and Jack to follow them. I'm sure they're all goin' to different locations. Jack, you take Hiram with you and try to follow LaPorte. He's single so he may go somewhere else after the warehouse party. Torrio and Capone will probably go home with their wives. All I want are addresses. Home addresses."

"Once we get their addresses?" said Sylvester.

"Then come back here and get a good night's sleep."

"What are the rest of you going to be doing?" Tommy Johnson said.

"We'll be sleepin'. At 5:30 a.m., I'll wake y'all up. You four will stay here on the rooftop with your Springfields. It'll still be dark at 6:00. I've got 24 sticks of dynamite. We're gonna wire each corner of that building with 2 sticks and use the other 16 to intersperse among the four walls."

"A New Year's Eve celebration?" one man said.

"Nope. New Year's Day. We're going to welcome it at sunrise."

"How about the men inside?" said Sylvester.

"As far as we know," said Bos, "nobody stays in the warehouse overnight. If anyone does come out of the warehouse before or after the explosion, only shoot if they look like a threat."

"You're big on sending messages, aren't you, Bos?"

"Messages are important. Now let's get some sleep."

The four men following Torrio, Capone, and LaPorte, picked up their Springfields and walked to the edge of the roof. One by one, they exited down the fire escape.

All four of them had been told how Torrio, Capone, and LaPorte had approached the warehouse. It was assumed they would leave by the same route. They positioned their vehicles accordingly.

On the rooftop, Bos opened up his cot. Under the cover of his tent, he hoped to get at least five hours of sleep.

Five in the morning came quicker than he thought. His sleep had been uninterrupted. When he exited the tent, he looked to see if Sylvester Scott and the others had returned. It looked like all four of their tents were occupied. He could tell by the noises coming from them.

He approached the tent of Scott and poked his head inside. He gently nudged Scott, who grunted.

"I know that's you, Bos. Nobody wakes me as gently as you do."

"How'd it go?" Bos said.

"I followed Torrio home. Not easy driving through this city with no lights on. He lives about thirty minutes from here. I got his address. For a man with all his money, it's not much of a place."

"How 'bout the other guys?"

"Yep. Mission accomplished."

"That's the way I like it. Now for the fireworks."

Bos proceeded to wake up the other men.

He had thought about having a lookout throughout the night. He figured that was futile. Somebody marching from post to post on this rooftop would probably just draw attention. All of the men had slept through the night. It wasn't much sleep, but it was more than many of them got in Northern France.

They loaded up the two trucks. The plan was to plant the explosive, blow it, and leave town. Shoot and scoot. Just what Bos and his brothers were used to.

Bos had figured that at each corner they would place one explosive at ground level and one along the roof. He had brought several grappling hooks for men to climb up to the roof and plant the explosives. All 24 sticks of dynamite were separately wired. His plan was to fire them in serial fashion. The first two at one corner would blow, and right after that another corner would blow, and then the third and fourth corner in sequence. Then, the intervening sticks along the walls would blow. Each man knew the sequence. As long as they maintained it, none of them should get hurt, and the warehouse should either be leveled or made unusable.

At 6:15, the first one exploded. Bos hated to think about military precision. In his mind, there was no such thing. In the military, almost everything that could go wrong, did go wrong. He had seen it all. What he hoped for in this case was that his men would just follow orders and blow the dynamite in the order he had directed.

That's exactly what they did. The first two explosions were ear-splitting. The later explosions seemed to be less percussive. Bos thought that it was because there were so many waves of explosion that they cancelled each other out.

Whatever it was, the fireworks were a sight to behold. All four walls of the warehouse collapsed. Within minutes, all 11 men were on board the two trucks, heading east.

West Virginia, here we come.

Chapter Twenty-Seven

Showdown in D.C.

January 17, 1920

Washington, D.C.

"We're gonna make 'em pay. They're gonna pay. They're gonna pay," Capone said.

He stood on the back of a truck talking to 15 men, all armed with shotguns or Thompson submachine-guns.

He had brought three trucks with him. They were stopped at a rail yard in Alexandria, Virginia. From that location, they could see the Washington Monument and the US Capitol. The White House was not visible.

"Over there," Capone said. "That's where we're goin'."

The crowd of men shouted back.

"The White House!"

"Their delivery arrives at 9:00 a.m. We'll be there to meet them. After all, we like Prohibition. We like the fact that liquor is not legal."

On January 16, 1920, Prohibition, as declared in the Volstead Act, had become the law of the land. Alcohol could be made or purchased for personal private consumption, but otherwise it could not be distributed.

At the White House, three truckloads of scotch and gin were being delivered for what the occupants called private personal consumption on government grounds. That was illegal. Capone knew it was. If he'd been the supplier, he would have been happy to be party to the illegality. But he was not so lucky. Bos Custer was. He had now become enemy number one for the Chicago outfit.

The three trucks left the Alexandria rail yard at 8:00 a.m. It was only a 10-minute trip to the White House. Bos knew that Torrio would be coming for him. A big boss like Torrio and a big mouth like Capone couldn't let the Chicago warehouse bombing go unanswered.

The delivery to the White House could have been carried out in a less showy way. Bos wanted what he was doing to be known by those concerned. He was bringing 10 trucks to the White House. Five of them were loaded with 10-gallon barrels of his alcohol. Gin and vodka were particularly easy to make. Scotch was more time-consuming. His scotch had aged for less than a year.

Two of Bos's trucks that were not loaded with alcohol were set up in the back with Lewis guns on tripods. Bos had reconstructed these trucks himself. The bed of each truck was surrounded on three sides with layers of two-by-eights laying vertically. The boards had all been compressed to be more resistant. Three feet off the floor of the truck bed was a two-inch hole that surrounded the circumference of the three sides. Each of the gunners in the back of the trucks could point their Lewis guns out of these holes and have a good shot at anything outside. The two-inch holes also served as sight holes for each gunner. The layered two-by-eights provided some protection. It wouldn't be perfect.

Bos knew that Torrio's men would come armed with Thompsons. The .45 caliber Thompson rounds would not penetrate the layers of his two-by-eights. However, the porthole for the Lewis guns was a problem. Any rounds that entered the truck through those portholes could be fatal to the shooters inside.

Bos wasn't trying to conceal anything. He was in the lead truck. All 10 trucks were heading south on 16th Street straight toward the White House. The plan had been that at K Street they would move up to 17th Street and enter the White House from the west entrance.

Bos had told Lee Ann what was coming. She had opposed his plan. She had no choice but to tell Mrs. Wilson. They made sure that the president was out of the White House. His recovery from his stroke had only been partial at that point. He understood what was going on around him but had lost any executive function. Decisions were now being made by Mrs. Wilson.

The Secret Service had also been alerted to what was coming. Since the president wasn't involved and wasn't even at home, they had conveyed to the Metropolitan Police that there may be trouble on 17th Street.

As he approached the White House, Bos could see Torrio's men lined up on Pennsylvania Avenue. His lead truck was not carrying alcohol. All it had in the back were two Lewis guns. Once they reached 17th Street, Bos told his driver to pull straight onto the sidewalk. On a Saturday morning at 9:00 a.m., the sidewalks were empty except for the shooters.

The truck pulled right up to the metal fence surrounding the White House. The driver jumped out with his Thompson and lay flat on the sidewalk under the truck, protected by its two rear tires. Bos got out from his side of the truck, jumped on the hood, and lay flat. He could see Torrio's men were confused.

The operators of the Lewis guns pulled the canvas covering off the back of their trucks and with short bursts began picking off the Torrio men.

The second truck in Bos's caravan pulled into the west gate of the White House. The third truck was a Lewis gun truck, and it pulled onto the sidewalk on the opposite side of 17th Street. The fourth truck in the caravan was loaded with alcohol.

Torrio's men, to their credit, stood their ground. There was no cover on 17th Street. There were trees to hide behind. There were no cars parked on the street.

Within minutes, all five of the Lewis gun trucks had positioned themselves on the sidewalk on 17th Street and had taken up their position. Some of Torrio's men had actually climbed the trees on 17th Street. Bos was puzzled as to how they had gotten up into the trees, since there were no low-hanging branches. They stood there on branches that were almost 20 feet off the ground firing their Thompsons. The machine-gun fire from the Lewis guns came in staccato bursts. The bursts were merciless and tore Torrio's men apart. What rounds didn't hit their target embedded either in the sidewalk or nearby earth.

The firefight lasted 60 seconds.

Bos was on the lookout for the man referred to as Scarface. Capone was nowhere to be found. Bos had counted the three Capone trucks that had parked on Pennsylvania Avenue. Capone was either inside one of them or had fled on foot. When the shooting stopped, Bos got down from the hood of the truck and directed his remaining liquor trucks to proceed through the west entrance of the White House. Only three of the trucks made it. The other two were disabled.

Bos approached each of his remaining trucks for a head count. Two of his drivers had been killed. All 15 of the Torrio men were dead and accounted for. Bos directed that all the bodies be loaded up.

The liquor from the two disabled trucks was loaded onto two of his other trucks and driven through the 17th Street entrance to the White House. All the deliveries were now secure.

Bos gave the order to head down to the 14th Street Bridge.

"We're headin' home," Bos said.

He jumped on the back of the last of the five trucks heading south to 14th Street. In the bed of the truck were the bodies from Chicago. Young men, nicely dressed. Somebody had bought them dark suits and white shirts and dark ties. They were all stained in red.

Bos thought about how stupid this setup had been. Whoever led these men had ushered them into a meat grinder. They had come to a gunfight with Thompsons, and they were met with machine-guns that could spit out larger pieces of lead with greater accuracy.

For a moment, Bos felt sorry for the men in the back of the truck. He would take them to West Virginia, identify who they were, and give them a decent burial.

He figured if Capone wanted to pick up these men, Bos would let him. He would even meet them halfway between Harpers Ferry and Chicago to exchange the bodies. He knew Capone didn't care about that. Capone would abandon the bodies. They meant nothing to him, just like the sacrifices they had made. All that counted to men like Capone was money. There would be plenty of that coming for him. Bos was determined that Capone wasn't going to make it on his turf.

Chapter Twenty-Eight

Taking Care of Basics

January 18, 1920

Harpers Ferry, West Virginia

Bos had built a porch on the front of the house, facing east. He had also built one on the back, facing west. Sitting there in the early evening watching the sun descend was inspiring.

"Did you know that's really an optical illusion?" Bos said.

"What do you mean?" Lee Ann said. "The sun is not really the sun?" She smiled.

"In a way. When we see the sun descending, what we're looking at is not really the sun, but the glare from the sun. The sun has already descended below the horizon. We're just seeing the glare from that descent."

"So, it is an illusion?"

"In a way it is. You might better think of it as a reflection of an event that happened just a few moments earlier."

"How'd you get to be so smart?"

"It's called reading."

The cat jumped up on Bos's lap. UA had been slowly acclimating to West Virginia. Bos thought he liked it since he liked being an outdoor cat. He also liked the protection of home.

UA nestled in Bos's lap. Lee Ann threw him the brush he used to clean the cat. He brushed the cat gently and UA began to purr. Lee Ann smiled. Bos was the only one who UA would let brush him like that. As he continued to brush, Bos encountered more and more tangled snarls. Ten minutes later, Bos had collected a big wad of cat hair. UA was still on Bos's lap, still purring.

"What are you going to do with all the bodies?" Lee Ann said.

"We'll treat 'em with respect. Most of the men have been identified. They all had wallets. Some of our men are out digging graves already. Others are building coffins. I have Torrio's home phone number. I'm gonna call him tomorrow morning and tell him I've got 15 bodies. I'll meet him halfway between here and Chicago. If he doesn't want the bodies, I'll bury 'em here. They'll all be marked with their names, which is more than he'd do for any of our men."

"Sylvester Scott was badly hit. Does he have family?"

"He's not told me about any. Is he upstairs?"

"Yep."

"It's funny. It's the same type of wound that Thomas had. Shoulder wound through and through," Bos said.

"Left or right?"

"Left."

"That's too bad. Scott was your only southpaw. He shot from his left side. He could hit a target at a thousand yards."

The descent of the sun continued. Soon there was just the orange glare.

"How long do you think you're gonna be here?" said Lee Ann.

"I hope to be here for at least two weeks. I need to take a closer look at the stills to get a better sense of how they're operatin' and check the quality of our output. Alvin's already begun the distribution."

"Something I've been meanin' to tell you," Lee Ann said.

"About Wilson?"

"Nope. About us."

"Don't tell me Wilson's going to run for another term?"

"Nope. I'm pregnant," Lee Ann said.

Bos stood up. His wife was leaning against the porch railing facing west. The sun had set and there was a smattering of orange light still in the west.

Bos kissed Lee Ann and picked her up in his arms. She still only weighed 120 pounds.

"Does this mean you might be puttin' some weight on?" He laughed.

"It does look that way," she said with a smile.

She hoped she wasn't being too presumptive with her husband. She suspected she was probably only several weeks pregnant. She could already feel something different inside.

Chapter Twenty-Nine

Liberators on the Loose
January 30, 1920
Potomac River

Alvin Morrison had found his calling. A Bachelor of Legal Letters was his goal. Once he had that in hand, he could practice law. His weekend employment with Bos Custer was turning out to be quite profitable and also lots of fun.

His estimate of his payload, though, had been a bit off. Each barrel weighed 83 pounds. Twenty of those barrels totaled over1,600 pounds.

Bos had thought that he would be able to carry 30 barrels, but Alvin disagreed. He wanted to maintain the maneuverability and speed of the Liberators. If he carried more than 20 barrels, it would put him over 2,000 pounds when he included the three men on board.

Those weights led him to reconsider. The two men he'd picked to help with the loading and to man the Lewis guns were Bo Louis and a man known as "Brooklyn." Each was tough as nails. They weighed no more than 160 pounds each. Alvin figured their combined light weight would compensate, at least in part, for his 220 pounds.

Bo Louis was especially proud to be on board. He tried to tell people he was a descendant of the maker of the Lewis guns. He was not. He didn't realize the name was spelled differently.

On Friday night, there was no traffic on the Potomac River. Alvin had learned the hard way to avoid the Potomac River after a heavy rain as it brought loads of debris into the river. That debris could be floating logs or, on rare occasions, floating bodies. Either of those could do some serious damage to his hull or propellers.

January 30 was a clear, cold night. There hadn't been any rain in a week. Alvin was afraid there were fringes of ice on the riverbanks, which might drift into the channel. As he proceeded south toward Fort Washington, it appeared to be clear sailing ahead. He could see small chunks of ice in the channel, but they did not pose a threat.

He shouted back to Bo and Brooklyn and told them that they might want to take cover on the deck. They had brought three mattresses with them. Alvin had tied his own mattress down to the area in front of the helmsman's perch. He thought it might get a little bit wet there from the water spray, but overall, it was protected. The two other men lay down on their mattresses in the exposed cockpit and covered themselves with blankets.

Alvin stood on the helmsman's perch, both hands on the wheel, and decided to rev it up. Even with 20 barrels of alcohol on board, he figured the boat was now cruising at about 50 miles per hour. He had decided to stop every hour and take a 15-minute break. Even with goggles on and a pullover hat, the winter wind was piercing.

Bos had unloosed the Liberators tonight. All 10 of them were following their distribution routes. Almost 600 barrels of alcohol were being delivered just tonight. That would fuel a lot of parties and clubs. Ten of the barrels Alvin was carrying were vodka. The other 10 were scotch. He thought if there was a way to do it without Bos detecting, he would tap into the scotch barrel. He knew better. He knew Bos was a good man. Bos could also be unforgiving. Alvin had no interest in seeing that side of him.

Tonight, the boat's first stop was in Colonial Beach, Virginia. Alvin pulled into that dock shortly after 10:00 p.m.

"Time to get up, sleepyheads!" he yelled to his two companions, who quickly got to their feet.

"Man, that was quick," Brooklyn said.

"It's gonna be quicker unloadin' this stuff."

Alvin could see a single green light on the dock 100 feet ahead.

The routine was to be the same at every stop. A green light meant safe landing. A red light meant keep going.

Alvin put small bumpers on the starboard side of the boat and brought it to a stop. He tied the back of the boat to a cleat on the deck. Bo tied the bow of the boat to a deck support beam.

"Custer delivery?" said a Black man on the dock.

"You got it," Alvin said.

"Twenty barrels?"

"Yep. That's all we carry."

Within 10 minutes, all 20 barrels had been unloaded.

"Sign on the bottom for 20 barrels of vodka," Alvin said.

He handed a clipboard to the man on the dock.

"Easy come, easy go," the deckhand said.

"What's your name?" said Alvin.

"Byron Washington."

"Everybody down here named Washington?"

"It is a popular name. That and Johnson."

"Where is the cash?"

"I was hoping you wouldn't ask."

Alvin counted the bills.

"It adds up."

"It better." Alvin paused to continue the counting. "See ya next week about this time," Alvin said.

He untied the back rope and began to pull away from the dock.

"Okay, back to D.C. to take on another load and then down to Sandy Point, about an hour from here," said Alvin. "You guys can go back to sleep if you want."

"I like this job," Brooklyn said. "I get paid for sleepin'?"

"Yep. That's the way Bos set it up."

He headed the boat back north, gradually got back into what he thought was the channel, and turned up the speed. He knew his final stop tonight was Hampton.

Sixty barrels a night, five nights a week added up to 300 barrels a week. Alvin knew he was only one of 10 delivery boats. He smiled. He acknowledged that Bos was quite the man.

Chapter Thirty

Nevin in Murfreesboro
February 5, 1920
Murfreesboro, North Carolina

The Meherrin River runs through the east end of the town.

"It ain't much of a town," Nevin said to himself.

Of course, he was used to Harpers Ferry, which wasn't much of a town either. The Meherrin emptied into the Chowan River, which Nevin had heard was part of the Inner Banks. He thought to himself if there were inner banks, there must be outer banks, but he'd never heard of them.

Rhonda Murfree's home was on the banks of the Meherrin. He had visited the house several times. He could never quite understand why someone built a house on the banks of a river when they knew the river overflowed on a regular basis.

The house was built on concrete piers that had been drilled into the ground. The bottom floor was actually four feet off ground level.

He pulled his Model T into the driveway. Rhonda was sitting on the front porch, reading a book. She looked up as soon as she heard the engine. Nevin could see the smile on her face. He turned off the ignition and set the brake. By the time he hopped out of the car, she was alongside the driver's door.

"Man, have I missed you!" she said.

She put her arms around him.

"The feelin's mutual."

They kissed for a good minute.

"Is this the part where your father comes out and beats me with a stick?" Nevin said.

"My parents are still workin'. They don't get home until 8:00 to-night. I told them you were comin' down and that we were goin' out to dinner together."

"You'll have to excuse me while I crank it."

Nevin went around to the front of the car and turned the hand crank one revolution. The engine fired up.

"Would you like to drive, my lady?" Nevin said.

"Us country girls don't drive. Although truth be known, I've been drivin' since I was 10," Rhonda said. "My daddy used to work for a white man who let him take a car home every night. If he'd known that I drove the car, my daddy would have been whipped."

"We won't talk about that."

"There's a little restaurant in town where we can eat. It's run by Black folk, and the food is good."

"I hope it tastes as good as you look."

"Well, aren't you sweet. You been drinkin' some of that scotch you been makin'?"

"Nope. None of us drink."

"I know. I heard that from Cookie. Of course, he also told me that none of you ate pork, which I know isn't true."

"Well, let's go. I'm hungry."

They hopped into the front seat of the old Tin Lizzy. Nevin backed around and pulled out onto the dirt road that served the small community where Rhonda's family lived.

"I've been meanin' to ask you, since your last name is Murfree, are you related to the Murfrees from Murfreesboro?" Nevin smiled.

"We *are* the Murfrees. Well, I should say, the white people who used to own my grandparents were the Murfrees. After the Civil War, my people stayed here. They were sharecroppers for close to 40 years. Finally, the Murfrees sold all of their 500 acres of land to my family and one other family. We still farm the land."

"What do you grow down here?"

"Mostly soy and corn. Some tobacco but not much. There's a large stand of apple trees on the northwest corner of the property. I'm in charge of the blueberries and strawberries. I like to think they are the most profitable crop we have."

"Pops always said you had a business head."

"Yep. That's what I like. Business. Unfortunately, not much of a future."

"You've already got a four-year degree from North Carolina A&T." Nevin looked at Rhonda.

"Not really. They wouldn't let me in. It was men only. I had my brother register under the name Rhondo. I attended all the classes myself dressed up as a boy."

"How'd you pass as a boy?"

"It wasn't easy. I had to put the stink on to make sure that nobody got close to me."

They both laughed.

"So I got a degree in Agricultural Economics in my brother's name. Even if it was in my name, what good would it do for a Black woman?"

"Use it to make some money off the land. Look at what my pop did."

"He was lucky."

"Ain't no luck associated with Pops. Just hard work and keepin' your head down."

The center of town was only about a mile away from the Murfrees' home.

"You can park on the street just up there on the right."

Nevin pulled the vehicle into an open spot. His car was at a 45-degree angle to the curb when a white man stepped in front of him.

"We're parkin' here," the white man said.

Nevin looked over at Rhonda.

"Just back up," she said. "We'll find another spot."

"That's not my way," Nevin said.

He brought the vehicle to a stop and opened the driver's door.

"And where be your vehicle?" Nevin said.

"It's comin'," said the white man.

"Well, this is a public street and parkin' is first come, first served."

"Not for you it ain't," the white man said.

"Well, I guess you may have to stop me."

At that point, two other white men came out of the nearby hardware store. One of them was carrying an axe handle. Nevin had two .45s with him, one on his right hip and one in the small of his back. He reached into the back of the bed of the converted Tin Lizzy and pulled out his own axe handle.

"Nevin, no! Get back in the car," Rhonda said.

"I told you, that ain't my way."

"And what do you think you're doing with that axe handle?" one of the white men said.

"I'm gonna stand here and admire it until you nice men get out of my way so I can park in this spot," Nevin said.

"You ain't parkin' anywhere. In fact, we may be disassemblin' this car."

"Educated too," said Nevin. He smiled at Rhonda.

"Yep. Educated enough to give you a lesson," one of the white men said.

The three of them approached Nevin, who figured that the man on the left was probably the most athletic one of the bunch. He didn't want to hurt any of them too badly, but he did want to teach them a lesson.

Nevin quickly thrust the axe handle into the man's solar plexus and then parried to the right to block the blow coming from the man on his right. Nevin brought the left end of the axe handle up into the jaw of the man in the middle who had been doing most of the talking. The man to his right came at him again with a full swing over his shoulder. Nevin parried again with his axe handle and stopped the blow and then came around with the left end of the axe handle and hit the man's forearm sharply, forcing him to drop his axe handle.

Now, Nevin had all three axe handles.

"We can call a truce here and everybody go on their way, or I can finish this off if you want," Nevin said.

Silence. He knew what that meant. He walked back to his car and put two of the axe handles in the back of his vehicle, keeping the other alongside him as he put his vehicle into reverse and backed up.

"You have to put up with this on a daily basis?"

"Not daily but often enough to keep us in our place," Rhonda said.

"Well, this ain't no place for you. I'm takin' you to a place where you'll be treated like a lady."

Nevin headed back to the route he'd followed into Murfreesboro. He and Rhonda didn't talk for almost an hour.

"Do you mind telling me where we're going?"

"We're going to Harpers Ferry, West Virginia, by way of Washington, D.C., *and* we're gonna get married."

Chapter Thirty-One

Cookie and Rhonda
February 7, 1920
LeDroit Park, Washington, D.C.

"I like that girl," Cookie said.

"I knew you would."

"Of course, I knew her before you did." Cookie smiled.

"That's right. She's one of your contractors."

"She knew how to distribute that pork. Murfreesboro is not that big a town, but she could sell more pork than any person I ever saw. She didn't limit herself to Murfreesboro either. She went into every other little town nearby."

"I know. She's a go-getter," Nevin said.

"She's more than that. She's got ambition. She did all that distribution with a horse and wagon. She didn't have no automobile."

"Did she tell you where she'd gone?" said Nevin.

"She just said she was goin' out for a walk. She wanted to look around the neighborhood. If she doesn't already, I bet she'll soon know all the neighbors. She'll know everything there is to know about us."

"Well, that's fine."

"I'm not sleepin' upstairs anymore," said Cookie. "These stairs are too much. That wound to the thigh is still throbbin'."

Nevin watched his father trying to get out of the chair. He could barely get up. When he finally stood up, he stayed there for a full minute until the dizziness went away.

"Man, those cobwebs are somethin'," Cookie said.

"They're more than cobwebs. If it takes you a full minute to get your bearings, that means your circulation is really slow. That's dangerous."

"Living here in Washington is dangerous," said Cookie. He smiled. "In fact, I'm not sure I've ever been far away from danger."

"That may be true. There are things they can do to treat those types of dangers now."

There was a light knock at the front door. Nevin turned around.

"You don't need to knock," said Nevin. He smiled at Rhonda. "This is your home."

"It'll never be my home, Nevin. As soon as I told people where I was stayin', people wanted to tell me the history of the Custer family. It was like it was all scripted. Everybody said the same thing."

"I hope it was good," said Cookie. He laughed.

"More than good."

"If you would like to go for a walk with me in the opposite direction, maybe we can find some people who will say some bad things about us," said Nevin. He laughed.

"Oh, there's plenty of them out there," said Cookie. He laughed along with his son.

"I doubt it," Rhonda said. "But I like your idea. Let's go for a walk down 7th Street. I've heard a lot about Howard University. I'd like to see it."

The university was named after a white general who was in charge of the Freedmen's Bureau, which had been formed to aid recently freed men. Part of that aid was education.

The campus was quite small. The interlocking roads for the most part had not been paved. As a holdover from the Freedmen's Bureau, the administration building was still the largest.

Neither Nevin nor any of his brothers had ever contemplated going to college despite their mother expecting them to.

Nevin had been born in 1890. When the United States entered the war in 1917, he was 26. Cookie's business, which his three sons had worked for all along, did not accommodate attending college. Nevin had no regrets, though. He had learned the pork distribution business as he grew up and helped his brothers run it. With the schooling and love of learning that his mother had instilled in him, he felt he had gotten a good education. He had always loved reading. Wherever he had lived, his rooms had been filled with books.

"Tell me more about your family name," Rhonda said.

"You mean you haven't heard the story? I can't imagine that my father has not bored you to tears recountin' the family history."

"He has not. He seems to be a private man. In fact, the apple did not fall too far from the tree."

"I get the message. You want to know more about me," said Nevin. "Fair enough." Nevin smiled at Rhonda. "You asked for it."

Chapter Thirty-Two

Rhonda Meets Lee Ann

February 8, 1920

Harpers Ferry, West Virginia

"Why didn't you tell me she was white?" said Rhonda.

"You never asked," said Nevin. "In any event, she's Lee Ann. She's not white. She's not Black. She's just Lee Ann. We grew up with her."

"She sure looks white to me. She's about the whitest, blondest person I've ever seen."

"Lee Ann is like a sister to us. I know she can be pretty blunt. She's protective of us, that's all. It'll take a little time, and she'll warm up to you." Nevin opened his arms and invited Rhonda in.

"I'll keep an open mind, Nevin. You want to know what I see?"

"I guess I'm gonna hear it."

"I see a woman who's used to havin' the three of you around her, and she doesn't want that to change. Where do I fit in that little quadrangle?"

"You'll fit just fine. I know you probably don't want me to do this, but I need to talk with Lee Ann. I need to tell her she has to back off and that's it."

"If you do that, she'll never talk to me."

"She'll do what I tell her to do," Nevin said. "She always does. She just wants us all to be happy."

"I'll trust your instincts." Rhonda smiled.

"Can I show you around?" Nevin said.

"Lead the way."

As they walked down the front stairway, they could hear Bos and Lee Ann talking in the kitchen. They walked out the front door onto the porch.

"You know what our family business is, don't you?" Nevin said.

"I know what it used to be," Rhonda said. "Pork production."

"We're expanding. We're now into liquor production."

"I know. Hogs are not real controversial. Liquor gets people fired up."

"You bet it does. Is that something you can live with?"

"You need to give me more facts."

"We're makin' the liquor. In fact, most of it is gonna be made here. There're two stills right behind the house. That big building you see halfway down the hill is the barracks. There're 25 men livin' there. They built the house and the still, and they're gonna operate it and protect it."

"I know you and your brothers fought in France. I know you're brave men, but are you bringin' the war home?"

"Nope, but you need to understand that the war may be comin' to us."

"You told me you were in D.C. on July 19th. Tell me about that."

"That was somethin'."

"Can you give me any details?"

"I can tell you there was a lot of gunfire. There were a lot of men gettin' hit with axe handles, and there were a lot of dead bodies."

"So far, it looks like the three of you have fared pretty well." Rhonda smiled.

"So far."

"So, what happens when you come home one day with a bullet in your chest or don't come home at all?"

"That's why I want you to understand what you're gettin' into, Rhonda. We don't go lookin' for fights, but our goal is to produce liquor and distribute it primarily to Black churches. What they do with it is up to them, but we get a two to three percent return over our costs. The hope is the Black churches use it to help Black folk and promote Black business."

"I know Cookie. I know he is a good businessman. He is an honest businessman. He treated me fairly. He's promised me his sons are all like him. Is he right?"

"You bet he is. Pops is a man of his word."

"Well, show me the rest of your fortress, then."

"Look behind you. There're actually two forts up there."

"They look like they're made of steel."

"They are. One-inch steel plating. See the holes that are on two different levels? Those are gun ports. We're fully expecting that one day the Chicago outfit is gonna come visitin'. We'll be ready for 'em."

"And where will I be when that happens?"

"See that hill about a mile and a half from here? Hopefully, you'll be safe and sound. That third hill further to the west is where Thomas may live. That is, if he chooses to get married."

"Any prospects?"

"Nothing right now, but he's always on the lookout."

"So, I'll be expected to live here?"

"That's up to you. We have our home in D.C. Mom and Pops used to live in D.C. Monday through Friday. On Friday evenings, we came out here. Lee Ann lived here with my father's partner, Joe Harper, and his wife. She was raised by them."

"But you said her maiden name is the same as yours. How is that?"

Nevin explained Lee Ann's connection with General Custer.

"We're goin' to D.C. tomorrow. Before we leave, I'll take you over to the hog farm. At heart, we're just hog farmers."

"I think you're a lot more than that." Rhonda smiled.

Both stills were in full operation. The water supply came from the stream about a thousand yards away. The water was pumped up through a canvas hose. Calpurnia Custer had developed a combination cotton and hemp thread that served as the main component of the hose. She had made hundreds of yards of it for her husband's hog operation. The hoses were used to drain waste and to supply water to the hogs. The tight weave Calpurnia designed made the hoses waterproof, although they sometimes bled small amounts.

Cookie had developed a simple hydroelectric system alongside the stream. He set up a paddle system where the movement of the stream moved the paddles and served as a generator. The movement of the paddles then moved the spinning coil of wire between two magnets, which generated the electrical energy to drive the pump.

Nevin explained the operation of the two stills. One of them was devoted only to scotch. The second still produced gin three days a week and vodka three days a week. Using the same still for both liquors had the benefit of giving the vodka some flavor.

Rhonda was fascinated by the early warning system that Bos had developed. She loved birds. She protested about keeping them in captivity. Once she understood that they were released every 30 days, she became more tolerant.

Anywhere from 10 to 30 birds were kept inside each net. The net itself was quite expansive. After a month, the birds in the net were let free. A new batch of birds was then put in. Each net had plenty of food.

They walked hand in hand around the property.

"Your dad is a smart man, Nevin. What are the chances of my marrying him?" Rhonda smiled at her joke.

"I could bring up the subject with him. Even though Mom has been gone for 10 years, he's still committed to her."

"I can see that, for sure."

Chapter Thirty-Three

Lady Monica
March 1, 1920
Harpers Ferry, West Virginia

"Bos, there're three men out here to see ya," Rhonda said.

Bos had been working in the back of the house reviewing income figures that Rhonda had compiled.

"Who are they?" Bos said.

"They said they're miners from Tucker County, West Virginia. If I had to guess, I'd say they want your help with something." Rhonda paused. "Are you going to talk to 'em or not?"

"Okay. Tell 'em I'll just be a minute."

Bos finished what he was doing and walked to the front of the house. He saw three Black men who looked like coal miners. Their short, cropped hair was filled with dust. Their clothes looked like they'd been crawling through dirt. The shoes on their feet had strange scuff marks on their toes.

Bos opened the front door of the house and stepped outside. One man stepped forward and extended his hand.

"Mr. Custer, I'm Jacob Foster."

"Bos Custer. How can I help you men?"

"In case you haven't noticed, we're coal miners. We came here to ask for your help. This man to my right is Joe Williams. The other is Fancy Hart."

Bos smiled. Fancy Hart was one of the few men Bos Custer had met who was larger than his own father. Fancy was at least six feet eight and had to weigh 300 pounds.

"I'm surprised a man your size would fit in a mine." Bos smiled.

"That's how he got his name. More times than I can count, he's gotten himself stuck in a crevice, but he always had some fancy way of getting out of it," Jacob Foster said.

"It's a pleasure to meet all of you. What can I do for you?"

Foster took the lead. "We've heard that you're a good man and that sometimes you try to help people. Well, we need some as soon as possible."

"I've got a business to run and a growin' family. I'm not sure I need any more problems, but tell me what's up."

"We work in a small mine in Tucker County, not too far from here. The mine is called Lady Monica. It's owned by a local company. It's one of the few mines anywhere that employs Black men and has them working alongside white men. Of course 100 feet underground, we all look Black. The mine was recently taken over by a new company. They have not only segregated us, but they have put all the Black workers in the portion of the mine that is the most dangerous."

"How many miners are there?"

"There're about 60. Black and white. They are about evenly divided. We barely scrape out a living. We all live side by side, white and Black."

"I'm not exactly a labor negotiator, you know."

"We know you're not, but the owners brought in some roughnecks from Pennsylvania with axe handles. They're bustin' the heads of any miners who refuse to work according to the new work rules. We're all hard men, but we can't stand up to these guys."

"So, you want me to come to your mine and rough them up?"

"We know these new owners have money. They can afford to improve mine safety. The Black and white miners have gotten along for as long as I've been there, which is more than 10 years. We just want to work, protect ourselves, and take care of our families."

"I should have invited you men inside. My wife might have a second thought about that given the amount of coal dust you brought along. Have a seat here on the porch, and I'll get you something to drink."

Bos brought back a pitcher of cold lemonade and four glasses. "I'd offer you some beer, but I'd probably have to charge you for that. I hope lemonade will do?"

The three men smiled. Bos brought over a chair and sat down with the three of them.

"You may have come at the right time. We're busy with our production here but things have been somewhat quiet for the last couple of weeks. My men could probably use some excitement. Tell me what you have in mind."

The four men talked for 30 minutes. Bos was impressed.

"How far is your mine from where we are right now?"

"It's close to 100 miles. In this beat-up old wagon we came in, it's taken us close to two days to get here. I understand that you have cars and trucks."

"So, we're looking at a four- to five-hour trip to get there. It's four in the afternoon now. I suggest you men spend the night here with us. We got plenty of beds for ya. Are these guys with the axe handles gonna know we're comin'?"

"As far as I know, the owners don't know what's up. Most of these owners are so used to gettin' their way, they couldn't imagine any miners fightin' 'em."

"How many of these hooligans with axe handles are we talkin' about?"

"About 15."

"We'll take two trucks. I'll bring a total of 10 of my men with me, so with you three we'll make 14. My men all know how to use axe handles, but they also know how to use firearms. Just to be on the safe side, we'll bring both."

"Mr. Custer, we appreciate whatever you can do for us."

"We need to start by you callin' me Bos, short for Boston, and not Mr. Custer."

The three men stood up and shook hands with Bos Custer.

"We leave tomorrow morning at 6:00 a.m. Plan on arriving before noon. Let me show you where your bunks are. Dinner is served at 6:00. No alcohol."

The three men nodded in agreement.

Chapter Thirty-Four

Road to Monica

March 2, 1920

Lady Monica Mine, Tucker County, West Virginia

Bos had calculated that they could make it to the mine by noon. His calculations were wrong. The road to Tucker County was anything but groomed. The detours and obstructions were endless. A little after 2:00 p.m., they pulled into the mining camp.

The 30-plus ramshackle houses were within eyesight of a large hole in the ground that had a sign with the name "Lady Monica" on it.

The houses were where most of the miners lived. Many of them had families. Some of the men were single and lived in group homes. There were Black and white children everywhere. Bos got out of the lead truck and motioned to Foster.

"Lead the way," Bos said.

"I'm sure they saw us comin'. No doubt they'll be here shortly."

Bos addressed the 10 men he had brought with him.

"Keep your axe handles close. Keep your .45s holstered 'til it looks like there's gonna be gunplay. If I can talk some sense into these people, that would be my preference, but I suspect that's not gonna work."

The men stood by the trucks for nearly 30 minutes.

The mine was a hole in the side of a large mountain. Bos had never been inside a mine, but he envisioned that the horizontal portion eventually led to a vertical portion that went into the ground where the richer coal was deposited. He could hear one large coal car rumbling on the tracks coming out of the mine. As soon as he saw that coal car, he heard trucks rumbling in the distance coming toward the mine. Then, two trucks appeared, loaded with white men who did not appear to be miners.

"What can I do for you boys?" The man who had been riding shotgun in the lead truck spoke first.

Bos stepped forward to meet them.

"Mr. Foster and his friends came to visit me yesterday and said they just want to work in peace for a fair wage in a safe environment."

"Well, isn't that interesting? That's exactly what we want, but we don't want coloreds here."

"I understand these Black men have been workin' with white men for many years. They get along, they live together, and I assume it's been a profitable experience for everybody. Why can't that continue?"

"It can't continue because the new owner says it's not going to continue. Now, you need to get back on your nice new truck and get out of here."

"Sounds like you're not gonna even offer us lemonade," Bos smiled.

By this time, the 10 men Bos had brought with him had gathered around him in a semicircle. Each of them had strapped their Springfield rifles on their backs, and they were leaning on their axe handles as if they were canes. They also purposely exposed the .45s that each of them carried on their hips.

"Looks like you boys came prepared," a white man said.

"We came prepared to make peace. If you want something other than peace, we'll give it to you."

Five of the white men rushed forward with their axe handles on their shoulders as if they were expecting to step up to bat. Bos stepped forward and met the lead man with his own axe handle. He stopped the horizontal blow that the white man attempted to lay on him. He then stroked the man upward with one end of his axe handle, breaking the man's jaw and leaving him on the ground, groaning in pain.

Nevin quickly stepped forward and poked one of the white men with his axe handle right between the eyes. The man went down flat. Nevin then hit another one of the men on the back of his left thigh with such force that it sounded like the axe handle would break. It didn't. The white man on the receiving end of the blow fell to the ground, holding his left leg. He approached the other two white men who had charged forward. They had made the mistake of standing in close proximity to each other. Nevin swung a horizontal blow, hitting the first man in the chin and the second, shorter man on the top of his head. Both men fell to the ground, bleeding profusely.

When Nevin saw the leader of the group start to get up, he kicked him in the gut and put his boot on the man's neck. "This is just the appetizer."

"We didn't come here to hurt your boys," said Bos. "We came to make sure that Foster, Williams, Hart, and the other Black men in this minin' town continue workin' like they did before. You just met my little brother. He's a one-man wreckin' crew. He's nothin' compared to the other nine I brought with me."

"I might disagree with that," Nevin said.

He and Bos smiled at each other. Bos stepped over to the leader of the group.

"So what's it gonna be?"

"We've got plenty of work here for everyone," the man said. "I guess we can go back to the old system. If that's what these men want, that's what we'll give 'em."

"It's not just what they want. It's what's fair. If you're not prepared to do that now and in the days to come, let me know. I don't want to have to come back here, but if I do, we won't be carryin' axe handles and rifles. We'll be comin' back with Thompson submachine guns."

"We can live with that," the white man said.

"I'm glad to hear that. Just to make sure that we all know what we're gettin', I'm gonna put that in writin', and you and Mr. Foster are gonna sign it. Can I assume you know how to read and write?"

"I do."

Bos looked at Foster but didn't get a response.

"I just happened to bring my own paper and pencil."

Bos walked back to the truck and wrote down what he said was the agreement.

"I need your name," he said.

"Ebeneezer Green."

"You might have to spell that for me. The first name that is. I can probably spell the last."

Bos put the finishing touches on the one-page document, read it out loud, and then directed Mr. Green and Jacob Foster to sign it.

"Foster's gonna keep this document. I'm only a few hours away. If he or anyone else comes and tells me that you violated the terms of this agreement, I'll be back to enforce the agreement, not to renegotiate it. Do you understand?"

"I understand."

Chapter Thirty-Five

Lee Ann Delivers
September 1, 1920
LeDroit Park, Washington, D.C.

"I'd like to deliver this baby in a hospital," said Lee Ann. "I know the family tradition may be to deliver at home, but I'd feel a lot safer at Freedmen's."

"You're in charge," said Bos. "I know I can be controllin'. This is new ground for me."

"Same here." She smiled.

Two hours later, Lee Ann was starting to feel frequent contractions. Bos said he would go across the street to ask Mrs. Roybal to come over. Bos was reluctant to ask for help. He didn't know what the contractions meant. He knocked on the door of the Roybal residence. He saw the smiling face of Mrs. Roybal.

"I was hoping I might hear from you. How is she doing?"

"Contractions. She says she's havin' a lot of contractions."

"That's good. That's what comes first. Let me come over and try to help. I can let her know when it's time to go to the hospital. My husband would drive her but he's out getting some groceries."

Mrs. Roybal invited Bos inside. It had been many years since he had been in the Roybal home. He had fond memories of playing with their older son and of Mrs. Roybal making cookies for the boys. Bos knew that Cookie had helped the Roybals out financially. He and the Roybals were too proud to make any mention of it.

Mrs. Roybal entered the Custer residence. She walked to Lee Ann who was sitting on the living room couch.

"Lots of pain, dear?"

"Not that much, but the contractions are comin' pretty close to-gether."

"Have you been timing them?"

"Not precisely, but I think they're about two minutes apart."

"That's good. That means you're close." She looked at Bos. "Young man, I think you need to take this young lady to the hospital. You go out and get the car ready. I'll help her get her things together, and we'll be out."

The Custer family was familiar with the new 278-bed Freedmen's Hospital. Cookie had been a patient *and* a benefactor. They liked him better as a benefactor. The feeling was mutual. Cookie didn't like hospitals. He had seen too many men die in Civil War hospitals. If you entered a hospital during war time, you didn't come back.

The staff of the hospital greeted Lee Ann at the front door. Bos felt like his wife was in good hands. He drove his car back to the house in LeDroit Park and left it there. He then proceeded on foot back to the hospital. Mrs. Roybal insisted on staying with Lee Ann.

She came out to the waiting room to give Bos periodic updates. He appreciated what she was doing. Her consideration made him think of his own mother. She would be doing the same thing if she had still been alive.

Bos thought for a moment about the hundreds of men he had killed over the years. He had no remorse. No sorrow. They were combatants. They knew what they were getting into. Maybe, just maybe he could make amends for all the death he had caused by bringing a healthy baby into the world. He smiled at the thought of this circle of life.

Two hours later, Mrs. Roybal came through the door from the obstetrics area with a big smile on her face.

"You're the proud father of a 10-pound baby boy." As she hugged Bos, she thought she felt this huge, powerful, good man cry. "Have you thought of a name?"

"I have. What do you think of Harper?"

"From Harpers Ferry?"

"Yep. Let me check with Lee Ann."

Bos walked down the corridor to the obstetrics door, thinking about how this new addition to the family was going to change things. He knew Lee Ann had thought it through, but up until then, he hadn't. Now the reality of a new baby scared him.

Chapter Thirty-Six

Lee Ann in the White House
February 15, 1921
Washington, D.C.

"He will not be seeing anyone today," Lee Ann said.

She was addressing the president's chief of staff. Only she and Mrs. Wilson had direct access to the president. Most of the time, he stayed in the private quarters. Sometimes, he would venture out. Mrs. Wilson discussed issues with him and tried to make sure that she was following his directive, but she was the decision-maker. She and Lee Ann.

Lee Ann knew better than Mrs. Wilson how the president thought, what he preferred, and what direction he wanted to go. The president could express all those ideas, but he tired quickly, and he had no ability to follow up.

As a result, all meetings with congressional leaders had to be spaced out. More than one or two such meetings a week exhausted him.

He had hoped to be nominated for the presidency a third time. At the Democratic National Convention, electors refused to endorse him. They picked Governor James Cox and Assistant Secretary of the Navy Franklin D. Roosevelt as their ticket. Their opponents were Senator Warren G. Harding and the governor of Massachusetts, Calvin Coolidge.

Cox won all of the southern states but did not win a single northern state. Although Cox had endorsed Wilson's policies, he ran a defensive campaign. Harding endorsed a return to normalcy, arguing that America needed to focus on America and not European affairs.

The White House in early 1921 was a somber place. Lee Ann spent her workweek in Washington and her weekends in West Virginia. The trek northwest to Harpers Ferry had become familiar. She didn't mind the trip, especially with the baby. Bos always came on Friday and picked her and the baby up at 3:00 on Friday afternoon. They drove to Harpers Ferry on a two-lane road through Loudoun County, Virginia.

Bos loved to talk about the liquor operation. He could sell his scotch now that it had aged for a year. To the connoisseurs, that wasn't much, but it was better than being only six months old. He was distributing more than 3,000 barrels of liquor per week.

Rhonda had become the chief bookkeeper and financial officer. She kept close tabs on who was receiving, how much, and their payments. When the payments slowed down, the distribution to those churches slowed down. She had developed pen pal relationships with almost all of the pastors up and down the East Coast. With every distribution, she sent a letter confirming how many barrels they had received and how many they had paid for. She demanded that with each delivery the pastor note on the bottom of her letter how much cash was being returned. That made her bookkeeping easier and also kept her delivery personnel honest when it came to controlling inventory and handling money.

In late January, Mrs. Wilson announced that when she and the president left the White House, they would be staying in Washington. She had picked out a townhouse in the Kalorama section of the city. The president had decided that he would open a law practice with the former secretary of state, Bainbridge Colby. Wilson was not a lawyer, but he would be the magnet that would draw in the business, and Colby would be the one who practiced law.

To Lee Ann's surprise, Mrs. Wilson had reacted well to her newborn. As a woman raised in the segregated South, Mrs. Wilson had specific notions about the separation of Blacks and whites. She had reacted with joy to the news of Lee Ann's pregnancy. Even knowing that her child would be Black.

Lee Ann went into the kitchen that was on the lower level of the White House. This was a place she had frequented, so the staff noticed her right away when she entered.

"As you know, I'll be leaving shortly. The president's last day is March 4. On that day, you'll have a new president in the White House. I'm hopeful that President Wilson will come down here and speak to you and say goodbye. You should not be offended if he does not. I wanted all of you to know how much I appreciate what you have done for me and for the president over these eight years. Most of you know my husband. You have seen him around. Even to this day, he has to come in the back entrance."

She smiled. The staff that had congregated was all Black. They smiled back at her.

"Race is a difficult issue to talk about. My husband and I frequently discuss it. I'm aware of the humiliations he suffers on a daily basis. He suffers them in silence. I know you do the same. I do not have to endure those humiliations. But someday, I will. Our children are not and will not be blonde haired and blue eyed like me. You know that since you have cared for our son for the last several months."

Lee Ann smiled, and the staff nodded.

"I expect that as my children grow, I will experience many of the humiliations that my husband does. I will experience them through my children. I want you to know that when I leave this house, I leave with my head held high. I know that my husband and I have served this president well. In his own way, President Wilson is a good man. I don't agree with a lot of his policies. I don't agree with a lot of his thinking. But there is more I agree with than I disagree with. That is part of the reason why I've stayed with him. I know that you don't have any reason to get into those policy-type issues. I do know, however, that you have been loyal to me and to him. For that, I thank all of you."

She embraced each of the 10 kitchen workers, one by one. These good people had taken care of George Custer, the baby of Bos and Lee Ann for six months, ever since he was born. Bos's hopeful name of Harper had not passed muster with Lee Ann. Each day during that time, Lee Ann arrived early at the White House, usually driven by Bos or one of his brothers. She entered through the service entrance with her baby boy. The kitchen workers had been loyal, kind, and caring. Lee Ann would not forget them. They would not forget baby George. He was named after Lee Ann's great-uncle, the general.

Chapter Thirty-Seven

Lee Ann Is Pregnant Again
March 4, 1921
Washington, D.C.

The stroke he experienced on October 2, 1919, had left Wilson paralyzed on his left side with only partial vision in his right eye. The stroke also left him with impaired impulse control and difficulty making decisions. Through the remainder of his term, he was physically disabled. In October 1919, Wilson had vetoed the Volstead Act but Congress was able to override the veto.

On March 3, 1921, he met with the man who was to succeed him. Senator Warren G. Harding had won more than 60 percent of the popular vote in the 1920 election. Because of his declining health, Wilson was not able to attend the inauguration, but now they were meeting for tea in the Oval Office.

"Mr. President, Senator Warren G. Harding, the president-elect, is here to meet you." Lee Ann made her announcement as she entered with the incoming president.

Wilson was seated in a chair opposite his desk. He did not stand up to greet Harding, who had been briefed on the president's condition. He offered a gracious smile and a warm handshake to Wilson.

By this time, Mrs. Wilson had been reported in the press as being the de facto president of the United States. She chose to refrain from meeting Harding because she found the man distasteful. Lee Ann was the stand-in.

Two of the presidential attendants brought in tea and cookies for the soon-to-be ex-president and soon-to-be new president. They conversed briefly about the effect that Prohibition was having on the country. Harding commented that the enforcement efforts were being strengthened. He projected that Prohibition would not only be effective but that the liquor trade would soon be brought to a halt.

Wilson looked at Lee Ann and winked.

The meeting between the two men was cordial. As the president-elect left the Oval Office on his way to the inauguration, Lee Ann walked him to the door, where a single Secret Service agent met him.

Lee Ann walked back into the Oval Office.

"Mr. President," Lee Ann said to Wilson. "I have a surprise for you."

He pulled his head up and smiled.

"I hope it's good news."

"It is. I'm going to have another baby," Lee Ann said with a big smile.

Wilson returned the smile.

He looked at her quizzically.

"Have I met your husband?"

"You have. He's a fine man."

"Is that the young fellow from the Bureau of Investigation?"

Lee Ann smiled.

"No, it's the young man who helped you and your wife about 18 months ago with the battle here in the Oval Office."

"Oh yes, I remember."

Clearly, he did not remember.

Mrs. Wilson came into the Oval Office and addressed her husband.

"We're all packed and ready to go, dear."

"Okay. I'm going to miss this place. Lee Ann, are you coming with us?"

"No, Mr. President. I have a new job."

"She's about to become a mother again," Mrs. Wilson said. "Did she tell you?"

"Yes she did. It's great news," Wilson said.

He stood up slowly. Mrs. Wilson took his right arm and led him to the door.

"Well, Lee Ann, I guess you're the last one out," Mrs. Wilson said.

"We couldn't have made it this far without you," the president said.

"Oh, I think you could have. I think you'll do quite well in your new home."

The presidential couple turned and slowly walked out the door.

Lee Ann walked behind the presidential desk. She knew in a couple of hours that a new president would occupy this room. The issues had not changed. No doubt the approach to addressing them would.

She was going to miss Washington. She knew that she would be back in the city but not as a presidential advisor. She would no longer have access to the White House, but she would see the people who worked there, such as the unnoticed ones who cut the grass, cooked the meals, and cleaned the bathrooms. Those people would stay on and continue to be Lee Ann's conduit to the seat of power.

Chapter Thirty-Eight

Year-Old Scotch
April 5, 1921
Harpers Ferry, West Virginia

"Why don't you sample it," Bos said.

"You said it's 200 proof," said Lee Ann.

"Well, that's what we tell people, but it couldn't possibly be 200 proof. That would be 100 percent alcohol. That's impossible. It's got other ingredients in it. But it's got some kick to it."

"I'll take a sip of it, but I want it in a glass filled with ice. That should dilute it nicely," Lee Ann said.

"You know we don't have ice here. What we do have is mountain-cold water. That spring water is probably not more than 45 degrees."

"That'll do."

Under other circumstances she might have walked down to the stream herself to get the water.

"You stay here," said Bos. "I don't want you fallin' down the hill and hurtin' that baby."

Ten minutes later, he came back with a canteen filled with cold stream water. He filled the glass and added a touch of scotch from the barrel. The water turned golden.

"It looks good," she said.

"It's only a year old so technically it's not scotch. But the barrels we got from Kentucky give this a lot of flavor," Bos said.

She put the glass to her lips. "It's an acquired taste." Lee Ann smiled.

"That it is. Acquired by many and acquired by many very quickly." Bos laughed. "Let me try it," he said.

He picked up the glass and took a sip.

"Well, for a man who's not a drinkin' man, it tastes pretty good," he said.

"I suspect that people who imbibe are not purists," Lee Ann said.

"That barley you've been bringin' us is the real deal."

"I'm not so sure it's the barley itself. It's the way you've been treatin' it. It looks like from everything we've read, the way you're steepin' it and then tossin' it is allowin' it to germinate properly."

"The thing that amazed me is when we put it into the kiln for dryin'. None of it gets singed."

"That's because you're using the peat in the fire. That gives the barley the flavor and creates all the smoke," Lee Ann said. "Where have you been gettin' that yeast from?"

"There's a farmer about 20 miles east of here. He started growin' the fungus about 10 years ago. He said there's probably fifty stills within 100 miles of his place. All of them get their yeast from him."

"Is that legal?"

"Yep. Yeast is just a fungus. In this case, it causes the fermentation, which produces the alcohol."

"I thought we might be able to do with one copper still. Now we're up to 10."

"Is Sylvester still your chief distiller?" Lee Ann said.

"You bet he is. He's able to run all 10 of these stills. We built this house thinkin' it would be our home and there would be only one still here. Now, we've got 10 stills and we're the center of production."

"I'd leave it as is, Bos. I like being in the center of everything."

"Do you think that single warehouse is large enough to hold all these barrels?"

"Probably not. After all, we are a growing family." Lee Ann looked down at her belly and smiled.

"Have you been talking with Rhonda at all about our income?" said Bos.

"No. I've been occupied with other things."

"The numbers are amazing, Lee Ann. We can't keep up with the demand. The money is flowin' like you wouldn't believe. I'm thinkin' we need a second barracks to accommodate all these men."

"All these single men here and no women. Is this gonna work?"

"You mean all these Black men?"

"No. I mean all these men."

"I know. I was just teasin'. I'm thinkin' we can rotate these men in and out: 30 days in and 30 days out. When they're out, they would be free to do as they wish and go where they want. I would pay them up-front for those 30 days. If they chose not to come back, then so be it. If they did come back, they would stay on the payroll. That gives everyone a little breathin' room."

"I like that idea. Give the men the type of freedom they need."

Lee Ann smiled. Bos looked at her and nodded his head.

Bos extended his hand to his wife. They both stood up and walked to the stairway in the middle of the porch. They walked down together.

"Kind of like our wedding day," Bos said.

Lee Ann didn't respond.

"Penny for your thoughts?" Bos said to his wife.

"I'm concerned about what you're doin' with this alcohol. The reason that Congress voted for Prohibition is because of the problems with alcohol. Too many men gettin' drunk, spending their paycheck, beatin' up their wives. What are you doing to the Black community? Aren't you just promotin' that same kind of behavior?"

"I thought about that. Black men are Black men. If they want alcohol, they're gonna get it. They're gonna get it from whatever source they can. Maybe I am makin' it easier for them to get it. But I'm relyin' on these Black pastors to practice what they preach. To enforce what our goals are. Our goals are to generate wealth so they can have a better life. That's my goal. That's my only goal."

"Aside from gettin' a return on your investment," Lee Ann smiled.

"Aside from gettin' a return on my investment," Bos said.

"I wouldn't be countin' much on the pastors practicing what they preach. You know what Lincoln said. He was once asked if he was a religious man and if not, why not. He said he hadn't yet found a preacher who practiced what he preached. He said that once he found one he probably would have found religion."

Chapter Thirty-Nine

The Weakest Link
April 9, 1921
Colonial Beach, Virginia

Bos thought he could get away with a year-old scotch, when three years of curing is the minimum. The alcohol was there. Some said it was too much, and Bos was inclined to agree. He knew that could be altered with water. Cookie had taught him that the solution to pollution was dilution. Battle wounds, wounds from wrestling hogs, cuts and scrapes from farming could all be cured with enough water. This problem with the scotch could also be solved with water.

Bos had made many of the first deliveries himself. He had waited for the sampling. Most of the time they produced smiles. Sometimes not.

The late-night Friday run to Colonial Beach was cold. The boat was loaded with barrels. It was just Bos and Alvin Morrison. The two helpers had been given the night off. Mid-April could still be cold. Forty-five degrees running at 40 to 50 miles per hour tested the body's insulation. Bos had come prepared with layers of clothing and a rain slicker to fight off the cold.

He enjoyed Alvin. They shared their experiences in northern France. Alvin had volunteered for combat there, but it took six months before he saw any. His unit was a group of Black cooks and kitchen staff who were armed by the French and put into the trenches. The kitchen staff knew how to slice and dice. Alvin was the senior noncommissioned officer.

"That first day in the trenches turned us upside down. The French did not have enough rifles for us, so they gave us bayonets. They didn't know we could improvise," Alvin said.

"What do you mean?" said Bos.

"That first day, two platoons of Germans came over the top. There were only ten of us. The lead Germans jumped into the trenches. They had no idea we were there. We hacked probably 20 of them to death. At that point, we had their Mausers and handguns."

"They probably thought you were white guys in black face."

"I didn't care what they thought. After that first wave, we had plenty of rifles and ammo. We attacked the remaining Germans. It was blood and guts all over. We had no mercy."

"One of the French officers had given me his side arm. You won't believe what it was. It was an American-made Smith and Wesson .38 six shot. Almost worthless in the trenches because it took too much time to reload."

"Pretty stupid."

"I had a pitchfork that I had picked up in one of the open fields. I put it to good use. If you can imagine, I'm spearing these guys with a pitchfork and the rest of the guys are shooting the Germans or cutting them up with bayonets."

"Sounds like you taught 'em a few things."

"I doubt it. That night, they put all of us back in the kitchen. I insisted our men carry their Mausers strapped to their backs and keep on their bloody uniforms. We served 100 French soldiers looking that way. They had no clue what we had done."

"Did they ever?"

"The day we left France, one of the French officers came to me and offered his hand. He had tears in his eyes. He apologized for the way we had been treated. I think he was really sorry, but he still didn't get it. My guys may have been uneducated and barely able to utter a sentence, but they fought like hell day after day and never got any recognition."

"We had a little different experience but not by much," said Bos.

"Funny," said Alvin, "the French had trouble saying pitchfork. For the rest of our stay in France, I was known as the BEETCHFORK." He smiled.

The lights ahead indicated they were coming up on Colonial Beach. Alvin had keen eyes. "I can see the whites of their eyes and their skin. I don't like what I see, Bos. Plus, there is no green light."

"I'll get two of the Lewis guns ready."

Bos wasn't sure how accurate Alvin's eyes were. What he saw on the deck as they approached were three figures. Two were holding long barrel guns. He saw no clue as to their skin color.

The first shot rang out as the boat was about 50 yards from the deck. Bos didn't hesitate. The Lewis gun began chattering. Bos purposely aimed low. He didn't realize that the deck platform was supported by only two vertical piers. Both of them broke off. The deck platform began to sink. The three men on the deck slid into the water.

"Bos, isn't it time to get out of here?"

"Nope. We need to see what happened to the men who were supposed to greet us."

Bos told Alvin to pull straight in to where the deck had just been standing. He was concerned about the water depth. From the bow of the boat, he was able to jump on what was left of the deck platform.

"Pull into deeper water and just idle. You know where the Thompsons are. Keep one ready. If any shootin' starts, back off. No heroics. This boat is more important than I am."

Bos unholstered the .45 on his right hip. As he moved ahead, he saw what appeared to be two men tied to a tree.

"Jackson, is that you?" Bos said.

The reply was muffled. Bos could see that the two men had something over their mouths. They couldn't talk. Bos smiled as he approached.

"I told you to be on the lookout. Word has gotten around about my fine scotch. You're lucky they didn't lynch you."

He removed the tape from their mouths. Both men shook their heads.

"Nobody told us we would get kidnapped before we even got here," Jackson said.

"I told you there's a lot of interest in my product, and it ain't friendly. I expected better," Bos said.

"Where are the three guys on the deck?" Jackson said.

"The current at this point is pretty swift," said Bos. "Unless they are good swimmers, they're probably still floatin' down the river or swimmin' with the fish, as they say. That's not my concern. Are you able to help us unload our barrels and get them back to your distribution point?"

"We will, Bos. We work for the preacher. He said you're a man of God. We are too."

"I don't care much about being a man of God. I'm just distributing liquor, and I want it done right. Did they steal your weapons, too?"

"Looks like they did."

"Have you ever fired a Thompson?"

"Never."

"I'll leave one of mine with you. As soon as Alvin pulls the boat in and we unload, I'll give you a quick lesson."

"That would be nice of you, Bos."

"My little chain here is only as strong as the weakest link. Right now, you're a weak link. I can't afford weak links. You get the message? Another outcome like this, and we'll be skippin' Colonial Beach."

Bos wasn't smiling.

Together, they unloaded the barrels. Bos turned over one of the Thompsons with two drum magazines. He gave a quick lesson, shook hands, and headed back to the boat.

Bos looked at Alvin.

"Next trip down this way you need to be careful," said Bos. "These boys, they mean well, but I'm not sure they're up to the task. You follow?"

"I do. Our green light system worked," said Alvin. "Maybe it should be a flashing green light so that we know the guys on shore are with us."

"I like that idea. I'll pass it on to Rhonda and have her tell all of the preachers in the river and shore communities that the lighting system will be changing."

"I hope these boys don't get hijacked with the liquor."

Alvin smiled and Bos nodded.

"I hope they don't get lynched when those three bodies wash up on shore."

Chapter Forty

Funding the Investment
April 20, 1921
Baltimore, Maryland

Bos had gotten to know Sylvester Scott, who was a man of few words. Just like Bos. He knew his rifles and his Thompson. He knew the .45 he carried in the small of his back. They were all kept spotless, well-oiled, and ready for action, just like the stills he managed for Bos in Harpers Ferry.

Scott had grown up in the hills of Western North Carolina. His father was a sheep farmer. The mountain lions and other cats of that area had no mercy on the sheep. It was not unheard of to lose 100 head in the course of a year. Teaching the cats to keep their distance was part of the rancher's calling. It not only thinned the herd of cats but also sent a message to them as to where the permitted perimeter was fixed.

"Each March, my daddy and I'd go out for a week," Scott said. "We each had a Winchester and a .45. Two knives. One strapped to the right leg and one to the left. We both knew that if it came time to use the knives for defense, the fight was over. The big cats are too fast and too ferocious for any delay. You only get one shot and it better be at the center of mass. The goal of each was to kill ten big cats. It was eat what you kill. With cats, though, with their long, stringy muscles, the meat was tough and sinewy. Tasteless and dry. But we always showed our respect for these animals. They were predators. We knew that. After we killed one, my father and I would say a prayer over the body of the fallen. You couldn't help but admire them. They were warriors. Ruthless warriors. I never forgot that lesson."

Bos nodded.

"It sounds like we were raised by similar men," he said.

"So what's my job here today, Bos?"

"Protection. I'm meeting with some local preachers. I think they're good men, but I'm not in a position where I can trust people. I want to know who's watchin' me and who might be comin' into this church. I plan on being the first one to enter."

"Why don't we drive around for fifteen minutes and get a sense of the landscape. Do you know how many entrances there are?"

"Not sure. But I intend to close off all of them except the front one after I enter."

They drove for 20 minutes with Scott observing.

Bos finally parked two blocks from the church. Scott picked up his Mauser.

"Give me 20 minutes to find a good observation point. Then you can enter the church."

Bos followed the man's instructions.

"Good morning, Pastor Johnson," Bos said as he approached the entrance of the church.

"Mr. Custer, it is good to see you," the pastor said. "I think we're the first to arrive."

"We are indeed. I got here a bit early."

The pastor opened the front door of the church. They both entered. Bos had been in the church before and knew there were other entrances.

"You are punctual. I like that in a businessman," the pastor said.

"No sense in delaying. I might as well tell you I'm not happy with the return on my investment. I was hoping that you could help your community, and I would get a return, but I'm not seeing it."

"I hear ya. We're trying to do better."

"You've seen enough of me to know that I don't much care about effort. I care about results. I'm not seeing them."

"Should we wait for the others to arrive?"

"No sense in waiting. I've said all I have to say."

Bos extended his hand. He had made sure that they stayed in the back of the church so he could keep an eye on the side exits. He had not seen any of those doors open. He had no sense that anyone else was inside.

The pastor opened the front door. Bos sensed that something was wrong. He didn't know if the pastor was the setup man. He wouldn't be surprised if the Torrio gang had gotten to him and offered him better terms.

Bos unholstered the .45 on his right hip. He held it by his leg as he approached the front door. Bos stayed behind the cinderblock pillar just outside the door. He figured the pastor was not in danger. He was wrong. A shot rang out from the right and hit the pastor in the left shoulder. He fell back into the open door. Bos pulled him further inside.

Bos heard two more shots in quick succession. They sounded like Scott's rifle. There was something distinctive about the Mauser. It had a very crisp clap.

"Do you have any idea who the shooter is?" Bos said to the pastor.

"No."

"I don't know if they're gunnin' for me or you," said Bos. "We have an interest in workin' together on this."

"I know. I was not expecting this. The fact that my fellow board members have not shown up makes me suspicious."

"I have a man outside who can take care of the problem, but I need to know if this was a setup."

The pastor was failing. Bos believed the pastor was telling the truth. The other church elders who were supposed to show up had not. Bos assumed they were in on the ambush. He pulled the pastor further into the church and asked him if there were any tunnels leading outside.

"No. The best way to get out front without being seen is to go through that side door. It is covered and leads to the side building where you can enter and then exit on the far side."

Bos took him at his word and followed that route. When he got to the far side of the building, he had no clue where Sylvester Scott was. He had parked his car two blocks away. He figured his best bet was to get to that car. Scott would find him.

When Bos got to the car, he saw that the two front tires had been punctured with a knife. He knew this had to be the work of Torrio's gang. He saw a glint in the distance. He knew Scott would not let that happen by mistake. The reflection was intended. It must be Scott telling him his location. Bos smiled. He walked toward where the reflection was coming from and circled around. Scott had positioned himself on top of a four-story building where he had a clear view of the church. Bos climbed up the exterior fire escape.

"What the hell happened here?" Bos said.

"The shooter was on that building at two o'clock from here," Scott said. "He had a clear shot of the front door. Once he took it, he stood up and exited. You probably didn't hear my shot. I got him in the back as he was preparing to go down the fire escape."

"Why are you still here?" said Bos.

"Just waiting for you. I thought there might be another shooter waiting for you at the car. There wasn't. Just two local kids. They must've hired them to puncture your tires."

"Did you see the shooter go down the fire escape?"

"He didn't. He's still on top of the roof," Scott said.

"Let's take a look."

They walked a block to the other building.

The man had to be part of Torrio's gang. Torrio had a dress code. White shirt and black shoes.

Bos felt his neck for a pulse. Nothing.

"I'm gonna take one of his shoes. I'll send it to Torrio. He must've thought the preacher was me. Unfortunately, we all look alike." Bos smiled.

"How is the preacher doing?" said Scott.

"Let's get back to the church and tend to him."

Bos walked away from the dead man and back to the church with Scott.

Chapter Forty-One

Black Churches Burn

May 1, 1921

Harpers Ferry, West Virginia

"This is now 10 churches that have burned," Bos said.

"You know who's doin' it," Nevin said.

"I do. It's got to be Torrio," Thomas said.

"So what are we doin'?" said Cookie.

"You don't do anything," Bos said.

"I can help out," Cookie said.

Cookie stood up.

"Best thing you can do is to stay here and make sure Lee Ann is safe," Bos said.

"They didn't like our little warehouse fire. I think we need to take it closer to home," Nevin said.

"What do you mean?" Bos said.

"I mean we take it straight to Torrio's house," said Nevin.

"That means he'll retaliate against West Virginia or our LeDroit Park home," Bos said. "Do you really think we're ready for that?"

"We went into this knowin' there were no boundaries," said Nevin. "If you want to start drawin' boundaries now, we might as well change our focus. We're not mass murderers, but these guys know no limits. We need to play by the same rules. I say we destroy Torrio's home."

"If they're going to burn down churches, even at night, they're not just trying to send a message," said Cookie. "They want to break us. We need to break them."

Bos walked around the dining room table. He never took more than a few seconds to make a decision. This time, he was hesitating. After three revolutions around the table, he made up his mind.

"I agree with Nevin. It's all-out war. Torrio and Capone know nothing less."

"When do we start?" said Thomas.

"First thing in the morning. We have Torrio's home address. We'll draw the wife out during the day, make sure no one else is inside, and then level the house," Bos said.

"Some horrible times comin'," Cookie said.

"I know. I know it well," Bos said.

"I don't see where we have any choice," said Nevin.

"We better get movin'," Thomas said.

Bos waved to his brothers and father. Without saying a word, he proceeded upstairs. Lee Ann was waiting at the top of the stairs.

"Do you know what you're gettin' into?" she said. She had heard the conversation.

"No idea." Bos smiled. He put his arm around Lee Ann, and they walked into the bedroom.

"You've seen what the Chicago mob will do, Bos. They know no limits. You do. The two don't mix."

"I don't know if any other response would work. In the war, we only knew one response. That was attack. Attack. Attack. Attack. There was no alternative."

"You're not in France anymore. We have laws here. We have rules. We follow them."

"No laws and no rules for these guys. They call them Wise Guys for a reason. They make their own rules. They set their own laws. There are no exceptions."

"You know times have changed. This is not wartime. You have a family. You need to consider those things."

"I know. But times have not really changed. All that has changed are the characters."

Bos smiled and embraced his wife.

His sleeping baby was now eight months old. He knew he had to protect that baby. He also knew he had to protect his business.

The baby began to stir. He wasn't yet fussing, but Bos suspected that was coming.

"Why don't you get some sleep. I'll keep an eye on him."

"He's well-fed so he shouldn't need any food."

Lee Ann put her head on the pillow. Within seconds she was asleep.

Bos remained by the baby's side. George must have sensed that somebody was nearby. He continued to stir and opened his eyes. Bos reached over into the bassinet and rubbed the baby's head. That always made him smile.

The fussing became louder. Bos picked him up and held him in his arms and rocked him. He moved over to the rocking chair.

After an hour, little George was back to sleep. Bos laid him back in his bed. He slipped back in bed next to his wife.

Chapter Forty-Two

Confrontation with Lee Ann

May 2, 1921

Harpers Ferry, West Virginia

Bos arose at 6:00 a.m. It had been a short night. Lee Ann was stirring. She lifted her head up.

"I barely slept last night."

"I know. I had the same problem. Little George was talkative."

"We need to talk."

"I thought we did that last night."

"No. We did what we always do. Talk around the issue. We need to talk *to* the issue, which is your reckless behavior. I just finished readin' Jack London's *Call of the Wild.* You're like Buck. You're called to the wild. There may be no escapin' for you. I'm not called to the wild. So, there is an escape for me. I just don't want to go it alone."

"How do I get out of an attack mode when I am being attacked? The people around me are being attacked. The churches I grew up in are being attacked. I can't turn my back on that. It's not who I am. You knew that when you married me."

"What I knew when I married you was that you were a good man who would protect his family. I wasn't bargainin' for some type of vigilante who wants to right wrongs. If that is what we are gettin' into, I can't live with that."

"I'm sorry, Lee Ann, but I can't change my makeup. You know my father. You know what he's like. You know what he has been through. If he were standin' here, he would do the same thing I am about to do."

"How do you take the wild out of the dog?"

"You don't."

"Maybe you're right. It's bred in. It's part of your fiber."

"Now you're seeing the picture, Lee Ann."

"I'm not seein' any picture. What I'm seein' is the young boy who would chase a deer until the deer dropped or was tackled. You can't give up. You can't back down. I respect that, but you need to respect me, Bos Custer. That's not in my fiber. It may be in yours but not mine. When you get back from Chicago we need to talk further and set some limits. I'm not livin' in the Wild West and raisin' my children in Dodge City."

"I know you're concerned. I am, too. I know the warfare can't just go on and on, but Torrio needs to understand he cannot toy with us."

"Your little child doesn't want to grow up without a father. You and your brothers always had a father. You know what it's like. What you don't know is what it's like to *not* have a father. Don't you let that happen to our child who is here or the one on the way."

She got out of bed, walked into the bathroom, and closed the door.

Bos walked over to the mirror and stared at his own reflection. He wondered if he was doing the right thing. He knew a lot was at stake with his family and the business. He recalled a time when he and his father had been out hunting for a bobcat that had been raiding the farm. They had lost nearly 20 pigs. The cats were ruthless. He and Cookie walked shoulder-to-shoulder. Cookie carried a 10-gauge shotgun loaded with rifle shot. Bos carried a .30 caliber rifle. They each knew that there would only be one shot. The cat might be hiding in wait or might make a run at them. The fight would be over in seconds. There would only be one victor. That was the type of fight he was involved in now with Torrio. There was no turning back. No way out. The only thing he could do was attack.

Chapter Forty-Three

Road to Chicago
May 3, 1921
10:00 p.m., State Route 10, Ohio

Bos figured he would take his best guns with him—Alvin Morrison, Sylvester Scott, and Joe Taylor—aggressive marksmen who had served in Northern France. They were killers, just like him.

He positioned one of them in each of the trucks. Three men in two of the trucks and four in the other. Most of what was being transported were arms. Bos had some dynamite that he had used in West Virginia for clearing the mountaintop where the house was being constructed. He wasn't sure he would use dynamite. Kerosene and gasoline might be just as effective. Either way, he wanted to make sure Torrio got the message.

He had called ahead to two of the Black churches in his network. They agreed to provide accommodations, if needed. Bos was undecided if he would stop long enough for sleep. He wanted the men rested when they arrived, but he also knew that the secret to success was to strike fast and get out of town. He would play that by ear. He knew the longer he was away the more Lee Ann would worry.

Morrison and Scott did not see eye to eye on many things. They cut a wide swath around each other. Bos liked that. Each had enough sense to recognize they didn't mix with each other. Scott was going to be the shooter. He would set up away from the house. Morrison would be the torch man. He would burn it or blow it up, whichever method fit the circumstance.

Both men were single. Bos could see Morrison married one day. He was studying to be a lawyer. He'd be a good courtroom brawler. Scott didn't have such aspirations. He liked his guns, his women, and his booze. Pretty much in that order too. He had once told Bos he could be happy just sitting on his front porch with his beer and a Springfield, shooting at targets in the distance.

Bos brought plenty of food. He knew that getting food on the road could be a problem. Many stores wouldn't sell to Black people. He had loaded up with pork, steaks, chicken, potatoes, and beans. The men would be well-fed and rested by the time they arrived in South Chicago.

The three trucks stopped on the side of the road. They built a fire pit and prepared dinner. Joe Taylor was in charge of the cooking. After dinner, the 10 of them sat around the fire pit.

"You remember the time we went into Paris and those white girls were strutting up on stage with almost no clothes on?" Joe Taylor said.

"You bet I do," Sylvester Scott said.

"That African soldier got up on the stage and started dancing with one of the girls. Two of the Frenchmen grabbed hold of him. He was drunk out of his mind. He threw them both off the stage and kept dancing. The French appreciated us. They fought alongside us, and they let us get alongside their women. You can't ask for more than that," Taylor said.

"They were also pretty quick to throw us in the sewers. Remember when the city was overrun with rats? I guess the Germans must've driven them out of their fox holes. They came straight to Paris. The sewers were clogged with them. They had us down there shoveling rat carcasses," Scott said.

"I didn't mind. Once we finished a day's work, we had all the women and wine we wanted. Just think, if that was here in the US, they'd give us that shitty duty and then we'd be locked in the barracks all night. Not in France," Taylor said.

"Enough of the war stories," said Bos. "You two tell more stories about your war exploits and female conquests than any two men alive. You'd think you two have been alive for 100 years. How did you ever pack so much action into such a short time?"

Bos laughed.

"You were there," said Taylor. "You know what it was like."

"Not Bos," said Scott. "He's a clean-living man."

He laughed. Bos smiled right back.

"We'll do our laughing tomorrow. I should say our revenging."

"We know what you're saying, first sergeant. We need to get some shut eye." Scott winked at him.

"I agree. I'll drive for two hours. Who wants to take the second shift?"

Taylor agreed to do the next shift. Bos moved over to the other truck to set the shift schedule. Scott followed him. He knew it was not a good idea for him to sleep in the same truck with Morrison. They had their mattresses and were ready for a good night's sleep.

Chapter Forty-Four

Meeting of Capone and Torrio

May 3, 1921

Chicago, Illinois

"I told you these bastards wouldn't go away," the little man said.

"I know. I know," said Torrio. "You told me so. For a new guy, you are getting kind of big for your britches, aren't you?"

"The only way to deal with these coloreds is to cut them off at the knees. If you don't do that, they just keep coming at you," Capone said.

"I'm not looking for a war here. We got plenty of money coming in. If they make some money, who cares?"

"Wasn't that Big Jim's position? Isn't that why we got rid of him?"

"I guess I'm next. Is that it?"

"You know it's not. I owe you everything. But the name of the game is to expand. You know that. We got to keep growing in order to survive. If we don't, they keep chipping away at us. Is that what you want?"

"No. I'll put you in charge of this. Do what you think is best. How many men do you need?"

"Twenty."

"Twenty? What the hell are you gonna do with 20 men?"

"My spies tell me they have a regular fortress in West Virginia. That's where they're making their booze. We need to attack and destroy. These guys are all veterans. They fought in France. They got skills our guys don't have. We need to hit 'em hard and fast. I may need more than 20 men."

"You pick the ones you need. I'll support you. Just bring them back alive. These are good boys. They're loyal to me. They'll be loyal to you if you treat 'em right."

Torrio raised his glass of water to Capone in a toast.

Neither man felt the connection. Torrio knew what was coming. Capone didn't want to wait. He viewed Torrio as another Big Jim Colosimo. Clipping his coupons was not the way Capone envisioned things. If he couldn't grow the business, he wasn't gonna run it. Both men knew that.

Capone knew which men he wanted. Most of them were Sicilian. They had it in their blood. They had grown up in the hills around Syracuse. The bloodlines were thick. But they were killers at heart. They would kill anyone the boss told them to.

Capone didn't understand the mentality. He had never been to Sicily, but he knew how they operated. They were loyal to the man next to them. They were loyal to the boss. But the loyalty extended no further. Everything else was business. That's all they cared about.

Torrio came back into the room.

"I forgot to tell you that Anna and I are going away for a few days. We need to. She doesn't understand the business. She doesn't like having a house surrounded by my men. We've been married almost 10 years. I thought she'd get used to it, but she hasn't. We have a little place on the Upper Peninsula. We'll be there a few days. I know you got your hands full. Who are you going to leave in charge?"

"I'll give that some thought. I'm taking all of my own men with me." Capone said.

"Sounds good. I guess the ship will still be upright when I get back?"

"You bet, boss." Capone smiled.

You bet, boss.

Even the phrase annoyed Capone. According to him, he was the boss. Not Torrio. He knew he had to wait his turn. It would come. He didn't know when, but it would come.

Capone thought about the attack. He knew he would lose a lot of men. He figured he would take the ones most loyal to Torrio. If they didn't come back, they were just a casualty of war. Nobody could blame him. The fact that they were put on the front line was coincidental. They might be cannon fodder, but they would also fight to the death.

He had read some things about Sicily. The people living there were thought of as Italians. They really weren't. They had been dominated over the centuries by many empires. Their loyalty was to the local warlord, each of whom had his own dominion. Each warlord paid homage to someone higher in the pecking order. The men below the warlord knew that their survival and sustenance was dependent on that warlord.

Right now, Torrio was the local warlord. He didn't have the warlord mentality. He was too concerned about pleasing people. That's not what kept you on top. What kept you on top was the recognition that you had to dominate. That would protect those loyal to you. In return their loyalty was steadfast.

You had to show your dominance. The men expected that. They respected that. If you showed any weakness, someone would pounce. To Torrio's credit, a year earlier he had imported his friend, Frankie Yale to kill Colosimo. Killed him in his own restaurant in the middle of the day.

Capone knew what he had to do.

Chapter Forty-Five

The Burnout
May 4, 1921
Chicago, Illinois

"I saw him leave about two hours ago with the wife, kids, and all of the bodyguards," Sylvester Scott said.

"How many bodyguards?" said Bos.

"I counted eight," Scott said.

"What's he doing with eight?"

"These guys know security."

Bos looked at him with disbelief.

"Remember the way we did it in France. Like the spokes of a wheel," Scott said. "Guys would go out from the center. If anyone didn't return as scheduled, we knew there was an intruder. Pretty simple system, but it worked. Kept guys on the move. Nobody fell asleep."

"Okay, so it sounds like they've got some veterans in the ranks," said Bos. "Curious to see if they come with them to West Virginia."

"The good news is nobody is home. You don't need to worry about Mrs. Torrio. They're all gone," Scott said.

"With Torrio out of town, we need some fireworks," Bos said. "Blow all four corners of the house, and then torch it."

"A little overkill, isn't it?"

"No such thing. Like I said before, this is about sending a message. Torrio will get it. Capone will react like a hot head. We saw guys like him in France. They didn't last long. They were all show. No planning. No strategy. No regard for his men. Just plunge ahead."

"Okay, Bos. You call the shots. I'll set the dynamite. I need two men to help run the wire. That is, two men who know how to follow instructions."

"How long will it take you to set up?"

"No more than 30 minutes."

Bos ran back to his truck. Two of his best men were Joe Taylor and Alvin Morrison. He told both of them what he needed. Neither one of them liked Sylvester Scott but they would follow orders. Together, they ran back to Scott.

Scott set up the dynamite. The house was not that big. Four sticks of dynamite would blow all four corners. The interior of the house would fall in on itself. Bos had brought two cans of gasoline. Once the dynamite blew, his plan was to run in and spread the gasoline. Once he lit the match, there would be no waiting around. They would hit the road east.

Scott set the sticks so they blew about one second apart. The explosion was rhythmic. The first one shook the house and almost dislodged the second stick. Scott had anticipated that and set the sticks in such a way that the prior explosion would shake the house but not be enough to interfere with the next explosion.

Bos and his brothers had blown a number of munition dumps in France. Most of the time, they did it with gasoline. Sometimes they had explosives. The army had given him the one-hour course on dynamite explosions. Bos was a quick study but even he felt the course was lacking. Sylvester had a lot more experience with explosives, so Bos let him run the show.

Bos ran toward the house after the fourth explosion. He got into the middle of the rubble and emptied the two cans of gasoline. He exited the same way he had entered the debris and lit the fumes.

He had to turn around to admire the handiwork. Torrio's home was ablaze. He would never live there again. He would never want to either. Bos knew that Torrio could be rattled. Capone would not be shaken so easily.

The message had been sent. Torrio would prefer restraint. Capone would call for vengeance. Bos had seen how this played out in France. The party wanting vengeance almost always won out, but not with good results.

Bos knew that vengeance had no place on the battlefield. The battle was just about winning. It wasn't about extracting vengeance. That pursuit was for the foolhardy. A real warrior had no time for that.

Bos gave some thought to making a visit to Capone's house. That had been part of the original plan. He decided he would save that for another day. Capone knew that Bos knew where he lived. Capone knew he was vulnerable. Bos knew that Capone had a small child. He could identify with that as a father, so that was not a viable option.

Chapter Forty-Six

Capone Visits
May 6, 1921
Washington, D.C.

"Nothing like seeing the sights," the little man said.

"You've been here before, haven't you, Al?" said Frankie LaPorte.

"Sure. I've been everywhere. All over. You name it, I've been there," Capone said.

"What are we looking for?"

"I want to see their home in LeDroit Park."

"We can go there. I ain't got no map, but I understand it's north up 7th Street."

"Somebody told me the city's pretty simple. What do you expect in a government town?" Capone laughed.

"Take a left here. This is 7th Street." LaPorte directed the driver, and in a few minutes they turned right on T Street.

The home at 520 T St. NW was impressive. Three stories high. A small front yard. An alley on the left side as you face the house.

"There it is on the left," LaPorte said.

"I like it," said Capone. "Maybe someday I'll own it. Either that or blow it up. Johnny doesn't know yet what happened to his home in Chicago. He won't know how to react. He'll say he wants to protect his wife. He really wants to protect himself."

"So, where do we start?"

"I think maybe we start here. It looks like there's no one home. They seemed to enjoy attacking Johnny's home when there was no one home. We'll mimic them."

Capone laughed.

"You're a copycat, Al."

"Let's drive by there again. This time, turn into the alley."

The driver made a U-turn at the next intersection. A Metropolitan D.C. police officer saw them and pulled up next to Capone's vehicle in his Model T. The officer had a Sam Browne belt and shoulder strap. His service weapon was a Smith and Wesson .38. What he didn't know was that Capone had three Thompsons covered up on the floor. The officer looked in the back at Capone and LaPorte.

"You from around here?" the officer said.

"No sir, officer. We're from Chicago. Just touring."

"No U-turns at intersections."

"I didn't know that, officer. In Chicago, they're allowed," the driver said.

"Somebody important in the backseat?"

"Nope. Just some Chicago boys on a vacation."

"I'll give you a pass this time. But in D.C., no U-turns at intersections. You have a good day," the officer said.

"Thanks. It won't happen again."

The driver pulled away.

"You handled that well. What's your name?" said Capone.

"John LaPorte," he said.

"I thought he looked familiar. A brother?"

"No. Just a cousin," LaPorte said.

"Take a right into the alley," Capone said.

They surveyed the house and then headed west onto U Street where they circled around and took another pass by the house. The cop car was sitting in the alley. He noticed the car come by again.

"Let's get out of here before he stops us again," Capone said.

"I'd say we hit it tonight," LaPorte said.

"I agree."

"Do you remember how many sticks of dynamite we brought?"

"I don't remember the exact number. I do know they are fresh. None of them have been sitting around for any period of time. Johnny doesn't care much for dynamite. I do. If you're careful, it gets the job done."

"The cop who stopped us should be off duty by midnight. I'd say we come back around 2:00 in the morning."

"We think alike."

Al Capone smiled.

When they got back to their hotel on 23rd Street, Capone told John LaPorte to get some sleep. It was going to be a late night.

Capone asked Frankie LaPorte about his cousin.

"You can see he's a big boy. Six feet two, 220 pounds. He fought in the war. Good boy. Knows dynamite. He's worked in a quarry since he came home from France. Works with dynamite every day. He moonlights with us when we need him," LaPorte said.

"He can set the dynamite. It's a standalone. There's no connecting house. We'll just blow it and run. No need for a fire," Capone said.

"I say we relax for a few hours, have dinner, and then begin the fireworks," LaPorte said.

"Sounds good to me."

Their third-floor hotel room on 23rd Street had a small balcony. They both sat out there smoking cigars.

"Springtime in Washington is pretty," Capone said.

"It'll be a lot prettier once we blow up their house. They won't know what hit 'em."

What they didn't know was that Bos, his father, and two brothers had seen Capone and the LaPortes. They didn't know when the Chicago boys would be back but figured it would be that same night. Bos had been careful not to alarm the neighbors. When he saw the D.C. cop stop Capone, he figured all their plans would unravel, but they didn't.

They had vacated the house, knowing that Capone was coming for his inspection. Tonight, they would be there, lying in wait. None of the neighbors would be endangered. Cookie had insisted on being part of the operation. He would be stationed on the first floor of the house with a Springfield and his .45. Nevin and Thomas would be on the porch of the third floor. Bos would be roaming.

They set up their defenses shortly after dark. Cookie was given a mattress to lay on. The boys knew he would fall asleep.

They waited. At 2:15 a.m., Bos saw two vehicles coming up 6th Street. One of them looked like the car Capone had been riding in earlier that day.

Bos ran back to the house to wake up his father. Nevin and Thomas had taken shifts. They were ready in no time. Bos figured his best line of fire was straight down 6th Street. He returned there.

What no one had accounted for was that John LaPorte anticipated danger. He had the same instincts as Bos Custer. He hadn't come in the two vehicles that Bos saw coming down 6th Street. He had low crawled from U street to the front of the Custer home and inserted a stick of dynamite at each of the front corners. He ran the wires all the way back to U Street.

From his position on 6th Street, Bos had a clear shot at the two vehicles traveling side-by-side. He fired for the front wheels. The bolt action felt good. Four rounds. Two disabled vehicles. Bos was looking for the big guy who had been driving the vehicle earlier that day. He didn't see him. Bos knew something was not right. He ran home. He saw what LaPorte had done. He knew he had seconds to react.

As soon as John LaPorte heard the gunshots, he lit the fuses.

Bos ran through the front door. He saw his father by the living room window. He grabbed his feet and pulled him on his belly to the back of the house. At the same time, he shouted out to his brothers to get to the back of the house.

"Dynamite! Get to the back of the house."

The explosion was deafening. The front of the house shook. Cookie was now on his feet as Bos pushed him out the back door. He had no idea where his two brothers were.

Bos knew he had miscalculated. This was a different type of adversary. John LaPorte had anticipated the actions of Boston Custer. Bos had not anticipated the actions of LaPorte. His anger at his own bad judgment would have to wait.

Chapter Forty-Seven

Saving the House

May 6, 1921

LeDroit Park

"What happened?" said Capone.

"Part of the house blew," said LaPorte.

"I can see that. But it's still standing."

"Let's go find John," LaPorte said.

"I know he's your cousin, but he's on his own. They shot out our tires. Get the Thompsons out of the backseat and get out of here," Capone said.

"You go with the guys, Al. I'll catch up. I need to find John," said LaPorte.

Frankie LaPorte began walking toward U Street. He looked at the front of the Custer house and was amazed that it did not appear to be damaged. He knew that John understood blasting. Two blocks away from the Custer house, he saw John LaPorte leaning against the back wall of a single-story building.

"You look shell-shocked," LaPorte said.

"I am. I only had time to get two sticks in the ground before the shooting started. Two sticks should've been enough to drop the front of that house, but it didn't seem to move."

What neither of them knew was that Cookie Custer had spent a full month with 10 men reinforcing the foundation of that house. Additional concrete had been put in the front section because of deteriorating brickwork. The back part of the foundation had also been reinforced, but not as much as the front. When the dynamite blew, it was met by an immovable object.

Neither of the LaPortes had any idea what the other two Custer brothers looked like. The two Black men approaching didn't deserve a second look. When they got within 20 feet, each unholstered his .45.

"You tried to blow up the wrong house," said Nevin. "Nobody told you that our daddy reinforced the foundation. Ten sticks of dynamite would not have made a difference. Now, you're going to have the pleasure of confirmin' that. We're puttin' both of you in the basement right by the blast site."

Frankie LaPorte charged at Thomas. Nevin kept his .45 leveled at John LaPorte. He didn't move. Thomas reached out with the butt of his .45 straight at Frankie. The crack of metal against bone was sharp. Frankie kept coming at Thomas. Thomas struck him with the barrel of the .45 on the left side of his head. Blood gushed. Frankie was unfazed. He tackled Thomas. Both went down hard. Thomas rolled away. He came back at Frankie and put the muzzle of the .45 in his mouth.

"Keep on fighting, and I blow your head off," Thomas said.

The blood from the two head wounds was so thick it was blinding Frankie.

"Let me get the stuff out of my eye," he said.

"Get up and behave yourself. Try that again and I shoot you," Thomas said.

"Let's go. We're going back to the house you just tried to blow up," Nevin said.

"I heard Bos talking to Pops. He must be okay," Thomas said.

"We need to tie these two cowboys up tight. When Capone realizes he's lost two of his men, he'll be coming back," Nevin said.

"I'm not so sure. I think he's movin' on. He has no loyalty to these guys. He has no loyalty to Torrio. He's just about money," Thomas said.

"I don't think he knows what he's gotten himself into."

When they got to the back of the house, Cookie was sitting on a bench in the backyard. He looked beaten.

"Looks like your foundation held." Nevin smiled.

"It wasn't made to withstand dynamite. But it did anyhow," Cookie said.

"Hats off to the builder," Thomas said.

"Never mind the praise. Capone is heading to West Virginia. We need to meet him there," Bos said.

Chapter Forty-Eight

Back to West Virginia
May 7, 1921
LeDroit Park, Washington, D.C.

"We ain't got no time to waste," Bos said.

"These two boys look like hard cases. I say we tie them up in the basement," Nevin said.

Bos and Nevin led the two men to the basement. Bos took a two-foot rusty chain from the workbench. He sat both men down by the iron vertical support column, wrapped the chain around their necks and the column, and secured it with a lock. The chain was tight enough that they could not get their heads out but not tight enough to choke them.

"It looks like they might have some trouble sleepin'," Nevin said.

"You're very considerate." Bos smiled.

"Always thinkin' of those lesser creatures."

"Well, maybe I should have you stay here and spoon feed them. Make sure they get a good night's sleep."

"Second thought, let's just tie them up and get on the road."

"Who's tellin' Pops he's stayin' here and watchin' over these goons?"

"You're the oldest, so the honor goes to you."

"Well let's git 'er done."

They finished restraining the two men. Bos gave instructions to Cookie on how to manage the two prisoners. He was not happy about being a babysitter.

"You're turnin' my basement into a prison. This is the second time you've put prisoners down there. Remember what happened to the Germans?" Cookie said.

"I do, Pops. I do."

It was already 4:00 a.m. Bos was determined to get on the road. He knew that Lee Ann would be worried. He was also concerned that Capone might get to Harpers Ferry first.

The road west was well-traveled to Leesburg. After that, the roads were rustic. Bos and his brothers had made the trip many times.

Bos knew that his father would stay busy picking up the debris from the explosions. He was proud of the fact that the foundation he had built years ago withstood those blasts. Not many homes would.

When the dynamite sticks were planted, they were planted in soft ground. The blast effect against the concrete structure had nowhere to go except outward into the soft ground. That explained why there was a large hole at the two front corners of the house.

The neighbors had gathered on the street in front of the house. Elmer Roybal had come inside to see Cookie.

"Cookie, you come and sleep with us tonight. You shouldn't be alone," Elmer said.

"Oh don't worry, my friend. I'm not alone. I have some important guests in the basement. You might say they're tied up." He smiled.

"You're not making any sense, Cookie. What's wrong with you?" Roybal said.

"It's a long story, Elmer. I appreciate your help. It will be easier for me if you let me do the cleanup here," said Cookie.

A police officer walked in through the open door at the front of the house. Cookie looked at the large white man with the badge and uniform.

"Good morning, officer."

"It looks like someone's had a bad morning. Are you the owner?" the officer said.

"I am. Nothing to worry about, though. We have everything under control."

"I don't doubt you do, but a few questions if you don't mind."

"You want to know what happened. All I can tell you is we're from West Virginia and there's a feud going on. You ever heard about West Virginia feuds?"

"I have. But people told me there was an explosion here."

"There was indeed. A West Virginia explosion. It didn't go well." Cookie smiled at Elmer Roybal.

"Well, since you're the owner, and it looks like you're not hurt, I guess no need for the police," the officer said.

"We appreciate your comin' by, officer."

The officer looked around the living room of the house and exited.

"Give my best to your wife, Elmer." Cookie led his neighbor to the door. He watched Elmer descend the stairs to street level.

What the devil have we gotten into?

Cookie smiled. He knew what his sons had gotten him into. He appreciated their enthusiasm. He decided to check on his guests in the basement.

As they approached Harpers Ferry, Bos saw an encampment off the road. He figured this was where Capone's men had set up. They were on Custer property. Bos was not going to stand on any formality. He knew that many of these men would be dead in the morning.

As they drove into their own encampment, Bos felt exhilarated. He could see that his men were at their stations. Alert. Well-coordinated. He waved to the men as he drove in.

Nevin had brought Rhonda to stay at the house in West Virginia so she could handle the bookkeeping chores. Over time, she had warmed up to Lee Ann.

Despite feeling more of the effects of her second pregnancy, Lee Ann was ready for battle. She and Rhonda had staked out a position in the basement. Around one of the doors, they had built sandbags emplacements. They left portholes for their respective weapons. Rhonda was not familiar with firearms, so Lee Ann taught her the art of reloading. She seemed happy filling that role, recognizing that Lee Ann was experienced with all types of weapons and knew how to use them.

Rhonda was amazed by Lee Ann. She had an eight-month-old baby being cared for upstairs. She was three months pregnant, and now she was getting ready for a gun battle with a bunch of Chicago hoodlums.

Chapter Forty-Nine

Battle is Joined

May 7, 1921, 6:00 p.m.

Harpers Ferry, West Virginia

"Man, you guys are ready," Bos said.

He looked at Rhonda and Lee Ann surrounded by sandbags and guns.

"I had no idea what kind of a family I was getting into," Rhonda said.

She smiled at Bos and Lee Ann.

"Oh, I think you did," Lee Ann said.

"It doesn't look like you need any help here," Bos said. "I'm going upstairs to make sure they're still awake."

He kissed his wife.

"The family that fights together stays together," said Lee Ann, "at least durin' the fight."

Bos smiled. As he proceeded to the second level of the house, he heard a gunshot. He could tell from the sound that the bullet hit the metal plating around the tower. As he entered the tower area, Nevin looked at him.

"They fired the first shot," he said.

"Let the firin' begin," said Bos.

"The shot must've come from some distance," Nevin said. "The birds stirred from that, not from any human movement."

Any movement that the birds could hear would send them flying. They had been quiet up until that shot being fired.

Bos looked through the eye-level opening in the metal plates. North of where he was standing, he could see someone who looked like Capone about 500 yards away. Whoever had taken the shot was a superb marksman. He hadn't hit anyone, but he did ring a bell for the Custers.

Bos picked up a Springfield from the corner. He couldn't tell the wind factor, but he calculated it at 5 to 10 miles per hour. He placed the Springfield through the opening and fired two rounds in quick succession. The figure standing on the knoll in the distance ran for cover.

"Who were you shootin' at?" said Nevin.

"I think that was the little man himself, Capone," Bos said.

"Did you get him?"

"No. I didn't want to. He's a known quantity. I like him. He's predictable. The person I want is the shooter," Bos said.

"I think I see him. Two o'clock to your last shot," Nevin said.

"I got it."

Bos set the windage and fired. The round hit the shooter in the head. Bos could see the head snap back and no doubt split open. He saw Capone, 30 feet away, jump up and run.

"I sent more than a message with that shot. The shooter won't be goin' back to Chicago. The bad news is that Capone's hotheads are really steamed at this point." Bos smiled.

"Are we done for the day then?"

"We have about an hour. I'm gonna go around and check on the men. They probably know what just happened. The attack will come straight on from where they were camped. I'll put Scott and Morrison over there. Any other thoughts?" Bos looked at his younger brother.

"No. Looks like you know the lay of the battlefield."

Bos smiled. "Thanks for bringin' Rhonda. It looks like she and Lee Ann are enjoyin' each other."

"That's important," said Nevin. "Lee Ann always tells me she prefers the company of men. I know she doesn't. She tolerates us. You got her figured out just like she has you pegged. So, tell me, big brother. Who's smarter?"

"No comment."

Bos smiled and went out to check his defenses. The first line of defense were the birdcages, which were the nets that had been placed at four different locations around the front of the main house. Each net contained about 20 birds of different types. The house backed up to a steep precipice. It was unlikely that any attacker would enter by that route.

The next line of defense was what Bos called a "pop-up." These were like the spokes of a wheel. Each spoke was an underground tunnel that led back to the hub. Along the spoke, a shooter could pop up out of the ground and lay down a line of fire. If the incoming fire became too intense, the shooter could close the hatch, retreat into the tunnel and go to the next pop-up.

Bos always put his best shooters in these six spokes. Fifty yards inside the farthest pop-up was a more secure defensive trench manned by three men who could lay down more intense fire with Thompsons and Lewis guns.

The field in front of the house had been cleared, which created clear lines of fire for both sides. It also created a no-man's-land where an attacking force would have to think twice about entering.

All of the men were awake and ready. They were glad to see Bos, who passed on to them what he thought would happen. He warned them to be on the alert over the next three hours for Capone's assault.

Capone was predictable. One hour after losing his best marksman, he attacked. All that was missing was Capone riding in on a horse. Instead, he came running in the direction of the first pop-up with his

Thompson firing. The drum magazine was loaded to capacity. In less than a minute, he fired off all 100 rounds. He reloaded with a new magazine and charged ahead.

Sylvester Scott was in the pop-up tunnel that Capone approached, armed with his Springfield and two .45s. He killed the six men who surrounded Capone. When Capone realized he was alone and almost out of ammo, he threw the Thompson at Scott who was 50 feet away. Capone ran back untouched because Scott understood that he was *not* to be killed.

When Capone got back to the encampment, he looked for Frankie LaPorte. Unbeknownst to Capone, the LaPortes were tied up in the basement of the Custer home.

Capone licked his wounds.

"How was it, boss?" one man said.

"Like taking candy from a baby," said Capone.

He debated whether he should return to Chicago and cut his losses. He knew that if he did, Torrio would never let him forget it. Better to stay put and try to draw some blood from the Custers.

Capone smiled. The enemy was surrounded. Neither side had any place to go.

Chapter Fifty

Cover of Darkness

May 7, 1921

Harpers Ferry, West Virginia

"Get some sleep," said Capone. "We're getting up at 2:00 a.m. We will be attacking at 3:00. I need two men to low crawl toward the house."

"Don't you see what they've done, Al? They set up the birds to warn them. You can't crawl toward the house. The birds will sound the alarm. That's how they knew we were coming."

Capone looked at Jackie Franco.

"How did you get to be so smart?" Capone sneered, but he knew the man had a point.

"I didn't grow up in the city," said Franco. "I grew up hunting in the country. We killed the meat we ate. If we didn't kill, we didn't eat. You learned quickly how to read the land and how to track animals. If you don't learn quickly, you go hungry. Plus, these guys fought in the war. I understand many of them are country boys like me. They grew up hunting."

"Well, ain't you so smart," said Capone.

"This ain't about being smart, Al. It's about staying alive. If you take these men into that firing zone, Custer will know you're coming before you even reach the tree line. You're taking these men on a suicide mission. Don't do it."

"Come over here and let's talk," Capone said.

Franco didn't know what to expect. He had seen Capone use an ax handle to beat up a brothel operator who was skimming money. Franco wasn't afraid of Capone. He carried a .45 on his hip and one in the small of his back, which was a common tactic. Franco went even further and wore an ankle holster.

"We got rules here, Jackie. You don't challenge me in front of the men. It's bad for morale. My morale too. Don't forget that."

Capone stared up at Franco, who stood at least six-foot-two.

"I understand, Al. I know you're Johnny's man. I don't challenge that. But I spent 18 months in Northern France. We were led by officers who loved to send us on suicide missions. I ain't going on no more suicides."

"So, what do you say we do?" said Capone.

"You can see what they've done," said Franco. "The house is built up against the edge of a cliff. He figures no one will come up the cliff. He's probably right. No one in their right mind would want to come up that cliff. It's about a 50-foot steep drop. In front of the house, he has cleared the entire area for nearly 200 yards. At the tree line, he has guys who can pop out of the ground with automatic weapons. Closer to the house, he has fortified emplacements. The guy is smart. The only way you get in is to try the unexpected, like climbing up the cliff."

"You gonna do it?" said Capone.

"If you want me to, Al, I'll do it."

"What's in it for you?"

"Good will."

"Good will," said Capone. "Never heard that one before."

Capone laughed.

"I brought ropes and climbing equipment with me," Franco said. "When we used to go hunting mountain lion, you never knew where they might be. Their lair might be on a mountain side. You had to be prepared. They were cats so they could climb. I brought one of my guys with me who can climb. We could get up there tonight, set some explosives, and be back by dawn. They'd never know what hit 'em."

"I like your style. You willing to do all this?"

"I am, but I want something in return."

"What?"

"I want my own territory in North Chicago. That's where I'm from."

"You got it," Capone said.

"Here's what we do, Al. I need to drive around to find the bottom of the cliff. There may not be a road nearby. We may have to do some hiking. My buddy knows explosives better than I do. We'll climb up the cliff, set the dynamite, and be back by dawn. If we're not, you know we either were captured or fell off the cliff."

"I like it. I like you. I think you're gonna go places."

Capone punched him in the chest.

The face of the cliff was 50 feet high. Franco's companion was named Ray Donovan. The Irishman from North Chicago was an experienced rock climber. He looked up at the face of the cliff.

"This is nothing," said Donovan. "I can be on top in 20 minutes. Probably best if I go it alone. When I get to the top, I can throw the rope down for you."

"I like your thinking," said Franco. "Just remember I got the dynamite." Franco smiled.

The climb was not that difficult. The rock face was filled with natural crevices and hand holds. Donovan had brought spikes and two hammers, thinking he would need to create his own hold points. He didn't have to. He had grown up in New Hampshire, living with his grandparents. Rock climbing was second nature in those hills.

When he got to the top, Donovan threw down a 100-foot rope. Franco tugged it twice as a signal to secure it. Franco began his own climb. He wished he had brought gloves. His hands had been hardened from combat and years of physical labor. These hardened hands were not used to intense rope burn.

It took Franco 15 minutes to make it to the top.

"Nice view up here." Franco looked at his companion.

"Remember that big tower in Paris? We only had the weekend off. We went up and down that tower at least 10 times," Donovan smiled.

They had met at Belleau Wood. Their marine commander had just finished chewing out his French equivalent. The marine was determined to hold his ground and attack. The Frenchman favored a strategic withdrawal, but the marines stood their ground.

"We'll place the dynamite along the back of the house. They probably aren't expecting any activity back here," Donovan said.

They each took three sticks of dynamite.

"How do we blow this stuff? It's not like we can set the fuses and scamper down the cliff," said Franco.

"We'll light the fuses when we are halfway down the cliff," Donovan said. "You did bring a second rope with you, didn't you?"

"I am always thinking ahead."

Donovan smiled. They placed four sticks of dynamite along the backside of the house.

What they didn't know was that they were being observed. UA had always guarded the perimeter of the house. Not a mouse got inside without his approval. When he saw the two men approaching the house from the cliffside, he knew something was wrong. He scampered to the bed occupied by Bos and Lee Ann. UA was not allowed on the bed. This time was different. He jumped on the bed. Bos awoke. The cat jumped off the bed and meowed. Bos knew something was up, so he followed the cat downstairs.

Bos had never really contemplated anyone climbing up the cliff. These guys had made it up the rock face. He had heard of troops in

Europe who were mountain trained. He suspected that's where these guys came from. They had the bearing of soldiers.

Once the dynamite was set, Franco threw the second rope over the edge, and they began to rappel down. As soon as they were over the edge, Bos began cutting the fuse lines. Franco and Donovan were at the base of the cliff seeking cover and holding their ears for an explosion that never came.

Bos picked up UA and gave him a good rub. The cat only purred when he was being handled by Bos. He knew he had done well.

"What would I do without you? You're better than a dog."

When he got back to bed Lee Ann was awake.

"What's goin' on, Bos?"

"Capone's guys tried the back door. What they didn't know was we have a guard cat. UA heard them comin' and got me. I was able to cut their fuse lines."

"You mean they tried to blow up this house?"

"Daring, huh?"

"No. Scary. How did these guys get so close? I thought your defenses could not be penetrated. I'm worried, Bos."

"I'm worried too."

Bos rolled over and brought his wife closer to him.

"We'll get through this. I promise. Besides, we have our guard cat."

He brought Lee Ann close to him and squeezed her.

"Our guard cat won't let us down."

Chapter Fifty-One

Dynamite Galore

May 8, 1921

Harpers Ferry, West Virginia

"There's an old Italian saying," said Capone. "'Come back with your shield or on it.'"

"I think that's a Roman saying," Franco said.

"Same thing," said Capone.

Franco and Donovan had explained to Capone that Custer must have seen the dynamite and cut the lines.

"I am not trying to be a smart guy, but we can't leave here without taking some blood," Franco said.

"I agree," said Donovan. "How do we get close enough to do that? I suggest we dynamite the birds, blow out their pop-up holes, dynamite their tunnels, and then see how anxious they are to fight."

"Your Irish friend is on the aggressive side," Capone said.

"That's why we get along," said Franco.

"So, you're saying blow up the birds, blow up the pop-ups, and blow up the tunnels. I like showmanship. When do we start?" Capone said.

"Right now," Donovan said.

"What I failed to tell you is that my Irish friend brought back more than 100 German stick grenades from the war. They're easy to throw and they explode four-and-a-half seconds after the cord is pulled. We're trying to find someone here in the US who can make more of these," Franco said.

"How did you get these things out of France?" said Capone.

"Easy. They said we could bring home one footlocker. Nobody looked inside. Mine was filled with German stick grenades that we had captured," Donovan said.

"Okay. How many men do you need?" Capone said.

"Four, plus Donovan and me," Franco said. "They've laid out six spokes in their half wheel. One man for each spoke. Everybody gets six grenades. One for the birds. One or two for the pop-ups, two for the tunnels, and two for the bunkers. Most guys can throw these grenades about 100 feet. So, what I need are guys who know how to throw a baseball or football and can throw it some distance."

"Okay. I'll round them up. Do you want me to go with you?" Capone said.

"Think of yourself as the general. You're too valuable to be on the front line. You need to stay back to oversee the operation," Donovan said.

Capone was really starting to like these guys. He could get the credit and avoid the risk.

Donovan and Franco explained to the four new men what was expected. Donovan gave each of them a stone and asked them to demonstrate how far they could throw. Some were better than others. All of them could throw the stone at least 100 feet.

They positioned themselves near the bird nests. Franco was by the bird nest closest to the encampment. He had instructed the others to throw their grenades as soon as they heard his grenade explode.

The first explosion was followed by more. All six of the men advanced to within 100 feet of what they thought were the pop-up tunnels. Within minutes, Bos's men appeared from the underground tunnels. They were met with two grenades thrown in quick succession at each of the tunnels. So far, the plan was working.

All six of the Chicago men advanced toward the pop-up locations. Franco found that the one man in his tunnel was dead. The tunnel was partially collapsed. Inside, he could see that there was a ladder descending to the horizontal tunnel, which still had an opening.

Franco climbed down into his tunnel and threw two more grenades. He heard the cracking of lumber and collapsing dirt. Tunnel number one was no longer passable.

It took close to an hour for all six men to regroup. All reported similar results. The tunnel occupants had been killed and the tunnels collapsed.

Franco and Donovan agreed that their mission was accomplished. The house was too well guarded and fortified to attack. There was no way they could capture it. That would have to wait for another day.

"Your guy's good. Johnny will appreciate this. I guess I'll be going home with my shield, thanks to you two."

"My advice is we hit the road now. Custer's not standing still for this. His reputation in France was that any German unit that spilled the blood of his men paid dearly," Donovan said.

"It might be wise if we split up on the way home. Do all your drivers know other routes?" Franco said.

"I doubt it," said Capone.

"Let's teach them other routes," Donovan said. "Each truck should have several Thompsons on board for when the Custers attack."

Chapter Fifty-Two

Attack He Did
May 8, 1921
The Road to Chicago

"The bastards killed Alvin and Sylvester," Bos said. "I asked both of them to spend the night in the pop-up tunnels, thinkin' Capone would attack. I didn't think that they would have potato mashers. I won't make that mistake again."

"I guess that means we saddle up," Nevin said.

Thomas nodded at his two brothers.

"The two guys who set the dynamite behind the house are vets. They moved like soldiers. They're callin' the shots, not Capone. We need to find them and take them out," Bos said.

"Should we take one or two vehicles?" said Nevin.

"I'm thinkin' two. We need to take Joe Taylor and Tony Johnson with us. Taylor's handy with a Thompson," Bos said.

"Don't forget his use of the meat cleaver," Thomas said.

Taylor had been put in the trenches with no firearm. Only a meat cleaver. He had done some serious damage to the Germans. This time, he would be well-armed.

"We could be lookin' at some hand-to-hand. Both of these guys fought with Sylvester. He thought highly of them. Tony is handy with a Springfield," Bos said.

"Let's take the two Model Ts. They maneuver a little bit better than the trucks," Thomas said.

Bos gathered Taylor and Johnson, who were happy to join.

"Let's do a weapons check. One Thompson per man. Fifteen drums. Everybody got a .45 on the hip and one in the small of the back. Three Springfields and three boxes of clips. No dynamite. It's too unstable. These crazies from Chicago brought theirs. They must've known that it could accidentally blow," Bos said.

"Nevin and I will drive first," Thomas said.

They loaded up. The Chicago outfit had a 30-minute head-start on them. Bos figured they could make up that time. From West Virginia, they traveled into Ohio and headed west. The roads were unpredictable. Some were paved. Many were just gravel or dirt.

Bos had always packed four spare tires for each vehicle. Flat tires were not just common. They were the norm. That made the Model T much more valuable. It was easier to change a tire on this smaller vehicle.

Bos had told Nevin he wanted to lead the way. As navigator, he would be on the lookout for one of Capone's trucks on the side of the road. They were 45 minutes into the trip when Bos saw lights ahead.

"Turn the lights off. Pull over," he said.

He got out on the side of the road and walked back to Thomas's vehicle.

"This may be them ahead. Turn your lights off. The three of us know the usual formation."

Bos looked at the five of them and told Taylor and Johnson they would be staying with the vehicles. The three brothers moved into the wooded area on that side of the roadway. Thomas took the point. He knew his range of fire was 45 degrees to either side. Forming the base of the triangle, Bos and Nevin had ranges of fire only to the outside of the triangle.

Thomas halted 100 feet from the stopped vehicle. The left rear tire had just been replaced. Three men were standing around admiring their handiwork. The cover had been removed from the back of the truck. Three more men were visible there. They were asleep.

Thomas picked up a stone and threw it at the truck. The three tire changers had no idea where it had come from. The area between the truck and the Custers was populated by tall pines with branches that began 20 feet up. This gave the Custers cover and a line of fire.

Thomas opened up a quick burst from his Thompson. Two of the Chicago men went down. The three in the back of the truck jumped up. Bos opened up with his Thompson. All three went down as quick as they had gotten up. That left one man upright.

"You're surrounded. If you throw your weapon down, we won't kill you. Otherwise, we're comin' in," Bos said.

The man knew he was dead either way. To his credit, he opened fire. The three brothers spread out. Two went right, and one went left. They now had the shooter in a crossfire. He tried hiding behind the left rear tire he had just replaced. The tire was flat again from the Thompson fire. His body fell in the street. Several rounds had hit the man's legs.

Bos approached him with his Thompson muzzle pointed straight ahead. The man was writhing in pain. He had dropped his weapon and was trying to stop the bleeding.

"I can help," Bos said. "First, I need to know which way Capone went and how many men he has with him."

"We all took different routes. Al didn't tell us which way he was going. We just knew the destination."

"Makes sense," Bos said.

Nevin and Thomas approached.

"I say we take this guy back to the house and tend to him. Capone is going to know he lost six more men," said Nevin.

"You and Thomas take him back," said Bos. "He needs to be tied up securely so he can do no more damage. Taylor and Johnson and I will forge ahead. I need to look Capone in the eye."

Nevin and Thomas looked at each other. They knew Bos was right. There was no sense in arguing.

Chapter Fifty-Three

The Chase
May 9, 1921
Greenburg, Indiana

The plan was to cut across Ohio in a northwesterly direction and continue through Indiana and into Illinois. Bos had no idea what route Capone had taken. He assumed it would be the most direct one available since Capone was no stranger to east-west travel.

Joe Taylor took the first turn at driving. Bos had figured that Capone would have the other trucks follow a different route.

Just outside of Greensburg, Indiana, on State Route 46, Bos saw a truck that looked like the other Capone truck parked in front of a roadside diner.

"Pull up and park in the back. We're probably not allowed to enter through the front door. Joe, why don't you go in through the back entrance and poke around. Capone's guys will stand out, so let me know what you see," Bos said.

Five minutes later, Taylor returned.

"It's them," he said. "There are six of them. No open firearms. They look pretty haggard. I didn't see Capone with them."

"Tony, check out the truck. Pick up any loose firearms and bring them here," Bos said.

Tony Johnson returned with an arm full of rifles, Thompsons and handguns.

"Looks like they left everything they had in the truck," said Johnson. "There was also a large wooden box. Probably had their grenades."

"Joe, you go help Tony bring back that box. We could use the fireworks," Bos said.

They waited 20 minutes. The first of the Capone group came out of the diner. His shirt was open, and he was staggering. No doubt the beer and alcohol had been aplenty. Bos whistled to him. He had no idea where the whistle was coming from.

"Over here," Bos said.

The drunk followed. Once he turned the corner, Taylor hit him in the kneecap with an ax handle and Johnson covered up his mouth. He whimpered and gasped.

"Where is Capone?" said Bos.

"Who are you?"

"You attacked my home and you don't know who I am?"

"Oh, that was you?"

"Yep, that was me," said Bos, "and my family, my wife, and all the men who are important to me. You killed some of them. Now, I want to know where Capone is. I won't be askin' again."

"We all took separate routes. I don't know where Capone is. He's not with us."

"Break his other kneecap," Bos said. "I don't want him to forget us."

"Now?" said Taylor.

"Let's wait for the rest of them to come out," Bos said. "I suspect the two with explosives experience are in this group. We'll find out soon enough. I don't want any of them killed. My hope is to get information out of 'em."

A few minutes later, five more of the crew came out and stumbled toward the truck. One of them noticed that all of the tires were flat.

"What the hell?"

He looked around, trying to figure out what had happened. He looked inside the truck for the first man who had come out. No sign of him.

"Gun up, everybody."

Most of the men were too intoxicated to understand the order. Bos and his two men walked around from behind the diner. Each was carrying a Thompson.

"Nobody move," Bos said.

"Who the hell do you think you are?" the leader said.

"You guys all seem to have the same question for me. As I told your buddy, you attacked my home and my family and killed some of my friends, and you don't know who I am?"

"We're just following Capone's orders," the man said.

"Well, I'm just followin' orders, too," Bos said.

He butt-stroked the man in the face with his Thompson.

"Anybody know where Capone is?" said Taylor.

No one responded.

"I guess we got a hard group here," Johnson said.

He pulled out a seven-inch knife from his left hip and drew a six-inch line of blood on the cheek of the man closest to him.

"I can do some serious damage with this. You boys need to answer our questions."

Bos focused on two of the men. They were both intoxicated but were the only two that had some semblance of military bearing.

"What's your name?" he said.

"Donovan. Ray Donovan. You're Bos Custer, aren't you?"

"I appreciate the courtesy of you at least recognizing me."

"We all know about you. I was in the Marine Corps at Belleau Wood. That ammo dump you guys blew up was meant for us. You saved our asses."

"And you pay me back by trying to blow up my house?"

"This is just business. I got a boss. You got a boss."

"Talking about bosses, I need to know where Capone is."

"All I know is, he is in front of us. We took different routes. At least that is what we planned to do. For all I know, we are all on the same route."

Bos looked over at Taylor and Johnson.

"I say we hit the road and let these guys walk back to Chicago."

"I like that idea," Johnson said.

"We got your guns. You got your flat tires. Good luck making it home," Bos said.

"You can't just leave us here," Donovan said.

Bos looked over his shoulder.

"We just did. Be thankful we're not breakin' your kneecaps. My instincts are tellin' me to do that. I suspect we will be meetin' again."

The three of them got into their Ford and continued their journey northwest to Chicago.

"Do you think we will catch up with them before Chicago, Bos?" said Joe Taylor.

"I think Capone is a privileged character. I don't think he is going to sleep under the stars. I suspect he has checked into some roadside motel," Bos said.

They were only 30 miles northwest of Greensburg when Johnson spotted the truck. It was the same type of truck as the other two.

"Pull around to the side so we can do a little reconnaissance," Bos said.

"You can tell where Capone is sleeping. He's got a bodyguard outside his room," Joe Taylor said.

"Joe, make like you're part of the cleanin' crew," said Bos. "Approach Capone's room and take out the guards. This is about sendin' a message, so use your knife. We'll find the other guys. I suspect they're sleepin' in the truck."

Tony Johnson walked to the truck on the other side of the motel. Three men were seated in the front and three were asleep in the back.

"This ain't gonna be pretty, Tony. I'm happy to do it myself. These boys ain't goin' home to their mamas."

Bos raised his Thompson and pulled the trigger. The circular drum began feeding .45 caliber rounds into the chamber. The Thompson was an effective killing machine. Bos was only thinking of what would've happened if the sticks of dynamite in Harpers Ferry had blown through the back of his house. Most of his family would have been wiped out. That wasn't going to happen.

The six men never knew what hit them.

Bos and Johnson walked toward Capone's room. The guard was laying on the floor on the balcony outside. Joe Taylor was inside, pointing his .45 at Capone's head.

"Hey what's up? You don't belong in here," Capone said.

He had his usual air of arrogance.

"I belong wherever my Thompson and Ka-Bar will take me," Bos said.

He ripped off the shirt Capone was wearing.

"You've already got scars on your face. I should probably give you a second one, but I prefer something more subtle. I'm going to give you two new ones."

Bos pressed the blade of the knife against Capone's right chest and let it bleed for a second and then did the same on his left side. Capone was left with two six-inch cuts.

"Have a nice walk back to Chicago alone."

He nodded to Taylor and Johnson.

Bos closed the door behind him.

Chapter Fifty-Four

Reporting Back to Torrio
May 11, 1921
Chicago, Illinois

"I gave you 25 men!" said Torrio. "You bring me back less than 10. The ones who do come back want out of the business. Tell me how this is a success story?"

"I told you that Donovan and Franco got in close to the house," said Capone. "They destroyed their six pop-up tunnels and came close to blowing the entire house. That's more damage than anyone else has heaped on these guys."

"I told you at the outset that I believe in staying close to home. Sticking with what you know. What we know is that booze from Canada sells, and whores sell themselves and a lot of booze. Let's keep it simple, Al."

"I hear ya, Johnny. I'll do what you say, but I still believe that for this business to survive it has to grow."

Torrio wasn't listening. He thought about his own house being blown up.

How could a bunch of novices from West Virginia cause so much grief?

He shook his head.

"So, what did I miss while I was away?" Capone said.

"You forget that I was away too." Torrio smiled.

"I looked at the numbers from the different houses. Business is up, so to speak."

"You're right. The numbers are up. The liquor is flowing. Our competition is the liquor coming in from Europe and also the Custers. They're small potatoes. We need to make sure they stay that way."

"So, you're saying to leave Custer alone and let New York deal with him?"

"Now you're getting the picture, Al." Torrio smiled.

"Maybe you're right. After all, how many barrels can you sell to churches?" Capone said.

"Check with Seagram. See if he can increase the flow. The demand here in the Midwest and farther west is unlimited. The sky is the limit if we stay focused."

Torrio looked at Capone. Capone looked at the floor.

Al Capone figured he'd bide his time. Torrio was too old school. He didn't understand competition. The only way to get a bigger piece of the pie was to take it from someone else.

Just growing the pie don't work. Too many people want their finger in.

Capone wasn't having that.

Custer embarrassed me. Custer will pay. Someday soon. Soon.

Capone decided to take some time to think about this. Big problems required big thoughts. Capone thought about some of the other big problems he'd had. When he was coming up through the ranks in New York, he'd been ordered to kill a guy. He did it with a splash. He killed the guy as he was paying off a New York cop for protection. The detective was an eyewitness. Capone knew the cop couldn't admit why he was present. Capone figured that he would play stupid and act like he didn't know who the shooter was.

The cop surprised him. He fingered Capone. Now, he had a big problem. It didn't take him long to decide that he had to go after the cop, who he knew was dirty. He knew the cop had been taking money for years. To all of a sudden now decide that he wanted to do what was right didn't sit well with Capone. He found out through a friend where the cop lived.

Capone knew the history of payments to this cop. He was able to get the amounts and the dates. He had a friend write up the chronology of those transactions. He slipped it into the cop's home mailbox and waited for a reaction. It came.

Capone had been arrested on the cop's say-so. He was out on bond. At the arraignment, two days after the mailbox drop, the cop didn't show. He was an expected witness. The prosecutor wanted Capone in jail, not on bond.

Capone hired his own lawyer. He knew enough about the legal system to know that he needed someone who was loyal only to him. Taking a lawyer from the South Side Gang meant the lawyer had split loyalty. Capone's big thoughts told him to stay away from those guys.

"State of Illinois versus Alphonse Capone," the court clerk said.

"Alphonse D'Amico for the defendant, your honor," said Capone's lawyer.

"Is the defendant present?" the judge said.

"Present, your honor," D'Amico said. He looked at Capone sitting next to him.

"This matter was set for 10:00 a.m.," the judge said. "The government is not ready to proceed?"

"That's correct. I am asking for a delay so I can call the witness," said the prosecutor.

"We have too many matters on the docket for that. Who is this witness?" the judge said.

"It's the arresting officer," said the prosecutor.

"They're supposed to know better. Request is denied and the motion is also denied unless the government wishes to otherwise proceed," the judge said.

"No, we cannot proceed at this time," the prosecutor said. He looked at Capone.

This was the first of many court appearances for Capone. He would quickly become a veteran. He sat next to his lawyer, looking at his fingernails as if they were the most important thing in his life. Without the cop, Capone knew the case would fail.

Big problems generated big thoughts. Capone liked that.

Chapter Fifty-Five

Layin' 'Em to Rest
May 15, 1921
Harpers Ferry, West Virginia

As Rhonda kept track of the numbers and came to understand the business, she became a force. Bos liked that. Business was good. Delaware, Maryland, Virginia, West Virginia, and North Carolina were showing nice returns. In South Carolina and Georgia, business was troubling. Too much noncompliance and a slow rate of payments.

Bos didn't want to hear excuses. All he cared about were results. Was the liquor selling and were the recipients paying? Rhonda understood that.

Alvin Morrison and Sylvester Scott had not yet been buried. Morrison had grown up in the city of Washington and lived on the streets. Bos thought he might have one or two uncles, but they paid Morrison no attention. He was just a street urchin. In and out of trouble. At age 17 he enlisted in the army and found his calling. They trained him, honed his significant fighting skills, and then set him loose on the battlefield. He proved to be a one-man wrecking crew.

Scott came from a similar background. He had a sister who lived in Montana. Bos wrote to her about Scott's passing. She replied with a nice letter, saying that she could not come back for the burial. She asked Bos to take care of any final services, and she would try to repay him.

Bos went back to the Baptist pastor in Loudoun County, Virginia. This was the same man who married he and Lee Ann. Bos asked him to preside over the final service for his two friends. The pastor agreed. The service took place at the Baptist church on Market Street in

Leesburg, the only Black church in Loudoun County. The crowd consisted of the Custer family and employees. It added up to more than 50 people.

Pastor Wilson preached to the crowd.

"I know the nature of this operation," said Pastor Wilson. "I may not fully approve of it, but Bos Custer has been honest with me and told me what was going on here and what is continuing to happen. I wish I could say it is God's work, but I can't. What I can say is that the Custers are good people. They treat their employees well. They are respectful, and they command respect. These men who we honor here today were friends of the Custers. That's good enough for me. They were good men, no doubt hardened by war. They knew fighting. They knew killing. This cannot be fully forgiven, but it is not our place to forgive. It is our place to understand. Bos Custer has helped me to do that. I would ask that we all try to understand and to look for a way to make peace. These two men were victims of war. First at home, then in Europe, and then back home again. It is our wish and our prayer that these men find peace and that peace finds them."

Bos felt like he had done the right thing for Alvin Morrison and Sylvester Scott. These men had been alone all of their lives. They found some peace in the US Army and found even more being a part of the Custer family.

All the men in camp knew Morrison and Scott. They knew that the two didn't see eye to eye and that they had fought. They knew Morrison had education plans for his future.

After the preacher spoke, Bos addressed the congregation.

"You know how much my family and I loved these two men. They were hard men who came from hard backgrounds. In the end, they were just friends that would do anything for me or my family. Either one of these men would've taken a bullet for me. Just as they knew that my brothers and I would do the same for them. Combat leaves you with a different view of the world. Whether you're in the trenches or the back lines. It makes no difference. Death was always around the corner. Not just lurkin' but attemptin' to pull you in. We all knew that. We saw it happen. These were two men who defied death. They defied the cruelty they grew up with and were surrounded by throughout their lives. Despite that, they were good men. Good friends. Good soldiers. My family and I will miss them."

Chapter Fifty-Six

Surveying the Landscape

May 25, 1921

Harpers Ferry, West Virginia

"I need to get out and meet the people we deal with," Bos said.

"I understand the need, but shouldn't you take one or two men with you?" Lee Ann said.

"That's a good idea. But you know a Black man travelin' alone is less menacin' than three Black men travelin' together," Bos said.

"You know best," said Lee Ann.

She rolled over in bed and kissed him.

"Good night."

"Good night. I love you."

Bos woke up the next morning at 6:00 a.m. He threw four spare tires into the back of the Ford. He was ready for anything. The men were up and operating the dayshift. Since the number of stills now operating had increased, he had spoken with the men and they had agreed to work two shifts of 12 hours, five days per week. On their two days "off," they simply maintained the defense perimeter. The open field needed to be kept open. The tunnels needed to be cleaned and refortified. The men all appreciated the work and knew that they were being paid more than double anything else they could make. Many of them only stayed for a few months. They were all loyal to the Custer family and felt like part of the family.

Bos headed straight back to D.C. He had left his father alone with two of Capone's men. Either they were dead, or they were eating well. He was satisfied that the two prisoners could not escape the chains around their neck. He hadn't given Pops any instructions on how the men were to relieve themselves. Hopefully, he had figured that one out.

When he arrived in LeDroit Park, his father was on the front stoop. Cookie had a drawn look on his face.

"Cheer up, young man," said Bos.

Cookie hadn't heard the Ford pull up. As soon as he heard Bos's voice, a big smile appeared on his face.

"How is the warden doing?" Bos said.

"The prisoners are fat and happy," said Cookie.

They hugged.

"Really?"

"Have you ever known me to lie?"

"Let's go check the goods."

As soon as Bos reached the bottom stair, the stench hit him. The two men were asleep. The vertical I-beam served as a cushion for their heads. Bos kicked the foot of one of the LaPortes, who opened one eye. When he saw it was Bos, he opened his other eye.

"Where the hell you been?" John LaPorte said.

"You're lucky you've been here safe and sound," said Bos. "Some of Capone's other guys didn't do so well. In fact, most of them are dead."

"If I stay here another day, I'm gonna be dead," LaPorte said.

"Let's unchain 'em," Bos said. "There's no threat. They won't be able to walk for at least 20 minutes. Two and a half weeks of confinement mellows a man."

Bos pulled the key off a nearby hook and opened the lock. Both men tried to move but were so stiff and weak, they couldn't.

"Take your time. You're young enough that there is no permanent damage. I'll take you downtown. Maybe you can get a train back to Chicago. I hope you got some money."

Bos smiled at his father.

It took almost 30 minutes to get the men out of the basement. Bos decided the safest way to get them downtown was to have them lay flat in the back of Cookie's truck with Bos seated in the back with them with his shotgun ready.

They dropped the two LaPortes near the train station.

"If I ever see you again, you're dead," said Bos. "Understand?"

They both nodded.

"Let's get out of here, chauffeur."

Bos looked at his father.

"Yes, sir, Mr. Custer."

On the ride home, Bos explained to his father what had happened over the last several days. There was no phone service at the house in Harpers Ferry. As a result, Cookie was in the dark as to what was going on.

"Pops, I'm spendin' the night here, and in the morning, I'm heading to Annapolis to check on the distribution there."

"I hope you haven't forgotten the pork distribution business, Bos. That's still the source of our wealth."

"I'll never forget that. My hope is to kill two birds with one stone. There is some overlap between the two businesses. Many of our preachers are also pork distributors."

"I never liked that mix but so far it has worked. I understand Rhonda is keepin' track of the books?"

"She is, and she's doin' a fine job."

"Let's make some dinner and talk more business."

The next day, Bos arose early. The trip to Annapolis would take less than an hour. The minister he wanted to visit oversaw a Baptist church near the Severn River. It was a Baptist church with a long history.

Bos now had six of his Liberators making runs up and down the Potomac. Nobody had boats as fast as Bos. From the mouth of the river, the liquor was distributed both north and south. His deliveries were all by water because he felt that was safer. There were too many chances for hijacking with ground transport.

The pastor of the church expected Bos at 9:00 a.m. His habit was to arrive one hour early and survey the church from a distance. This morning he arrived at 7:30. He parked on Chesapeake Avenue, almost six blocks from the church. As he faced the Severn River, the church was on his left. He could see water in the distance. He got out of the car and strolled toward the church. The neighborhood was a Black community. A Black man walking up and down the street would not be out of place. An address of 208 Chesapeake Avenue meant the church was two blocks from the waterfront. Convenient. He walked down toward the water. There were plenty of docking opportunities.

When he walked back to the church, he saw three men seated in a car on the opposite side of the street. All three were Black. They didn't fit.

For months, he had been thinking he was too lax with these pastors. If they could find a better deal, some of them would take it. He knew that within some of the congregations there were men who would be happy to supply the liquor without the limitations imposed by Bos.

He decided to take a left turn on First Street, walk over to Chester Avenue, and come around behind the parked car. He stood on Chesapeake Street and observed the car. At 8:15, the three men exited the car and walked into the side entrance of the church. Someone had opened the door for them.

Bos approached the car that had just been vacated and slit the two right tires. At least there would be no quick getaway. He walked around to the back of the church. From Severn Avenue, he could see the back door. There were no windows at ground level. Someone had left a wooden ladder on the ground. He propped it up against the side of the building and climbed up to the second level. The window was slightly ajar. He opened it further and looked in. There was no one in the room or nearby. He pulled himself through the window and lowered himself to the floor below. He walked alongside the wall to avoid any noise from a creaky floor.

Bos moved toward the stairs. Before he entered the hallway, he could hear voices.

"He'll be here at 9:00. He is supposed to come alone. That may not be the case. He is a steady supplier. We have an offer from some Canadians to supply higher quality and more quantity. The demand is unlimited. We could charge anything for this alcohol and people would pay it."

"Pastor, you may not know who you are dealing with. Bos Custer ain't your ordinary man."

Bos had heard enough. He unholstered the .45 on his hip and put it in his left hand and then unholstered the .45 in the small of his back. He proceeded down the stairs.

"I'm glad that at least one of you has a high opinion of me," Bos said.

He came down the stairs with both .45s pointed at the four men.

"If one of you makes a quick movement, I fire at all four of you."

"This must be the one and only Bos Custer," the pastor said.

"I'm disappointed that you didn't see fit to honor our agreement," Bos said.

The man to the pastor's left came at Bos as if to tackle him. Bos sidestepped the man and fired one round into his right hand as he hit the floor.

"Any other takers?" Bos said. "I'm a tolerant man, but I have little tolerance for those who profess to do the Lord's work but are really just doin' their own. I gave you an opportunity to help people in this community."

Bos re-holstered one .45 in the small of his back, removed the Ka-Bar from his left hip, and slashed the pastor's right cheek. The blood poured out profusely.

"Capone has scars on his left cheek. Now, the two of you almost match. Your distribution rights are hereby revoked. If any of your parishioners have any questions, they should contact me."

Bos backed away to the door and exited. He knew it would be difficult to replace this Annapolis church. Deliveries were easy given the proximity to the water. The demand was substantial, and the payments were on time. Bos knew of two other churches in the Annapolis area that might substitute. He would check with Rhonda to see if there were any contacts with them on the pork side of the business.

Chapter Fifty-Seven

The Baby Gone Missing
May 30, 1921, Memorial Day
Harpers Ferry, West Virginia

Joey LaDuca knew nothing about babies. He knew he had to impress Capone. He knew he had to impress Torrio. He knew that Franco and Donovan had climbed up the cliff that abutted the back of the house. If they can do it, he could do it. The fact that he weighed 250 pounds and stood six-feet-four shouldn't make any difference. At least not in his mind.

LaDuca borrowed the ropes and climbing equipment that Ray Donovan and Jackie Franco had used.

As Donovan had learned, although the cliff was 90 degrees, there were plenty of handholds and footholds. The climb was difficult, but it was doable. LaDuca actually made it in about 15 minutes to the top of the cliff. The back door of the house was open.

He knew the house was all new construction. The floorboards should not be creaky. In spite of that, he walked alongside the walls.

The first room he entered on the second floor was the baby's room.

LaDuca knew that if he could get the baby back to New York City, he had relatives there who could take care of him.

His harebrained plan was to use the baby as ransom to get the Custer family to bow out of the liquor distribution business.

He scooped the baby up gently in his arms and retreated the same way that he had come in, except he went out the front door rather than the back door.

For a big man, he could run nimbly and fast. He didn't hesitate in running the almost 500 yards back to where he had left his car. What he didn't appreciate was the early warning system. As soon as the birds heard his footsteps, they were all awake and moving. At 2:00 in the morning, the sound carried. It carried far enough to wake Bos up. He went into the baby's room. He knew that Lee Ann didn't have the baby because she was still in bed. He knew that whoever had the baby at 2:00 in the morning wasn't supposed to have the baby. He ran downstairs, opened the gun cabinet, and withdrew a Winchester lever-action and a box of .30 caliber shells.

He ran out the front door to the Ford that was parked in front of the house. He put the gearshift in neutral and cranked the engine. It turned over on the first revolution. Bos hopped in the car, turned on the lights, and began moving down the road. He could see some of the men coming out of the barracks, no doubt they were wondering who was driving off at 2:00 a.m.

Bos drove as fast as he could down the gravel road.

Several hundred yards ahead, he could see an automobile that was moving away from him. He tried to increase his speed.

Within three to four minutes Bos had pulled up behind the moving vehicle in front of him. He could see it was occupied by a large man. He seemed to have the same body shape as the man he had previously seen driving the Capone vehicle in LeDroit Park.

Bos had the Winchester on the seat next to him. He knew that it was not loaded. He put both knees on the steering wheel and picked up the Winchester and loaded four rounds.

If the baby was in the car, he couldn't very well kill the driver. He fired two rounds into his own windshield to break out the glass. That gave him a clear shot at the two rear tires of the vehicle in front of him. He fired off two rounds and the vehicle slowly came to a stop. Both tires were flat. He loaded four more rounds into the Winchester. He brought his own vehicle to a stop and got out. He could see the driver of the car in front of him lean to the right as if to try to pick something up. As soon as he leaned, Bos fired. The man's head exploded. Whatever he had been reaching for, he had not gotten. Bos approached the right side of the vehicle and could see that his baby boy, George, was laying on the floor crying. Some of the blood spatter was on the baby's nightgown. Bos picked up the baby, cradled him in his arms, and ran back to his own vehicle. He hopped behind the wheel, turned his vehicle around, and sped back home.

By the time he had gotten in front of the house, all of the lights were on, and everybody was on the porch or in the front yard.

Lee Ann ran to him crying.

"No. What have they done?"

"The baby's fine. The baby's fine," Bos said without thinking.

"The baby's not fine. I'm not fine. This family is not fine." Lee Ann grabbed the baby and held him close to her.

She slapped Bos across the face. "This has got to end."

She turned and walked into the house.

"It will end. It will end soon," Bos said to himself.

He didn't know how it would end. He didn't know where it would end. But he knew at this point Torrio and Capone had crossed the line. They'd crossed the line in the sand. They'd crossed the red line. There was no going back.

Chapter Fifty-Eight

Getting to the Source

May 31, 1921

Harpers Ferry, West Virginia

"Payback?" Thomas asked.

"He doesn't believe in payback. He believes in winnin'," Lee Ann said.

"You're right. No time for payback, but the rules have changed. Now it's just kill or be killed," Bos said.

"Poor Capone," Thomas said.

"We know they run their liquor into Detroit from Windsor, Canada," Bos said.

"So, what are you suggestin'?" Cookie said.

"You know very well what he is suggestin'," Lee Ann said.

Cookie sighed.

"You know that, and I know that, but I want to hear him say it."

"I'll say it," said Bos. "We need information about where their alcohol is bein' made. I intend to get to the source. Anyone who doesn't want to go there with me let me know."

Bos stood up. Nevin, Thomas, Rhonda, Cookie, and Lee Ann all looked at him. They had all learned over the years when it was wise to keep your mouth shut around Bos.

"We need to get into Canada and look around. It should not be all that difficult to find out where the alcohol is being made. I don't really care how they get it into the US. We're goin' to the source. We'll destroy their factories, their materials, and their vehicles. Capone and Torrio will be able to recover, but their cash flow will be pinched. I'm heading to Chicago next week. I need one volunteer other than Pops. I'm saving him for the trip to Windsor. You have never been to Canada, right?"

Cookie nodded and Bos smiled.

"I have never been outside the US. Now, I'm going to Canada?"

"You are, Pops, but we'll be sendin' some adult supervision," said Bos. "Nevin or Thomas can go with you. Maybe you can dress up as an old beggar and do surveillance in disguise."

"Who knows? When I was a boy, we used to do shows. We'd make a platform and use it as a stage and do performances. For some reason, I was always cast as the beggar. I was good. I think I still got that in me," said Cookie.

They all laughed.

"So, what are you going to do in Chicago with your volunteer?" Thomas said.

"We're going to shut down the moneymakin' arm of the Torrio family. They make their money off whorehouses. We're going to identify them and shut them down."

"Mr. Chairman, I have a question. Are you going to be samplin' any of the goods?" Lee Ann smiled.

"There will be no samplin', touchin', or oglin'. I promise. I'll even bring one of my brothers with me to keep me honest."

"In that case, I guess it has to be Nevin who goes with you since he is committed to one woman," Lee Ann said.

"Sounds like you have a lot of work to do," said Cookie. "You better get a good night's rest."

That night, Nevin and Rhonda finally had some time together. Their wedding date was a month away. There would be no honeymoon. They had barely spent enough time together to get to know each other.

Rhonda missed that. She wanted that alone time. She waited for her future husband to come to bed.

"Your family is pretty consumin'," she said.

Nevin laid down next to her and smiled.

"That's only part of it," he said.

"I mean it, Nevin. We need some time. Runnin' the family business. Constant contact with the family and no separation is not healthy."

"I agree. That's why we're buildin' our own house."

"You mean the house that the men are constructin' on the southern hilltop? I thought that was gonna be another still operation."

"Nope. That's our new home."

Rhonda moved closer to him and kissed him. Then, she poked him in the stomach.

"I'm angry at you for not tellin' me," she said. "I've been stewin' over this for weeks, and you just let me."

She smiled again and drew closer to him.

"I still want a wedding celebration like Bos and Lee Ann had."

"We will have that."

"But you know the baby havin' gone missin' changed Bos. He's different. I haven't seen him like this since we were in France. The Germans killed a good friend of his. For almost two weeks he was on a tear. It was scary, but he'll calm down."

Chapter Fifty-Nine

Staying the Course

June 1, 1921

Harpers Ferry, West Virginia

"You know what he's like. He's just like you. The kindest man you'd ever want to meet. But a harsh man. A hard man. A man who sets a direction and doesn't stray from it. He stays the course. That's the way you made him," Lee Ann said.

"I know. His mother and I both made him that way. No regrets about that. The day before she died, she talked about what a fine man Bos had grown into. Even back then she knew that one day Bos and you would be together. She just didn't know when, and she hoped that neither one of you waited too long to make it happen," Cookie said.

"I worry about him too. I thought he might be on the wrong course. The way things have happened, there's no turnin' back. I can't change the events. I can't change the man. All I can do is stand behind him."

"Sometimes you may need to stand in front of him. We put blinders on horses for a reason. His blinders seem to be homegrown. You need to take those blinders off so that both of you are lookin' at the same big picture."

"Big picture or not, my goal is to make sure I don't lose my husband. I will succeed at that, but I need your help."

"I know you'll succeed. You said before you can't take the wild out of the dog. You also can't take the warrior out of the man. Maybe I raised him too well. Maybe I raised him to be too much like me. I can't change that, but together we can help protect him from himself."

Chapter Sixty

Old Friends
June 1, 1921
Harpers Ferry, West Virginia

"I've been in touch with Brendan Burke who I met in France," said Bos. "He was a second lieutenant and led a group of American storm troopers. He was constantly asking me for ideas on how to attack the Germans at night. I shared my thoughts with him, and we stayed friends. He told me that his father ran the Irish mob in Chicago and Detroit. I believe him. I've asked him to identify all the Torrio whorehouses in Chicago."

Bos handed Nevin the list.

"There're almost 100 addresses here. How do we cover that many?"

"Ten a day. Starting at 3:00 a.m., we visit these places and shout 'Fire,'" said Bos. "There won't be any fires, but at least they will evacuate. We'll go through the place, make sure everyone is out, and then blow it."

"This borders on diabolical," said Nevin.

He smiled.

"You're close. But we're fighting the devil. By the second night, they will catch on to what we're doing. We'll come back home at that point for a week and then revisit Chicago for more sets of bombings. We'll have all 100 houses destroyed in no time."

Nevin laughed.

"Diabolical doesn't do you justice."

The train trip to Chicago had taken two days.

Chicago in June was warming up. Bos and Nevin agreed that they could almost get used to it. The wind off the lake did not seem all that bad. The houses they were looking at were situated along the perimeter of the city. They split up and looked at five houses each. They had decided to begin their work after 2:00 a.m. All the houses were easily accessible from a front or back door. Most of them were only two stories. It wouldn't take long to get everyone out. A stick of dynamite thrown through a second-floor window left open by one of the Custers, followed by a bottle bomb, would be quite effective in destroying the house.

Bos went into the first house on 19th Street, which was isolated. There were only three or four structures on that block that were occupied. The house had a waist-high fence in front with a gate that swung freely open and shut. Bos felt right at home as he pushed it open. He could hear voices on the first floor. He walked up the center hall staircase. The hardwood floor barely creaked as he ascended. He noticed that the handrail on each side was hand-crafted. Each rail was less than three feet off the stair. The handrails were wide enough to accommodate a large hand. In most homes, the handrail was not made for a large man with big hands. Whoever had built this place must have thought there would be large men going up and down the stairs.

When Bos got to the second floor, he could tell that the rooms were empty or the occupants were asleep. He started with the back room. The door was open, and he looked inside. Empty. The second room was occupied. When he entered, he could see what looked like a female form in the bed.

"Fire!"

The person in the bed began to stir, and when Bos yelled "Fire" a second time, she woke up, along with some others in the other rooms. Soon, they all began to exit.

Bos went downstairs and out the back door. He had confirmed that the second floor was cleared. He lit the fuse on a stick of dynamite and threw it into a second-floor window he had opened. Within a few seconds, it blew. The window was now much larger. He lit the rag sticking out of the bottle bomb and quickly threw it through another open window.

As Bos began to walk away from the burning structure, he heard a police whistle.

"Stop!"

A police officer shouted at him. Bos was not about to stop. The officer gave chase. Bos had no intention of getting involved in a fight with a Chicago police officer. For all he knew, the cop may have been getting protection money from Torrio.

The police officer was taller than Bos. For the first hundred yards, he kept pace with him. Bos turned up his speed and was soon more than a block away from the officer. He began to question how he was going to pick up his vehicle and move on to the next house. As Bos turned at the next intersection, he saw two police officers coming at him. This was not part of the plan.

Bos had fashioned his own stocking cap with eyeholes and a hole for his mouth. He took it out of his pocket and pulled it over his head. Neither one of the cops approaching him had pulled their service weapons. More than once in high school football he had been clotheslined. It was not a pleasant experience. He approached the first officer, who was about 10 yards in front of the other and extended his right arm straight out at neck level. The officer went down and did not get up. Bos extended his left arm and did the same with the second officer.

He made a right turn at the next intersection and hid behind the corner of a building. The trailing officer came around the corner and

Bos stuck out his foot. The man went flying forward into a parked car. Bos removed his stocking cap and walked away looking innocent.

He recalled that he had parked his car on 22nd Street, which was only a block away.

Back to work.

The next nine houses were less eventful. By 4:30 a.m., all 10 of Torrio's whorehouses were destroyed.

Bos and Nevin had decided they would meet at the train station. Bos arrived at 5:00 a.m. To his surprise, his brother was sitting on a bench inside. Bos felt certain he had beaten Nevin to the station since he didn't see Nevin's car parked in the area where they had agreed to leave their vehicles.

"Where the devil did you park, brother?"

"Right where we agreed," Nevin said. "I disguised my car a bit. I punctured the two rear tires and repainted the front hood. I figured that no one would want to steal it in that condition."

"So, how were the fireworks?"

"Quite entertainin'," said Nevin. "My first time in a whorehouse. Sounds like it won't be my last. The residents were quick to exit when they heard the word 'fire.' All the houses were standalone, so there was no chance of the fire spreadin'. I'd say I had a good night in deterrin' illicit sex."

Nevin smiled.

"How about you?"

"I had a brief encounter with the police," Bos said. "Remember the clothesline tackle? It came in handy tonight."

He smiled.

Chapter Sixty-One

Canadian Liquor
June 7, 1921
Windsor, Ontario, Canada

"Burke, you know you don't really have to do this," Bos said.

"I know. My old man encouraged me," Brendan Burke said. "He said anything that hurts Torrio helps him. He's not interested in helping you. He's just interested in hurting Torrio. I can't say I fully agree with him, but then I don't really disagree with him either."

"Well, at least you're honest. I can live with that. I guess you know Windsor," Bos said.

"Sure. We used to come here all the time in high school. No age limit on drinking. But now, the Canadians are the main source."

"I've been up here for two days. Just lookin' at the volume of traffic. It's incredible. How do they allow all this booze to enter the country?"

"They just don't have the manpower to enforce the new liquor laws."

"I guess that's good for us. Is liquor your main business?"

"It probably is now. Torrio has a foothold with his brothels. Get 'em drunk and then you own 'em."

"That's a good business model. I need to try that. My dad's business model was get 'em fat and then you own them. His business was pork."

"You have some sense of what Torrio does. He's bringing almost 100 trucks across the border every day. There are two manufacturing plants side by side in Windsor. There is only one bridge across the river. During the day, it's busy with car traffic. At night, it's reserved for trucks. There is no inspection. No police supervision. Nobody cares what they bring in. The Canadian government views it as a win-win. They get the taxes from the plants, and the workers are taxed by the Canadians. All they care about is the tax money. Prohibition makes no sense to anyone in the world except the Americans."

"All I want to do is hurt Torrio. I'm not interested in hurtin' the Canadians."

"You have to focus on his trucks. There may be a part of the distillery that is devoted only to Torrio, but I have no way of knowing that. The Canadians play everything close to the vest."

"Do you know how to identify Torrio's truck?"

"Easy. These guys are so crazy they mark their trucks with a big T on the front hood and both front doors."

"Easy pickings."

"Each truck has one man riding shotgun. Most of them are armed with a shotgun or a Thompson."

"Do they begin their caravan at the same time each night?"

"They start rolling about 10:00 p.m. We kept track of them for almost a month. They outgun and outnumber us. My dad just decided to stick with the business he knows rather than trying to cut into the Torrio business."

"Sounds like we have fathers with a lot in common."

"Sounds like we have a lot in common." Burke smiled.

They walked back to their vehicles.

"You've been a big help," said Bos. "How do I return the favor?"

"Don't get caught. Torrio will think it is us trying to break up his operation. His reach is long enough that he will find out quickly it's not us. Whether he'll identify you, I don't know. Just don't let anyone else know who is supplying the information. Torrio could crush us if he wants to. He brought in a guy from New York named Capone who shoots from the hip and asks questions later. He's dangerous."

"We've had some dealings with Capone. You're right. He is crazy."

"Hey who are you two?" A voice came from a distance.

"Sounds like we have a visitor," Bos said.

"More than one," said Burke.

Bos unholstered the .45 on his right hip. "Probably best to not be seen here."

"I brought you here. I'll leave with you," Burke said.

He pulled out a sawed-off shotgun from under his raincoat.

"I was wonderin' what was under there."

Bos walked toward the approaching men. He could see that they were carrying long barreled rifles. Each appeared to be bolt-action. He bet that none of them had chambered a round. Bos brought up his .45 and pushed the slide back to chamber a round.

He knew these were Torrio's men, so he figured there was no sense in wasting time. He fired the first round at the lead man, hitting him in the left shoulder and spinning him around. Bos pushed him into the other two who fell back. Then, he stepped in and picked up the other two bolt-action rifles and tossed them to Burke. Burke had seen what Bos was doing, re-holstered the shotgun, and grabbed both rifles as they came at him.

"I'll let you live on one condition," said Bos. "You don't say nothing about this to anyone. I've got a man inside your operation, so I'll know if you talk."

"Whatever you say, man. We won't talk."

Burke and Bos unloaded the weapons, pocketed all the ammunition, and checked the pockets of the men for any additional ammo. Each of them had several clips of .30 caliber rounds.

"You won't be needin' this ammo. We'll leave your weapons further up the trail," Bos said.

Both men backed away and began walking toward their cars.

"It almost feels like we're back in France," Burke said.

"Except we didn't kill the enemy this time," said Bos.

Chapter Sixty-Two

Gravy Train
June 7, 1921, 10:00 p.m.
Windsor, Ontario, Canada

"Change of plans, brother," Bos said.

"How so?" Nevin said.

"Rather than just takin' out the trucks, I think we need to go deeper. I'm goin' into the distillery. My plan is to blow it up. Burke didn't want it blown up because that's also his supply source. I respect that, but he has alternatives. I told him I'd be happy to sell to him. Our scotch isn't aged like what is coming out of Canada, but it's pretty damn good."

"So what's my role?"

"As soon as the trucks start rollin', you shoot out the tires and the gun man. Burke said there's a man ridin' shotgun in each truck."

"And I just keep movin' down the line?"

"That's the way I see it. You might be able to shoot out four to six trucks from one position. Then, just move down the line and shoot out the next four, five, or six of them. Once the distillery is blown, I'll start at the back of the caravan and drop grenades into the back of each truck. I don't imagine they'll have more than 20 to 30 trucks. That couldn't be more than a quarter to half mile. If I zig and zag between the trucks, the gunners left standing won't have any idea what's happenin'."

"No time like the present."

Nevin picked up a Springfield, and they moved to a position on the nearby knoll where they had a good view of the roadway from the distillery and still had some cover.

"If things go as planned, you should hear the boom in about 30 minutes," Bos said.

He walked off.

The distillery was alongside the waterway. On a Tuesday night, the brewers and mechanics had been given the night off. The still would crank up the next day to full power. At least that was the expectation. Bos didn't relish putting working men out of work, but he knew he had to give Torrio a strong incentive to stay away from his operation.

The structure was brick and block. Bos knew the usual configuration of a still, so he could locate its soft spot right away. The underbelly was like a drip pan. The alcohol that rested there would be highly flammable upon ignition. He set the dynamite sticks there on two stills. The operating area was empty. No one was minding the still. He taped the two sticks of dynamite to the larger belly and ran the fuse cords out 50 feet. That gave him well over a minute to get away from the explosion. He lit the two fuses, picked up the bag of 20 grenades, and ran toward the caravan of trucks.

Bos slipped on his pullover mask and reached into the bag for the first grenade. The driver's side truck door opened up, and the man jumped on the ground directly in front of Bos.

"Who the hell are you?"

"Your worst nightmare."

Bos threw the grenade into the back of the truck.

The trucks were easy to see with their headlights on. Nevin had no trouble shooting out the front driver's tire on the first four trucks. Hitting the man riding shotgun was more of a challenge. The trucks all had canvas roofs over the driver's compartment. He couldn't see the man in the passenger seat, so he estimated where he would be and fired. That left the drivers untouched.

Nevin could see Bos at the end of the caravan. He had been delayed at the first truck. He could see someone chasing Bos. Bos was unaware that someone was on his tail. Nevin took aim and hit the man in the center of mass.

Bos had no idea what his brother had just done. He continued to sprint. In front of the fourth truck, three men, probably drivers, had congregated. Bos ran right into them as the truck behind them blew up. One of the men had a shotgun, which he leveled at Bos and pulled the trigger.

"No shell in the chamber makes it difficult to fire."

Bos grabbed the muzzle from the man and struck him in the face with the butt. The two other men came at Bos. He put his other arm through the loop of the backpack that contained the grenades and raised the butt of the shotgun into the charging man's face. The second man was close behind. Bos used the unloaded shotgun to jam the muzzle into his belly. The man dropped to his knees, gasping for breath.

Bos threw the shotgun aside and continued the road race. There were 15 trucks stopped in line. When Bos got to the front, he could see Nevin 100 yards away on the knoll. As soon as he waved to him, he heard the crack of a rifle. Twenty feet away, a man pointing a Smith and Wesson .38 at Bos was grasping his neck, red with blood from Nevin's Springfield round.

Bos knew it was time to depart. He ran north, knowing that his brother was covering his backside. He heard two more reports of rifle fire from Nevin's position. Bos knew those rounds were taking down men who were aiming at him.

He smiled when he got to the top of the knoll.

"Good shootin', little brother."

Nevin smiled. "I guess I saved your bacon once again."

"No argument here."

Chapter Sixty-Three

Stopping Heroin

June 9, 1921
Washington, D.C.

"We know he has one other source of income," said Bos. "That's heroin. He justifies sellin' it by saying he's only sellin' it to Black people. I don't really care who his target is. I just want to stop the income. We've shut down his brothels. We've shut down the distillery in Windsor. Thomas is in Chicago as we speak, lookin' for Frankie LaPorte. He knows where the heroin is coming from. Once we know that source, we'll kill it, too."

"This sounds like it's becomin' a cause for you," Cookie said.

"You must be talkin' with Lee Ann."

"We talk several times a day. She's concerned about you. It's like you're obsessed with Capone."

"She's right. I am. I resent the baby being taken. I resent the guy sayin' 'he fought' when he didn't. He didn't go over there. He didn't put on the uniform. He didn't kill men with automatic weapons. He didn't smell the stench of rotting bodies. He didn't see limbs torn off. We did. He has no right to talk about it. So, you're right. I'm gonna hurt him. He's not gonna hurt us again."

"Are you expectin' a call from Thomas?"

"Any minute. He said he had a source in Chicago who could help us. As soon as we know who it is, I'll be on my way."

The phone call from Thomas came two hours later.

"Hey Bos, I'm hearin' that Torrio is not into drugs. His other source of income is gamblin'. That's all they do. Whores, gamblin', and liquor."

"Then who is selling to the Black community?"

"I don't know, brother. I do know we can't take on another enemy. Torrio is all we can handle."

"You'd be surprised how adaptable we are. But you're right. We have enough battles to fight. Is the gamblin' operation mainly numbers, or is it also gamin' tables?"

"My friend said it's mostly numbers. They're startin' the gamin' tables where they sell liquor. Torrio doesn't own many establishments other than the whorehouses. We know what happened to them. Torrio likes to joke that he's a family guy. He's into women, liquor, and gamblin'. He jokes that they promote happiness in the family."

"I could grow to like Torrio. If only he didn't have Capone around him, we might be able to do business."

"Runnin' numbers is too spread out. We'd need 50 guys to shut down the operation. That's not practical. My advice is, I come home and we try to protect what we've got. If Torrio makes another run at us, then we hurt him. He knows we can."

"Good advice. I'll see you soon."

Bos sat down. He was lucky he had people who gave him honest advice and not always what he wanted to hear. His liquor operation was self-sustaining. He didn't rely on outside sources. The pork distribution business was going better than ever. Most of his churches were spreading the gospel of enterprise. If he could build up wealth among these churches, he would help a lot of people. He smiled to himself. It was time to take a walk and reflect on what he had.

He went out the front door of the family home in LeDroit Park. He turned left on the sidewalk. At 8:00 a.m. on a Saturday morning, things were beginning to hum. The sounds of the city were just beginning. He walked by the Roybal home. He had known Clinton Roybal, who was a year older than him. He had volunteered at the same time Bos and his brothers did. He had seen Clinton the day he reported for duty with the US Army. They talked about the war. Neither young man was certain what the war was all about. The president had asked for volunteers, and Clinton and Bos had chosen to answer that call. It had to be a noble and worthy cause, otherwise the president would not have issued it.

Little did either of them know that the president had no idea what the war was about, what caused it, what was to be achieved by it, or how to stop it. But in the moment, it seemed like the right thing to do. The disillusionment would set in later.

Chapter Sixty-Four

Placating Burke
June 10, 1921
Washington, D.C.

"You didn't tell me you were blowing up the still. That's our source. Why'd you do that to me?" said Brendan Burke.

"I told you up-front what my goal was," said Bos. "I never told you I wouldn't blow up the plant. As far as I'm concerned, takin' the trucks alone would have done nothing. He would have just put more men on the route. I can't match his manpower."

"You owe me, Custer," Burke said.

"As a matter of goodwill, let me offer you 100 barrels. Fifty barrels of vodka and 50 barrels of scotch. I don't have the men to transport it. If you can send three trucks out to my place in West Virginia, I'll have it ready, and we'll load the trucks. Plus I'll give you $2,000, which should more than compensate for the cost of sendin' three trucks. I appreciate what you did for me, Burke, but I've got to protect myself."

"I appreciate that, Bos. I have a little more information about Torrio. This is really about Capone. He's beginning to act on his own. We have word that he is part of a big bank heist in Chicago. My guy who's inside the Torrio organization tells me that Capone is fascinated with this guy called the 'No Boundaries Bandit.' Capone wants his guys to start doing the same thing. He's decided that the first target will be the first Black-owned bank in Chicago. It's called the Binga State Bank at State Street and 36th Place. It's taking place in two days."

"You're full of information, Burke. I'll be on a train tomorrow with one of my brothers. Maybe we can help the Binga State Bank."

"Don't bother stopping by to say hello. My father doesn't hold you in high regard."

Bos hung up with Burke and called his banker at First and Merchants in D.C. He asked the banker to find out whatever he could about Binga State Bank. He called out to Thomas, who was still asleep upstairs.

"Let's get movin', Thomas. We're on our way back to Chicago. There is no limit to how much good we can accomplish in fightin' Capone. He's got a robbery scheduled two days from now of a Black-owned bank in Chicago."

Thomas came to the top of the stairs and called back.

"I know what you're going to say," said Bos. "You're right. But we're gonna do it anyhow."

He and Thomas ate a quiet breakfast. Bos figured they would each take a Springfield along with their .45s. Everything would fit in the wooden carrying cases he had made for their rifles. One of them carried four rifles. It was inconspicuous and looked so much like a suitcase that people frequently complimented him on it.

The ride to Chicago was something they had both endured in the past. The coach reserved for Black customers was at the back of the train. There were no white people in it, which was fine with Bos.

State Street and 36th Place was a busy intersection in the Black community of Chicago. The bank was not conspicuous at all. It had double doors at the front, but only one of them opened. The interior was quite small. The walls were colorfully decorated with a number of paintings.

Bos approached one of the people seated at a desk and announced that he wanted to open an account. He put down a $100 bill as his initial deposit.

Outside the bank, Thomas had already surveyed the area. It was decided that he would be on the rooftop across from the bank. Bos would take up a position across from the front door, acting as if he was the local hobo.

The following day, they both assumed their positions at 8:00 a.m. At 9:00 sharp, three carloads of heavyset Italian-looking men pulled up in front of the bank. Those in the lead car spread out through the intersection. The men from the second car stood guard at the door. The men from the third car proceeded inside the bank.

The group of nine men had rehearsed this operation. As soon as the three men came out of the bank, the firing started. From the rooftop, Thomas fired three rounds and all three intruders crumpled to the pavement. The satchel that one of them was carrying fell to the pavement. The other six men didn't know how to react. Bos stayed next to the cast-iron mailbox he had been sitting against, which he used to shield himself from the gunmen. Four of the gunmen hopped into the three vehicles and began their getaway. Thomas shot out the tires of the lead vehicle.

The second vehicle pulled away from Binga State Bank. The driver of the lead vehicle got out with a Thompson and sprayed the top of the building where Thomas was hiding. Thomas took cover behind a short parapet as the rounds sprayed everywhere. When he saw the muzzle of a Thompson pointed at the rooftop, Thomas laid flat. At that point, the shooter was 30 yards away from the mailbox where Bos was hiding. Bos took aim with his .45 and fired three rounds. The man went down. The other occupant of the vehicle hopped out and began to walk toward him.

The passenger in the second vehicle was armed with a Thompson. He had seen Bos, who at this point was crouching behind the four-foot-tall mailbox.

Thomas shouted at Bos to take cover. Bos bent down further behind the mailbox as the muzzle of the Thompson was pointed at him. Thirty rounds from the Thompson ricocheted off the cast-iron mailbox. Thomas took aim from his perch and unleashed a single round aimed at the shooter. The man's head snapped back as the round hit him.

The third vehicle veered to the left and sped away with three occupants.

Thomas came down from the roof. He had the carrying case in his left hand and the Springfield slung over his right shoulder with his .45 in his right hand.

"Should we make a withdrawal from the bank?" he said.

"My account only has $100 in it. I think I'll call the bank tomorrow and tell them to close out the account. I'll let them keep the balance," Bos said.

"Very thoughtful of you," said Thomas.

"Let's make a deposit." Bos picked up the satchel that one of the dead holdup men had dropped. He opened the door to the bank and hollered, "Merry Christmas," as he threw the satchel into the bank.

They ran to the train station to catch the train heading east. Neither one of them knew exactly how far it was, but it made no difference. They would not need their rifles. They dropped the carrying case with the rifles into a nearby trash can. Their biggest need was to travel light and fast.

"The Chicago PD is right on their toes," Thomas said as they ran to the train station.

"I think they'd been told to look the other way. After all, who's gonna miss a colored bank?"

"Just us coloreds."

Chapter Sixty-Five

Thomas Gone Missing

June 15, 1921

Harpers Ferry, West Virginia

"Didn't I say that no one leaves the compound alone?" Bos said.

"You know how he is," Lee Ann said. "He's just like you. He's gonna do things his own way."

Bos looked at Joe Taylor.

"But you said the car is still in the center of town. And Thomas has not been heard from?"

"That's so, Bos," Taylor said.

"Then the Chicago outfit has him. The question is where," Bos said.

One hour later, the phone rang. They had just gotten service that covered the Harpers Ferry area. Rhonda picked it up.

"I need to speak to Bos Custer," the voice said.

"He wants you, Bos," Rhonda said.

Bos took the phone.

"Who's callin'?"

"You've forgotten me already?" Frankie LaPorte said.

"Who is this?"

"The guy you kept chained in your basement. Remember?"

"LaPorte? How could I forget you?"

"Well, your little brother is a guest of ours. In fact, he's just hanging around." LaPorte laughed.

"Where is he?"

"You know what? I'm going to tell you because I'm hoping to see you again."

"I suppose you're callin' from Chicago?"

"No. We're here in Harpers Ferry. Just go north on Harpers Ferry Road. You'll see us."

Bos looked around at Cookie, Rhonda, Lee Ann, and Nevin.

"They've got Thomas," he said. "They want me. He said that they're on Harpers Ferry Road. That probably means they're on that first knoll by all the blueberry bushes."

"There's a back way into that knoll," said Nevin. "You have to cross the river at that point, but this time of year we can easily do that."

"He wants me," said Bos. "I'll approach from Harpers Ferry Road. That's what they're expectin'. I'll go in alone. You and Joe Taylor take our 10 best shooters and go in the way you mentioned and surround that north side of the knoll. I doubt his boys are gonna wanna get their city suits stained on the blueberry bushes."

"Our men will take Springfields with them. We'll be loaded and ready to go in 10 minutes," said Nevin.

"When is this going to end?" Lee Ann said.

She looked at Bos, but she knew well enough that she was not going to hear the answer she wanted.

"I know what you're thinkin', Lee Ann. I can't deal with that right now. I need to get my brother home safe."

Bos stood up and walked toward the gun cabinet in the front hall. He strapped a holster onto his ankle that he had custom made. He had also constructed one for each of his brothers. Strapped to the outside of his left thigh was an eight-inch hunting knife. He knew tonight was going to be a bloodbath.

Bos met Nevin in front of the house. Cookie was there carrying a Springfield. Bos looked straight at him and shook his head.

"No."

There was no more discussion. Nevin had loaded 10 men into two vehicles when Bos approached.

"I don't need to give you directions," Bos said. "We'll be takin' no prisoners tonight. You take the first shot whenever it presents itself. Don't worry about me."

Bos headed toward Harpers Ferry while Nevin and the men took another route. Nevin did not tell Bos that he was bringing two Lewis guns. LaPorte's men would probably be armed with Thompsons, so Nevin figured he might need something heavier.

As soon as Bos made a turn in the road, he saw something at the top of the knoll. LaPorte and two of his men were standing in the roadway 100 feet from the top of the knoll. Bos brought his vehicle to a stop.

"I thought you would come better prepared," Frankie LaPorte said as Bos approached.

"I'm always prepared." Bos got out of his car. "What's that on the top of the hill?" Bos said.

Bos envisioned that Nevin and his men had arrived at the Potomac River crossing. The water at that point was about four feet deep. The current was variable but passable. Carrying their weapons overhead, they were able to cross the river without incident. Two hundred yards in the distance, Nevin could see what appeared to be a cross with a man hanging on it. His stomach churned. It was Thomas.

Nevin figured that Bos would probably align himself straight on with the cross. If he fired at a 45-degree angle to that line, then Bos should be safe. It took about 10 minutes for his men to position themselves. Nevin had one of the Lewis guns set on a tripod. He fired at the base of the cross four to five feet below Thomas' shoes. The cross fell backward.

Nevin had instructed his men that they only fire at targets they could identify. The shooters at the two ends of the formation could fire randomly, putting the lines of fire in a crossing formation to avoid any chance of hitting Bos.

As the firing began, Bos walked closer to LaPorte. Bos had both hands up. He pulled the hunting knife from his left thigh and put it to LaPorte's throat as he spun the man around. His two bodyguards were caught off guard. Bos raised his right leg and pulled the .32 caliber pistol from the ankle holster and fired two rounds. Both men fell to the ground with bullet holes in their heads.

"Now, I'm gonna check on my little brother," said Bos. "If he has more than a scratch on him, you're dead."

Bos marched his prisoner up the hill, using him as a shield. As he got closer, he could see a figure on the ground, laying on a cross.

"I had no idea you were so religious," Bos said.

"Get me off this damn thing," said Thomas. "Who had the harebrained idea of shootin' this thing down?"

"That must have been your other brother. The smart one. I was going to shoot the ropes." Bos smiled.

Nevin trudged up the hill with the Lewis gun on his shoulder.

"I wasn't expectin' this," Nevin said.

"You know that Capone is going to want you nailed to a cross next time. I just tied your brother to this one," LaPorte said.

Bos pointed his .32 at LaPorte's head and fired two rounds.

"What?!" Thomas shouted, shocked by his brother's action.

"What are we doing? Are we becoming criminals just like these guys?"

"No. But these are bad guys," Bos said. "They've lost their right to live. I said 'no prisoners' when we came here. I meant it."

He looked around and saw more than 15 bodies lying on the ground. Most of them had bullet holes in their heads or chests.

Chapter Sixty-Six

Second Wedding
June 25, 1921
Harpers Ferry, West Virginia

Rhonda didn't want a big wedding. She wanted her family and friends present. She ended up getting more than she asked for or ever expected.

Bos still had 25 men who worked at the distillery and guarded the Last Stand. Many of them had married or had women who visited on a regular basis. All of them were invited to the wedding. Rhonda had no idea she had so many friends.

The wedding was set for the last Saturday in June. Aside from being the in-house accountant and bookkeeper for the pork and alcohol distribution business of the family, she had also become the lead gardener. The house was surrounded with roses. They thrived in the rich soil and moist environment. Rhonda had managed to produce roses in a variety of colors. The red and yellow ones dominated the exterior of the house. Inside, she had festooned the walls and flat surfaces with small vases filled with red roses.

Rhonda's family did not approve of her union with Nevin and the Custer family. Rhonda's oldest brother came to the wedding. He was well received by the Custers. Rhonda was disappointed that her parents did not attend. They had inquired about Nevin's employment. They were familiar with Rhonda having worked for Cookie and found that barely tolerable. Now, her becoming involved with a bootleg operation was too much. They did not want to hear about the benevolent purpose of the operation. To them, a bootlegger was a bootlegger. Concealment.

Underhanded behavior. Thievery. These were all associated with their view of the Custer enterprise.

Rhonda had tried to educate them as to what Bos and his brothers were doing, but they did not want to hear anything about it.

Rhonda was determined that the wedding would be joyous, beautiful, and fun.

"Do we have enough flowers?" said Bos.

"You can never have enough flowers," Rhonda said. "Can't you smell them? We need more of them around here. What we're doing is beautiful. We need to say that. I think you say it through your actions. Flowers are my action."

"I like that. I am an action figure. Some people think I'm too active."

"Well, the wedding is in an hour, so I guess I should get dressed."

"I'm sure everything will be beautiful," said Bos, "including you. Nevin is a lucky man. For that matter, we all are."

"That's important to know."

Rhonda walked toward the front steps and looked back at Bos. "I'm going to make you dance with me."

"I'm lookin' forward to it. You'll be my second dance after Lee Ann."

Bos was a lucky man. He had two women now who looked out for him and protected him, just like he did for them.

As the bride came down the front stairway, the aroma of flowers was everywhere. Bos was surprised to see the musical instruments. There had been no string instruments at his wedding. Rhonda must have put this together. He knew there were two violin players among the men who worked at the compound. What he didn't know was that there was also a cellist and a man who played the viola. He smiled as all four men, who Bos knew as roughnecks in his crew, played their instruments so well.

Leave it to Rhonda to find diamonds in the rough.

The cello player, Johnny Jackson, was also the vocalist. Bos immediately recognized Mendelssohn's *Wedding March*, as he had heard it played in Paris one weekend when he and his brothers were on leave. He had never forgotten it. The upbeat melody made everyone smile.

Nevin was waiting outside with his two brothers. Bos could tell from the look on his face that he adored Rhonda and she adored him. Cookie had agreed to walk Rhonda from the bottom of the stairway out to the porch.

To Rhonda's surprise, he decided to take a slight detour. At the bottom of the stairway, Rhonda looped her arm through Cookie's, and he turned to the right to walk her through the living room area and then around to the back of the house behind the stairway and then back to the bottom of the stairway through the dining area. Then, they exited to applause from everyone in the house, on the porch, and on the front lawn.

Rhonda leaned into Cookie. "What was that all about?"

"I wanted everyone inside, includin' the people cookin' food, to see the beautiful bride. You can't blame me for that, now, can you?"

"I don't blame you for anything. Everyone adores you except your competitors. I wonder why." She smiled at her new father-in-law.

"I guess I need to work a little harder on my competitors."

The same minister from Loudoun County who had performed the ceremony for Bos and Lee Ann had wanted to do the ceremony on the porch, but Pastor Wilson was overruled by Rhonda. She wanted the ceremony on the grass in front of the house under the small flower arch by the porch. The minister stood there waiting with Nevin, Thomas, and Bos.

Cookie was taking his time delivering the bride. It was like he didn't want to let her go. He knew that he wasn't letting go of anything. Instead, he was gaining a huge benefit through this young woman. That kept a big smile on his face throughout the ceremony.

In a booming voice, Pastor Wilson welcomed everyone. He knew that Rhonda and Nevin had already been married in a civil ceremony in West Virginia. The music from inside the house moved onto the porch. Cookie turned Rhonda over to his youngest son. This tall, slim man had matured into a powerhouse. He had found a wonderful woman to be his bride. He was able to keep peace among his brothers and the women they were committed to. Prohibition now presented a great opportunity for all three of Cookie's sons to spread their wings and fly.

Chapter Sixty-Seven

Refining Distillery
June 30, 1921
Harpers Ferry, West Virginia

"It just takes too long," Thomas said.

"But it's worth it in the long run," said Bos.

"What's the curin' time with Irish whiskey?" Nevin said.

"It should be three years, but we can still get good product in less time," said Bos.

"Are there any benefits in terms of production?" Thomas asked.

"The ingredients are probably not quite as expensive," said Bos. "The grain and the malt would probably be more economical than what we buy for the scotch. The main difference is the curin' time and the expense of the barrels. With Irish whiskey, we can get away with less time and barrels that are made of oak. We don't need to look for barrels that have previously cured with sherry or other liquors that are more flavorful. It's simply more economical and easier, and the end product is almost as good. And by the way, Irish whiskey is the drink of choice by the Irish. I don't need to remind you that there's a lot of Irish on the East Coast."

"Can we set up a new still and try the Irish whiskey?" Thomas said.

"There's no reason why we can't," said Bos. "The maltin' floor doesn't change. We have plenty of room on the floor to place the grain and turn it. There's plenty of peat down in the flatlands to complete the maltin'. We have all the natural ingredients nearby. The equipment is the same. The process is a little bit different than with the scotch. This whiskey is going to have more of a smoky flavor and not be quite as smooth as the scotch."

"I'm in favor of anything that streamlines the process," Nevin said. "The key to our success is going to be quantity and not necessarily quality. The people we are distributin' to, Black or white, are not used to high-quality liquor. They just want a lot of it. I say let's give them what they want."

"Who is responsible for the peat?" said Bos.

"Rodney has been down there diggin' it and cuttin' it. It takes about a week for it to dry. So far, he and the four men with him have been productive," Nevin said.

"Give them two more men and tell Rodney we need to increase production. We're going to need a lot more peat," Bos said.

"So, if we change the product, what do we say to the customer?" Thomas said.

"We just tell them the truth. We can deliver more quantity if we can make production more efficient and cut back on the cure time. I think they will like the idea," Bos said.

"I agree," Thomas said, "but what is Pops going to say? He's grown accustomed to the scotch. Is he going to give it up?"

Bos laughed.

"Truth in production doesn't apply to Pops. He probably wouldn't know the difference between the two. If he does recognize some difference, we'll just tell him we have upgraded the smoking process."

"Sometimes you treat him like he's a child," Nevin said.

"I don't mean to," Bos said, "but sometimes what he doesn't know won't hurt him. That doesn't mean we don't need his input and business sense but he's better off not knowin' about the small stuff. That's no different than the way Mom treated him. She knew what he could deal with and what he was better off not knowin' about. It's not about excludin' him or lyin' to him. It's about keepin' him focused on the big picture. That's where he can help us."

"Getting back to the details, do we have enough grain in the pipeline to make sure we don't have any slow down when the cold weather hits?" said Thomas.

Nevin nodded.

"We have three barns filled. Most of the grain is still in the field, cut and folded. We should have enough to get us through the next growin' season. But that assumes no big increase in production."

"We can't assume that," said Bos. "There will be a big increase in demand. We need to be prepared to triple production. We have never dealt with the local farmers. They're not going to take kindly to dealin' with Black men. Maybe we can get Joe Harper to approach them and buy their grain. Cash is not a problem. I'll talk with Joe and see if he can buy up double of our current supply. After all, cash is still king, regardless of your color." Bos smiled.

"What planet are you livin' on?" Nevin said. "Cash may be king if you're a white man. But not if you're Black. The color of your skin means you never get in the door to show your cash. Just because you married a white woman doesn't mean people are going to treat you any better than they treat the rest of us."

Bos approached his younger brother. "What does my wife have to do with all of this?"

"Nothing, other than you sometimes seem to forget who you are. You can have all the money in the world. You can be married to the most famous white woman in the world. But the world is still going to look at you as nothing but a Black man."

Nevin stood up. The two brothers looked at each other. Bos resented what his brother was saying, but he knew it was true. He nodded and walked away.

Chapter Sixty-Eight

Back to Murfreesboro
July 4, 1921
Murfreesboro, North Carolina

It was still just a sleepy town near the Virginia border. Rhonda loved walking through the center of the small town. All of the Black people in the town knew her. The white people knew that she had married the man who stood up to the white hooligans. White or Black, they all wanted peace, even if their respective ideas about what it meant were different.

"Welcome home, Rhonda. This must be the young man I have heard so much about," Joyce Washington said.

The 50-year-old Washington had lived in Murfreesboro all her life. She had seen Rhonda grow from a toddler to a young adult business-woman.

"It's great to see you, Mrs. Washington. This is Nevin Custer. In case you haven't heard, I'm now Rhonda Custer."

Joyce Washington reached for Rhonda's left hand.

"What a beautiful ring."

She smiled.

"You're both very lucky. So many of our young people find no opportunity. It looks like you've both made yours count."

"Well, we've had some good fortune," Rhonda said. "I married into a wonderful family. I'm coming home now to see if my husband and I can re-join my family."

"Rhonda, you need to be understanding of your parents. What you've done is so new to them. They expected you to stay here. Your living in West Virginia and marrying this man is just not something they have ever thought about. They need time. They'll come around." Joyce Washington smiled.

"I know. I just don't want them to take too long."

The two women hugged each other before Joyce Washington opened her arms to Nevin, and he gladly responded.

"Well, I guess you've seen enough of my thriving metropolis," said Rhonda. "Time to go see the folks. It might be a good idea if we bring a peace offering."

"I could go out and cut some flowers," Nevin said.

"Flowers are a way to my heart. Food will be more appreciated by my folks. You remember the diner where you had some trouble parking? Let's walk over there. This time, you won't need a parking space."

"I hope I don't need my axe handle either," Nevin said. He smiled.

They walked the block and a half to the small diner. Nevin could see there were two white men in the far corner. Rhonda paid no attention to them. The small business had always served both the Black and white communities of Murfreesboro. The Black folks sat on the side of the diner closest to their neighborhoods. The white folks sat on the side of the diner closest to their part of town. Never the twain should meet. But both sides did eat.

"Rhonda, so good to see you," Abi Hawkins said.

Hawkins and his wife had owned this small diner for more than 25 years. Sarah Hawkins also ran a seamstress shop two doors down. During the lunch hour and dinner hour, she came into the diner to help out. The rest of the day, Abi and one long-time employee known simply as Lionel served everyone who came in.

"Thank you, Mr. Hawkins. Let me introduce my husband, Nevin, to you."

"I've heard good things about you," Hawkins said.

He could see that the two men who had been sitting in the back were now on their feet and moving toward the counter. Abi Hawkins was a small man, but the broken nose and scarring on his neck suggested that he was someone who knew how to fight.

"Hello, Benjamin," Abi said.

Benjamin Rhodes looked directly at Abi. Then, he looked at Nevin.

"I remember you," Rhodes said. "Vengeance is mine."

"Vengeance is not part of my dictionary," said Nevin, "but self-defense is."

Nevin withdrew the .45 from the small of his back. As he pointed the muzzle toward the floor, he made sure that Rhodes saw the weapon. Rhodes and his companion didn't waste any time leaving the diner.

Nevin looked at Rhonda and smiled.

"I smell trouble," he said, "and it ain't comin' from the food in this diner. I'm gonna amble back to my truck. You wait out front, and I'll pick you up."

"I know you can take these guys, Nevin. But there are a lot more where they came from, and you can't fight them all."

"My hope is not to fight any of them. In France, we never had a racial confrontation. Everyone knew who we were and what we could do. They didn't like us, but they feared us. These boys need to learn that fear."

Nevin re-holstered his .45 and left the diner. His small truck was just over a block away. He sensed that he might be looking at more than just two men. Sure enough, by the time he turned the corner and saw his truck, he could see four other men walking toward him down the middle of the street. One of them was carrying a rifle.

Nevin unholstered his .45. He normally didn't have a round chambered. He pulled the slide back. He had never liked the seven-shot magazine. He had two more on his left hip. *Twenty-one rounds should be more than enough.*

He knew his best chance against at least six opponents was to do something stupid. Without hesitating, he fired two rounds in the air from his .45 as he charged the four men. He was able to cover that 25-yard distance in no time. The man with the rifle was so surprised he never raised the muzzle. Nevin snatched the rifle from him, put the .45 in his left waistband, and then approached the others with the Winchester .30 caliber pointing at them.

Nevin unholstered the .45. He could fire it as well from his left hand as his right, so he kept the Winchester in his right hand. He saw the two men from the diner coming toward him from an alley to his right. They were both carrying what looked like Winchester rifles. He wasn't much worried about a fair fight anymore. He knew he was outgunned.

"This doesn't have to be a bloodbath," Nevin said.

"You're right. You can just put down your weapons and we'll just give you a good old-fashioned ass whipping," Rhodes said.

"As you may remember from last time, 'ass whipping' ain't in my dictionary."

With the .45 in his left hand, Nevin brought up the muzzle of the Winchester to his left hand and butt stroked Rhodes using his right hand. Rhodes fell back and Nevin moved quickly to catch him. With the Winchester in his right hand and the .45 in his left hand, he spun the man around and used both of his arms to hold the unconscious man up. He addressed the other men.

"I can take out at least four of you, and I'll still have your friend as a shield. Those aren't ideal odds, but I'll take them."

The men looked at each other, unsure what to do next.

"At least four of you are not going home today," said Nevin. "Who's ready to join that group?"

The men were not experienced street fighters. Nevin wished they had been. Their conduct would've been more predictable. The problem with novices was that they did the unexpected at the most inconvenient times.

"There's more of us where we came from," one of the white men said.

"I don't doubt you. With the exception of your buddy, who I'm holdin', we can all walk away from this. I'm willin' to let bygones be bygones. But if I ever see any of you again actin' in a threatenin' way, I will break several bones in your body."

Nevin waited for a response. Rhodes was not the leader of the group.

"The man's right. Ben Rhodes is a friend," said one man. "But he's not worth dying for over this. No apologies. No hard feelings. We just stay on separate sides of the street."

"Thank you, mister," said Nevin. "I'll just lay your friend down here on the street real gentle. He has a busted face. I'm happy to pay for his medical treatment. He needs some attention today, as you can see."

Nevin gently laid Rhodes down, protecting his head as he laid him out on the street.

"I'll leave the Winchester in front of the diner," said Nevin.

He walked toward his truck, cranked the engine, and drove to the diner to pick up Rhonda.

"What took so long?" she said.

"I was engaged in conversation with some of your fair citizens. I think we have come to an understandin'. Or at least a standoff. We'll see if it holds." Nevin smiled.

"Something tells me you pulled that .45 from the small of your back again. I heard the gunfire, so I guess there's no need for me to inquire further."

Nevin got out of his Ford and took the Winchester with him. He placed it alongside the door of the diner.

The ride to Rhonda's family home took less than five minutes. Her father was out in front of the house when they arrived. He had bought a Model T. Rhonda had said more than once how proud he was of being the first Black man in town to own a car. As he approached, Nevin could tell that Rhonda's father was having some problems with the crank.

"Hello, Mr. Murfree. Can I help?"

"I just don't have the strength I used to. Maybe I need to have a young man like you around," he said.

Nevin put his right hand on the crank. Two quick revolutions had the car sputtering to life.

"I wasn't sure I'd be saying this, but I'm glad to see you both. "I've missed you. Both of you," Rhonda's father smiled.

Rhonda's mother was smiling as she came out of the house. She was a tall, statuesque woman. Rhonda shared her height and body build.

"You children are just in time. Your brother will be here soon. He told us all about the wedding. I knew you would be a beautiful bride."

The two women embraced.

"This ornery old man here wouldn't let us go to your wedding. But since then, he's had quite a reckoning."

"I ain't had no reckoning. I've just been beaten about the head and shoulders by an angry mother who wasn't able to go to her daughter's wedding. I have to admit this old coot was wrong. We should have gone. I'm still learning, but times are changing awful quick."

"We can tell you all about it," said Nevin. "Your daughter was the most beautiful bride ever. The wedding was outside in front of our home. The Baptist minister from Loudoun County presided. My brother, Bos, gave the eulogy."

Everyone laughed.

"You can see my husband has a sense of humor," said Rhonda. "Not many people appreciate it. I'm just learning, myself."

Chapter Sixty-Nine

The Pork Business
July 8, 1921
Harpers Ferry, West Virginia

"You know they're lookin'," Nevin said.

"Whose idea was it to cage the birds?" said Thomas.

"The Germans," said Bos. "Don't you remember at Belleau Wood when they set up birdcages? It was clever. They had small birdcages hanging from the trees. They put them around the perimeter where they expected the enemy, and it was like a relay system. The birds in the furthest perimeter position would stir and that would set off a chain reaction. The flaw in it was that there were too many alarms set off. One set of birds was always being spooked."

"So, your system cured that problem," Nevin said.

"Not completely. But birds have a military-like command structure. When they're all in the same net, they don't get spooked unless there is something there to actually spook them."

"Pure genius. Through and through."

Thomas laughed.

"Excuse me, but I called this meeting to get a better sense of how the pork business is doing," Bos said.

"Thanks to my new bride," said Nevin, "who should be here, the business is roaring. Sales are up, inventory is ever-constant, and profits are up. We have more than a thousand contractors working for us. Ninety-nine percent of them are Black men and women. We are the largest pork distributor now on the East Coast."

Bos looked at Nevin. "How many of those employees . . ."

"I didn't say employees," said Nevin. "They are all contractors. We don't have employees other than immediate family."

"And why is this important?" said Thomas.

"Incentive," said Nevin. "Everybody gets paid based on results. Nobody is guaranteed a paycheck. The more they produce, the more they get paid. Everybody except our sorry asses is paid on performance." Nevin smirked. "And it's my wife who is in large measure responsible for this. She converted everybody to a contractor. Production has gone up. Income is up for the company and also for the workers."

"You may want to keep an eye on that woman," said Thomas. "She may own the company one day."

"Oh, I keep a very close eye on the goods." Nevin smiled.

"We're lucky to have her," Bos said. "The pork business is always going to be our foundation. We should never forget that."

The brothers all nodded.

"What about our other business?"

"Next time you call a meeting, make sure you invite Rhonda," said Nevin. "She knows the numbers. At this point, we are just breaking even. She tells me that some distribution points are meetin' their objective of two percent profit. But most are not."

"No question we lost some time and production due to Capone and his antics," said Bos. "He got his nose bloodied. I doubt he'll be comin' back for more. But there's no question that we can expect to see him again with one of our deliveries. He likes to make a splash, being the showboat he is. I suspect he'll hit us at the White House in two weeks. We have a big delivery at that time. President Harding likes his lubricants."

"Who is your contact at the White House?" said Nevin.

"Lee Ann goes in one day per week to help out with the transition," Bos said. "She likes Harding. He's even asked to meet me. Imagine that. The president wants to meet a Black man."

"I'd say keep your guard up," said Thomas. "He may want to put an apron on you."

Bos and Nevin laughed.

"Lee Ann says he's different than Wilson. She says he talks about some ways to make things better for Black folks. She thinks he means it."

"Maybe he does, Bos, but that ain't gonna help our business. We need to help ourselves." Nevin looked at his brother, who nodded.

"So, what about this attack at the White House?" said Thomas. "When is the delivery, and what's the amount?"

"It's the first major delivery," Bos said. "Off the books, of course. Harding is payin' cash. It better be our best stuff. He knows it's not Canadian or European. It's homegrown. Lee Ann says he seems to like that idea."

"What is Lee Ann doin' at the White House?" said Thomas.

"She doesn't have a specific task. She still has the same office that she had with Wilson, right next to the Oval Office. She has immediate access to the president."

"If this is where Capone is gonna hit us, then we need to do some plannin'," said Nevin. "Next time Lee Ann goes into the White House, we need to go with her. We need to pre-arrange an early delivery of the liquor. The delivery trucks need to be stocked with our armed men. Capone's boys need to be set back on their heels again."

"Lee Ann goes into the White House next Wednesday. Why don't the two of you drive in with her?"

"I like that," Thomas said. "That will give us a chance to walk around the perimeter. We don't need to go inside. Despite what Lee Ann says about Harding, I suspect we're not welcome."

Nevin leaned in. "Do you know if the deliveries are made to the East Wing or the West?"

"Probably the East," said Bos. "That's where most of the supplies come in."

"When we go in with Lee Ann, let's look at rooftops and any place Capone could put his shooters," said Thomas. "We need to be prepared to take them on, no matter where they are. The rooftops around the White House are mostly government buildings. Do we know if Capone could have any insiders who might be able to get up there?"

"I'll bring that up with Lee Ann. You can explore it further with her. She may have to check with the Secret Service about this. How much information do we want to give them?"

"I would suggest you have her inquire," said Nevin. "We don't want the Secret Service involved. Otherwise, they take over the operation. We need to handle Capone ourselves."

"It sounds like Team Custer is on it," said Bos. "Let's remember that our strength is down the middle. Based on our last encounter, they're going to be expectin' trucks loaded with shooters. If we can keep it simple, this can work. I would suggest we put steel plating around the back of our trucks. That way, our men are better protected. That raises the question, though, of how we protect the drivers."

"Same way," said Thomas. "Steel plating on four sides. It doesn't need to be the heavy plating we have at the house. It can be quarter inch all welded together. The plates can have eye slits that also serve as gun hole openings. The front will have a sight opening that is slanted to give the driver visibility but will prevent any rounds from enterin'. The roof can just be a solid piece of quarter inch steel."

"Where do we get all this?" said Nevin.

"Same place we got the other pieces," Bos said. "Pittsburgh. I'll call my contact there and have the pieces delivered. Let's get them fitted today so we can give the precise measurements. The side pieces in the back of the truck need one-inch gun holes for the Thompsons."

"Sounds like we're makin' progress," Nevin said.

"I like that," said Thomas.

"Pops would like that, too," said Bos.

Chapter Seventy

The White House Revisited
July 11, 1921
Washington, D.C.

Warren Harding was a kind man. He grew up in Ohio Boss politics. He let the real bosses set policy, and he became their mouthpiece. That worked well because he looked and acted presidential. In fact, he fit the part in all respects except an ability to make decisions.

Lee Ann was in an unusual position. The president had surrounded himself with aides beholden to the bosses who had elected Harding. He also knew that Lee Ann had no real loyalty to him. She was an insider who knew how government worked. She could make it work for him. Harding liked that.

He knew that Lee Ann was married to a Black man. That did not bother him. If Wilson had known that, she would've been fired. Harding, unlike his predecessor, not only was tolerant on racial issues but was supportive of fair treatment for all.

Lee Ann tried to repay that respect by being loyal and honest with Harding. He rewarded her for that by keeping her in the same office she had occupied for years, right next to the Oval Office. Despite being badgered by senior aides who wanted Lee Ann's office, Harding held firm, and Lee Ann stayed put.

Lee Ann tried to help him navigate all the drama.

"Mr. President," she said, "you are much too indulgent. You need to lay down the law to some of these secretaries. They are filling high-level positions in government with people who know nothing and have no concern for governmental ethics. They simply want to line their own pockets."

Harding leaned back in his chair and stared at the ceiling. He was the first sitting senator to be elected president. He had conducted a clever campaign, called "The Front Porch" campaign. People came to him rather than him going out seeking votes. He ran on a message of returning to normalcy, seeking restoration instead of revolution, adjustment over agitation, healing instead of heroics, serenity over surgery, and equipoise in lieu of experimentation.

Lee Ann thought that Harding was all of those things: normal, adjusted, well-heeled, serene, dispassionate, and balanced. He just couldn't make up his mind. She had been used to working for Wilson, who was the opposite. He deferred to no one. He made decisions promptly and without remorse. He loved being in control. Harding did, too. He just didn't want his hands directly on the wheel.

His appointment with Herbert Hoover was set for 2:00 p.m. It was now 2:05, and Lee Ann was meticulous when it came to keeping to the daily schedule.

"Should I show Mr. Hoover in?" she said.

"What?" said the president.

"Mr. Hoover. He's waiting."

"Oh yes. Show him in."

Lee Ann got up from her seat and walked to the door. Secretary of Commerce Hoover was waiting in the ante room.

"Mr. Secretary," Lee Ann said. "It's a pleasure."

Lee Ann liked Hoover. He was a self-made man, honest, kind, and competent. He had been the food czar during World War I. Instead of imposing food rationing on the American people, he let them impose it on themselves by coming up with the ideas of Meatless Mondays and

Milkless Tuesdays. The rationing worked, and people felt good about complying. After all, it was self-imposed.

Hoover had also led the relief effort in Northern Europe. After the battle of the Marne, with armies bogged down in trenches, the British blockade of Belgium was designed to strangle the Germans. They refused to take responsibility for feeding the Belgian population, claiming that the British should relax the blockade and allow food to flow. As a result, food supplies dwindled. On October 22, 1914, Hoover established a neutral organization with diplomatic protection to obtain and distribute food to the Belgian people. The British allowed food to pass. Germany promised not to seize the food. The Belgian people survived.

Hoover, a 40-year-old international mining engineer, was living in London at that time. He had dreamed of a career in public service. During this period, he controlled a mining operation, which employed more than 100,000 men. Not satisfied with just making money, he threw himself into public service, and one thing led to another as he ascended the ladder of American politics.

Hoover had never been in the Oval Office. Harding approached him as he entered.

"Herbert, it is so good to see you," Harding said.

"It is a great honor to be invited, Mr. President," said Hoover.

"You've met Lee Ann? If you don't mind, I'd like to have her sit in with us."

"Of course."

Hoover was one of the few cabinet appointees who was not full of political bluster. He was a technocrat and knew how to manage people and get things done. He had no trouble making decisions. His appointment as Secretary of Commerce was a victory for Lee Ann. He was someone she had identified as a qualified cabinet secretary. The political bosses had been too busy filling other government slots and ignored the fact that a qualified individual was appointed to Commerce.

"Herbert, the reason I asked you to come here today is to discuss the high unemployment rate among our returning veterans," the president said.

Harding knew next to nothing about the unemployment rate of veterans. Bos and Lee Ann discussed the issue with some regularity. Now, it had become a presidential topic.

"Mr. President, you're lucky to have this young lady working for you," said Hoover. She called me last week to set up this appointment and told me the agenda. I have prepared a detailed plan focused on the employment rate of returning veterans. Let me explain what I have in mind."

His presentation was short and precise. Hoover didn't mince words. He was a mining engineer. Orphaned at age 10, he was raised by relatives. He enrolled at Stanford University even though he failed all the entrance exams except mathematics. His brilliance and his conservatism set him apart from many. He believed in self-help, that the government must allow people to either succeed or fail on their own. It is their initiative that must be controlled.

"Mr. President, I believe this plan can work, but we need to let the veterans oversee it, implement it, and ensure its success."

"Lee Ann, do you have any questions?" said Harding.

"I do. Mr. Hoover, you know that many of the returning veterans are Black men. Will they be part of this?"

"There is no reason for them not to be included. I know my predecessor wanted strict segregation. I see no reason for that," Harding said.

"I agree," Hoover said.

"Well, that's settled then," said Harding. "Can I offer you a drink?"

"This Prohibition thing is putting a damper on imbibing," said Hoover.

Harding smiled.

"Not exactly," said the president. "We have a secret weapon here. It's called the Custer family. As you know, Lee Ann's maiden name and married name are both Custer. Her husband is a combat veteran from France. He also runs a successful pork distribution business. As a sideline, he distributes alcohol to churches for religious reasons." The president smiled. "You know that spirits lift the soul," he said.

"I know that well," said Hoover. "I was raised as a Quaker. I have been schooled in temperance and tolerance. The two don't always go together."

Hoover smiled.

"Let me introduce you to some Irish whiskey produced by the Custer clan," said Harding. "I find it's quite good. It has definitely livened up some of the White House parties. We need to keep all of this hush-hush. Our parties are not exactly religious experiences."

Harding smiled.

"With ice, Mr. Hoover?" Lee Ann said.

"Please."

Lee Ann prepared three drinks. Hoover smiled as he tasted the Irish whiskey.

"I'm not a connoisseur of whiskey," said Hoover, "but one thing I like is the smoky flavor that the Irish has. Very nice."

"So, when can you get started on this employment plan?" the president said.

"Immediately. Can I use your husband as a possible resource, Mrs. Custer?" said Hoover.

"He'll be thrilled," said Lee Ann. She gushed.

"Lee Ann, I assume you live locally?" Hoover said.

"We do. LeDroit Park."

Lee Ann looked for a reaction. There was none. Most people in Washington knew that LeDroit was a Black community.

"Well, this has been refreshing. I know you all have important business. I enjoyed the Irish. And for the record, we'll call this a revival."

Hoover stood up and bowed to Lee Ann.

After Hoover left, Lee Ann returned to where they had been sitting.

"You need more men like that in your administration, Mr. President."

"They don't make many like him. He's all business. Just what America needs. Unfortunately, I am saddled with political warhorses who know nothing about business or government administration. All they know is how to line their pockets. If I'm not careful, this will be my downfall."

"It doesn't have to be."

"Oh, yes it does. I've set my course and there is probably no changing it."

Harding looked out at the South Lawn.

"You know Mrs. Wilson used to keep sheep out there."

"I had heard stories of that. Are they true?"

"You bet they are. Edith Wilson was her own person. Sheep on the lawn. Sometimes sheep in the White House. She set unusual precedents."

"Well, your husband should be happy about this. We actually got something productive done today. Hoover is apolitical. I expect him to have this up and running within weeks. He'll brook no interference from the politicians. I'm sure I'll get plenty of feedback on that." The president smiled at Lee Ann.

"Why don't we finish our drinks?"

"I'd like that."

Lee Ann thought about what President Harding would say if and when he met Bos. He had seemed to be an even-tempered man. He wanted to help all Americans. He had been appreciative of the contribution of Black veterans in the war. Still, she questioned if in his mind helping all Americans included Black Americans.

Chapter Seventy-One

White House Imports
July 12, 1921
Washington, D.C.

"The point of entry is gonna be the West Wing," said Lee Ann. "There is a driveway that leads to the basement delivery dock. You can get there from 17th Street."

"There is not a lot of cover between here and 17th Street," Bos said.

"How many trucks do you figure you are bringin' in?"

"Three trucks of liquor. But there will be three others loaded with something else, which means we need a backup plan. I have no idea how many men Capone will stage. We need to be prepared for the worst. My brothers will be in two of the trucks. I'll be roamin'."

"You not only need a backup plan; you need some human backup. How about a pregnant lady who can shoot?"

"Only if she's as pretty as you."

"I could be up on a second-floor window of the White House. Or perhaps on the roof. I'm sure the Secret Service would let me up there."

"Look into that. We may need it. I suspect there's a leak in the Bureau of Investigation. I'd like you to make some inquiries with your friend at the bureau and also the director of the Secret Service. Those questions will generate enough paperwork for many eyes to see this."

Lee Ann looked at her husband. "What did you mean when you said you would be roamin'?"

"I've bought an Indian BGE motorcycle. My plan is to ride it behind our trucks. Capone's men won't know what to make of it. Most of them have probably never seen a motorcycle."

"Where did you get it?"

"The last time I was out in Chicago visiting Capone, I took a detour to Spirit Lake, Iowa, about 300 miles northwest of Chicago. I visited their headquarters. I bought the BGE and rode it home. It was not an easy ride."

"What does BGE stand for?"

"I think it stands for beyond good and evil."

"Isn't that something Nietzsche said?"

"You're right. He was beyond good and evil. He was pure force."

"Kind of like you." She hugged him. "Pure force. Unfortunately, sometimes little intellect," Lee Ann said.

"That's where you come in. The intellect."

"No. Where I come in is that I work in the White House and have access to information. That's true, intellect or not."

"When do I see you next?"

"Tonight. I'm cookin' dinner at 6:00. Nevin and Rhonda are comin' over, and Thomas will be here. I've also invited your neighbors from across the way. I forget their names."

"That's the Roybals. When were you thinking of lettin' me know?"

"I know you like surprises. Cat's out of the bag now."

"Nevin and Thomas are waitin' outside on 17th St. Three Black men comin' into the White House would draw attention. No need for that. I'd like to walk around this place for about 30 minutes. Just want to get a better lay of the land. They won't try to put an apron on me now, will they?"

"Don't worry. They don't have any big enough for you."

Lee Ann poked Bos in the stomach.

The west end of the White House grounds was a busy area. Vehicles delivering goods pulled up to the loading dock there all day long. Bos followed the driveway to the street level on 17th Street. Somewhere along there, Capone would set up his men. There were a number of buildings along 17th Street, and second-floor windows would be prime spots for a shooter.

He walked to the guard post on 17th Street. The guard looked at him like he was an intruder. Of course, he was. Bos exited the White House grounds. He moved north, walking on the east side of the street. This gave him a better perspective of where shooters could hide inside or on top of the buildings on the west side of 17th. He walked two blocks more and then came back on the other side. It was a wide street. It could accommodate horse-drawn and motor-driven vehicles. Bos had fought here before and observed that 17th Street was as good a place as any for open warfare.

He liked the landscape. On a motorcycle, which afforded him good mobility, he could use the trucks as cover. He'd have to practice firing the Thompson with one hand. He had grown accustomed to using two hands to keep the muzzle down. He knew he had the strength to fire with one hand. Loaded with a drum, he would be able to put down plenty of lead and yet still be an elusive target.

He smiled to himself.

Nevin and Thomas walked up behind Bos and tapped him on the shoulder. Bos instinctively stepped forward and spun around quickly. When he saw his two brothers, he smiled.

"I thought you had gotten a better offer."

"We did but we rejected it," Nevin said.

"So, how is it in Casablanca?"

"Lovely. Especially if you are married to a presidential aide," said Bos.

"Let's walk around for a bit. We've been here before, but sometimes things look different when you have a new perspective," Nevin said.

"Good idea. Let's split up. That way, we draw less attention. I'll take the front. You two take 15th and 17th St. Let's meet back here in 30 minutes," Bos said.

Bos thought about going back to see his wife. He demurred. No need to get more tongues wagging.

Thirty minutes later, the three brothers met in front of the White House. They sat on a bench in Lafayette Park. Unbeknownst to any of them, their father and Jack Sanders sat on the same bench more than 50 years ago. Cookie Custer and Jack Sanders had reminisced about their days fighting for General George Armstrong Custer. Cookie and Jack had spent most of their time under the command of General Custer's brother, Thomas, who had only achieved the rank of captain but had won two Congressional Gold Medals for heroism.

Cookie Custer, Jack Sanders, and the other men who fought with Thomas Custer viewed Captain Custer as a man who fought with reckless abandon. He never exposed his men to any danger he wasn't willing to face himself. He led from the front. Unlike other Union commanders, he had adopted the battle philosophy of Robert E. Lee: "attack, attack, attack." Cookie and Jack had a good laugh over that, recollecting how the Confederate battle tactic was being used by Union forces.

"Our trucks are comin' down Pennsylvania Avenue and turnin' right onto 17th Street," said Bos. "We need to expect that Capone's men will be on Pennsylvania and 17th."

Thomas nodded.

"Yep," said Nevin. "We need to give this some thought. Meanwhile, I need to get back to my wife. See you back at the house for dinner."

Chapter Seventy-Two

Capone Plots
July 12, 1921
Chicago, Illinois

"Good work," Capone said. "Where are you getting this information?"

"Do you really want to know?" said John LaPorte.

"That's why I asked," Capone said.

The basement of Capone's Chicago home was well-equipped. The bar in the corner had a highly finished surface. The deep colored wood looked like mahogany. The lip at the near edge of the bar was nicely beveled. The brass pole along the edge of the bar was highly polished. Each stool was covered with smooth leather, which gave them a rich appearance. Capone liked his basement office. It was quiet, and it kept him close to his wife, Mae.

Mae Coughlin was two years older than Al. She had been raised in Brooklyn on the edge of an Italian American community. She was Irish and Catholic. At the time, it was a step up for an Italian American to have an Irish-Catholic wife. They were wed at Saint Mary's Star of the Sea Church in Brooklyn. Three weeks before the marriage, Mae gave birth to a son, named Albert "Sonny" Capone. Sonny was born with hearing issues that plagued him and his parents throughout his life. Al was always devoted to the child.

The two men heard Mae's footsteps upstairs. They could afford a housekeeper, but Mae insisted on doing all of that work herself.

"How's the little guy doing, Al?" LaPorte said.

"He's progressing. I don't know about the hearing, but he's been seen by some of the best. Mae forever prays for him. I'm not much into that. It is what it is, you know. Life is what you make it. If the kid has a problem, he has to overcome it. I mean, look at you. You don't have a brain, and you overcame that."

Capone laughed. LaPorte laughed almost as hard. He'd only heard the same joke 100 times.

The two men understood each other. LaPorte knew that the only person Capone would ever be loyal to was his son. He loved Mae, but he also loved the ladies. Just as LaPorte knew that Torrio was expendable, he also understood that he was expendable. He needed to figure out a way to make himself more essential.

"You got a beautiful family, Al. That's what counts."

"You're right. But this small talk ain't getting us anywhere. We need to stop Custer, and I want to do it with a big splash."

"Well, I got a splash for you. This guy has balls so big he is delivering the hooch directly to the White House. Harding loves his booze. They serve it at most of the functions there. Right out in the open too. Everybody knows about it, but nobody says anything. Harding obviously doesn't invite the people enforcing Prohibition."

"So, maybe we could interrupt the supply to the White House. That would make a splash, right? I think I tried that once before. The result was not pleasant. So, what's your plan?"

"We know they have a delivery coming this Saturday. It's scheduled for 8:00 a.m. I'll need 25 guys. We need to check the place out first. I'd like to get down there on Wednesday or Thursday and get to know their routine. On Saturday, things should be slow. Not too many people on the street that early."

"You've seen the Custers before. You know they're tough. These guys know how to fight. We're not going to beat them man-to-man. We need to overpower them. Are 25 men going to be enough?"

"I think so. Let me get down there and check things out. I'll take five guys with me. The others should plan on arriving tomorrow. As soon as we finish these guys off, we leave town."

Capone picked up a glass of wine from the bar.

"Here's hoping you're able to leave town."

Chapter Seventy-Three

White House Revisited Again
July 14, 1921
Washington, D.C.

"Second time I've been here," John LaPorte said.

"I'm not impressed," Rocko Fischetti replied.

"You're not impressed by anything because you've never been anywhere."

"I've been around. I fought in France."

"I'm kidding. I know. We've both been there. I respect that. I do. Now, let's keep our eyes peeled. What we're looking for are patterns."

"Most of these guys are military. They know patterns are dangerous. But military guys like routine."

"We're looking mainly at 17th Street. That's where they bring the booze in. Custer won't change the routine. He likes routines, but he also likes surprises."

"It's 7:00. Let's give it an hour and then meet down on 15th Street. You take this end of 17th, and I'll take the other end."

"Sounds good."

Both men were familiar with surveillance. They both were trained by Torrio, who was big on keeping track of his enemies. They liked Torrio, but they knew he was too old school. Capone wanted expansion, and he was going to get it. Either with or without Torrio.

They kept their attention on the entrance to the west side of the White House. Trucks began rolling in shortly after they arrived. Between 7:00 a.m. and 8:00, more than 15 trucks had entered and exited, bringing supplies and laborers. By 8:00 a.m., the flow of trucks had slowed.

What they didn't notice was a guy on a motorcycle wearing goggles and a French beret. Both men were used to seeing motorcycles. They were common in the Italian community in Chicago. No big deal.

What both men did notice was the presence of men on the roof of the White House. LaPorte thought they would be carrying rifles, but none of them were. It was hard to tell, though, if they had sidearms. He had noticed that the guards at the gate on the street were carrying .38 revolvers. Not much of a match against a .45.

LaPorte observed one guard walking around the perimeter of the White House. He covered the 18 acres in 30 minutes. Two revolutions per hour.

"What do you think?" Fischetti said.

"Not what I was expecting," said LaPorte. "You saw the guys on the roof? No rifles. If they have weapons, they're probably .38s. Totally useless. Looks like they're mainly lookouts. The guys at the gate appear to be old guys. Not much."

"I agree. Let's go down to 15th Street and take a look there."

The motorcyclist sped by again, still unnoticed. Bos thought these must be the guys. He had seen both of them before. In fact, one of them had been a guest in his basement. He was surprised Capone had sent this same man again. He had been easy pickings before. Maybe this time he was smarter.

Chapter Seventy-Four

Battle at 1600
July 16, 1921
The White House

"So, how are you getting the liquor into the White House?" said Lee Ann.

"It's being brought in on the Liberators and will be delivered at the watergate," Bos said. "There are three trucks there that will pick it up and deliver it to the 15th Street entrance. It's 6:00 a.m. now. The liquor should be delivered by 7:00."

Bos wondered for a moment if the others knew the significance of the watergate. It had been the arrival site for visiting dignitaries to Washington coming in by water. He also wondered if it had been the site where enslaved people arrived as they were delivered to the city of Washington.

"It sounds like you've thought of everything?" Lee Ann said.

"I'm only as good as the people around me," said Bos. "That includes you being on the second floor at the kitchen window with your .22 rifle. I know you've fed the information to the Bureau of Investigation and the Secret Service. I'm sure that's been passed on to Capone's spies by now."

"You're only as good as your weakest link," said Lee Ann. "That may be you."

She smiled.

"Would you like a ride to the White House on the back of my motorcycle?"

"Nothing like the humid Washington air to curl my hair."

They continued getting dressed. UA jumped up on the bed. He looked at Bos as if to say, "you're not leaving again?" The cat had been a fixture at their Washington home and in West Virginia. He liked the more defined environment of the city. That was because the mice were more plentiful there.

The cat looked at Bos as he strapped on the .45 to his right hip and put the other one in a holster in the small of his back. The cat sensed a battle was brewing.

The motorcycle ride down 7th Street to the White House took about five minutes. Bos delivered his wife to the 15th Street entrance. Her pregnancy was in full bloom. In just a few months, they would be parents again.

They kissed. Bos sped off to the watergate. The three Liberators were docked at the bottom of the steps.

"Good morning, big brother," Nevin said.

"Yeah, good morning to you too," said Bos. "Let's get the liquor movin'."

It took about 30 minutes to load the barrels onto the three trucks. Thomas would drive one of the trucks. Nevin would be in the lead since he had already run the route to the 15th Street entrance of the White House. There, the liquor could be unloaded and placed in the basement. Lee Ann had made those arrangements.

Thomas and Nevin would then run several blocks to the other three trucks.

Bos headed back to the White House. The three trucks that were armor protected and loaded with three men with either a Lewis Gun or a Thompson were six blocks away and waiting. Shortly before 8:00 a.m., they would move toward the west entrance.

Bos pulled up in front of the White House and got off his motorcycle. He parked it on the north side of Pennsylvania Avenue. He walked through Lafayette Park, looking for people who didn't belong. As a Black man in an increasingly Black city, he fit right in. He sat on one of the benches. At this hour on a weekend, the only people about were alcoholics who had spent the night on park benches and the people who worked at the White House in service capacities.

Bos did not notice anyone out of the ordinary. What he didn't realize was that on the third floor of the nearby Hay Adams residence, Capone had staged all his men who were ready to fan out across Lafayette Park once the Custer trucks began rolling.

Bos waited until 7:45 a.m. and walked back to his motorcycle. He took another look around. On the far west end of the White House, he could see movement behind the second-floor kitchen windows. That was his wife getting herself into position.

He hopped back on his motorcycle and headed toward 23rd Street and G Street, where his brothers had staged the three trucks.

"How come we have to run, and you get to ride a motorcycle?" Thomas said.

Nevin smiled.

"You need the exercise," Bos said. "I don't know where they are, but we'll go about our business and see what happens."

Thomas and Nevin jumped into two of the trucks and took the steering wheels. They were not big trucks, but with heavy iron plating and three men in the back they were sluggish.

Bos came alongside the three drivers' doors.

"I don't know exactly what to expect other than the unexpected. My guess is that Capone's men will be on foot. We just don't know. He came into D.C. with several carloads of men. Where they went, I don't know."

The third driver looked at Bos and asked what he should do if they threw a hand grenade into his truck.

"Bend over if you can and kiss your ass goodbye," he said. "I wish I had some way out of that situation, but I don't. I don't foresee these guys having hand grenades, but you never know."

"We're taking 23rd down to L and making a right turn there. Then it's down to 17th Street. We'll be there in 10 minutes," Nevin said.

"I'll see you there. I'll be the crazy guy on the motorcycle," said Bos.

Capone's men had begun exiting the Hay Adams house and were moving toward the park. Black raincoats in June made them stand out. Bos saw the first of them when he reached 18th and Pennsylvania Avenue. He turned around on his motorcycle and proceeded back up Pennsylvania Avenue to 23rd. He stopped the lead truck in the caravan, which was driven by Thomas. He told the three drivers to get out and gather around him.

"Capone's men are on foot. There's no need for the automatic fire. Tell the men in the back that they may be better off using handguns or rifles. There will be less chance of ricochet."

"You're heading back to 17th Street?" Nevin said.

"Yep."

Bos put the motorcycle in gear and sped off.

The east side of 17th Street was occupied by the massive State, War, and Navy Building, which was set back less than 50 feet from 17th Street and Pennsylvania Avenue. Bos stopped to get a better sense of where the attack would come from. Several of Capone's men had set up behind benches, trees, and other fixed objects in Lafayette Park. Bos decided that his best vantage point would be to attack from the rear. He sped down 17th Street to Constitution Avenue and made a left on 15th. He came up toward Lafayette Park, approaching from the rear of Capone's men. As soon as he reached the intersection of 15th and Pennsylvania, he could see the three trucks making a turn onto 17th Street from Pennsylvania Avenue. Bos had his Thompson strapped over his back, concealed by a rain pouch.

He unstrapped the rain pouch and removed the Thompson. His backpack contained several drums of ammunition. With his gun at waist level, Bos unleashed several short bursts. The park had cleared. Anyone in the park had sensed the raincoats on a clear day were not a good omen. Capone's men didn't know how to react. They had been expecting easy pickings. Now, they were confronted with fire from the rear. Several of them had been hit by Bos's selective fire.

The three trucks approached the West Wing of the White House and came to a stop. The drivers exited from the passenger doors and took up positions behind the wheels. The men inside pulled up the canvas covers over the beds of the trucks and opened fire with their rifles and handguns.

Bos approached from the southeast corner of Lafayette Park, running from one covered position to another. The men in the park were now caught in a 45-degree crossfire. Sensing that the only people in the park were Capone's men, Bos chose to use automatic fire. The .45 caliber rounds were flying everywhere. Four of Capone's men recognized the crossfire and turned toward Bos and charged. Three of them had Thompsons.

Bos rolled over three times to get behind a large oak. He laid out fully prone. Using automatic fire, he took down two of the attackers. The other two men had spread out and now had Bos in a crossfire.

Bos low crawled over to a public metal trash can about 10 feet away, but it provided no better cover. He heard a sound coming from the White House that sounded like the crack of a .22 rifle. The attacker on his left went down screaming and grabbed his right knee. Bos looked at the second-floor window on the west end of the White House and could see the barrel of a rifle. He smiled to himself, thinking of Lee Ann.

The gunfire that Bos was receiving from the right side continued. He rose to his feet and dashed to a nearby tree for cover. He pulled another drum magazine out of his backpack, released the drum magazine in place, and inserted the new one. He ran further to his right, hoping to draw more fire from the attacker, which he did. Bos reversed and ran back to his left, hoping to confuse the other man. He let go a steady burst from the Thompson. The .45 caliber rounds struck the man hiding behind a park bench. Bos could hear him go down. As he approached the bench, he could see the man drawing up the muzzle of the Thompson toward him. Bos lowered his weapon and fired a three-round burst, which entered the man's gut.

Bos moved toward where the three trucks were parked. Nevin was laying on the front hood of the lead truck with a .45 in each hand.

Capone's men had not had much training with their Thompsons. Their fire frequently went high. That was especially the case with those who were hiding behind fixed objects. They couldn't securely get a hand on the front stock to keep the muzzle down when they fired. Nevin felt comfortable laying on the front hood trying to pick them off one by one.

Bos positioned himself directly across from the front entrance to the White House. He had slung the Thompson over his shoulder and took cover behind a metal trash can on the edge of Lafayette Park. He unholstered his .45 and took aim at the man who Nevin had been shooting at. He fired two rounds in succession, and both landed in the left flank of the attacker.

The four remaining men from Capone's contingent continued to stand their ground. Three of them had used up all of their rounds from the drum magazine of the Thompsons. No one had thought to give them replacements. They now resorted to their .38 pistols. The Smith and Wesson was a tried-and-true weapon, but it had limited range and stopping power. From inside the three trucks, the gunfire continued. Those four attackers were now the exclusive targets.

Bos heard another crack of a .22 rifle behind him. This time, he could see Lee Ann's blonde hair. A man with a Thompson fell.

"You three men can throw out your weapons, or I'm comin' to get you," Bos said.

No response. Thomas was standing behind one of the trucks. He let out a long burst from his Thompson. As soon as he stopped firing, one of the men stood up and threw out his .38.

"How about the other two," said Thomas.

"We're coming out," someone said.

Nevin jumped down and approached the three men.

"You can run back to Capone and tell him he has one hour to get out of town. Otherwise, we're comin' for him."

"Hold on before you let anyone go. We know he is stayin' at the Hay Adams house," Bos said.

"Let's go pay him a visit," Nevin said.

"I like that," said Bos.

The three brothers, along with their prisoners, walked through Lafayette Park to the Hay Adams house on the north side of the park. As they approached, they could see Capone in a third-floor window. Bos raised his Thompson and fired around the window. The glass remained unbroken. Capone stood still in the window.

Bos shouted to him.

"Your name may be Cap One, but now it's Cap None."

He raised his .45 out of his holster and fired one round above Capone's head. The glass shattered as Capone disappeared from the window.

Bos turned to his two brothers and smiled.

"Should we go after him?" he said.

"I told Rhonda I'd be home tonight," said Nevin.

"I told UA you'd be home today too," Thomas said.

"I guess it's unanimous then. There's no turning back. Capone's got to die."

"Not so quick," a big voice boomed from almost a block away.

Cookie Custer strode towards them with a Winchester rifle over his shoulder. "I've been keepin' an eye on you boys."

The brothers smiled.

"Bring your trucks down to 14th and G. We'll see if we can get into the Ebbitt Grill and have some breakfast. I don't intend to walk in the back door either."

Cookie turned around and walked back toward the Ebbitt Grill that was two blocks away. His sons moved towards their trucks. Bos walked towards his motorcycle.

Cookie trudged through the front door of the Ebbitt Grill, an exclusive establishment that served Whites only. With the Winchester now on his left shoulder, Cookie looked at the bartender and said, "We'll need a large table in the back. We'll be inconspicuous," he smiled.

Cookie walked towards the left rear of the restaurant and put two tables together. He sat down at the head of the table.

His sons and the other men with them ambled in. As they walked through the front door, they could all see Cookie in the far back.

"Service here may be a bit slow, especially to us. Before we begin eatin' though, I want to ask my oldest son what's the meaning of that brand on his right shoulder. His wife has been askin' me."

"It's a circle. In the culture of the American Indian, everything is circular. There's no place to hide in a circle. There are no corners.

Everything is out in the open. Everybody works for the greater good. I had Stone brand me so that I never forget that. For the rest of my life."

About the Author

Brien A. Roche: After four years as a patrol officer with the Washington D.C. Metropolitan Police Department and 45 years as a trial lawyer in the Washington, D.C. area, I have "been around the barn."

Since being admitted to the practice of law in Virginia in 1976, I have tried more than 300 jury cases to conclusion and handled thousands of other cases of every conceivable type. In 1985, I became a partner with the firm of Johnson & Roche in McLean, Virginia. My practice has been principally litigation with a focus on tort litigation along with substantial involvement in commercial litigation, real estate litigation and domestic relations litigation.

My interest in writing fiction ties in with my interest in the study of history. The main character in the *Prohibition* series is not a historical character but he acts as part of some historical events including the race riot of July 19, 1919 in Washington, D.C. Most of the other events are purely fictional but many of the characters of course are not. The existence of the Liberator boats is fact-based as these water crafts were constructed as part of the U.S. war effort in Europe. The integration of fact and fiction is always tricky but hopefully these novels instill some further interest in the reader in this historical era and in further historical exploration. Visit www.brienrocheauthor.com

Upcoming New Release!

BRIEN A. ROCHE'S

THE COUNTERATTACK
THE PROHIBITION SERIES
BOOK 3

Al Capone has taken to the tunnels in Washington, D.C. He is on the run. Across the 14th Street Bridge and into the Potomac River. He finally makes it back to Chicago.

Bos and his brothers have followed him to 7244 S. Prairie Avenue in Chicago. It's a two story single family home. Capone's primary residence.

The Custers knew that Capone was the prize.

Bos decides that maybe the best way to deal with Capone is not to deal with him for the time being.

The Custers have bigger fish to fry.

Capone will come later.

For more information
visit: www.SpeakingVolumes.us

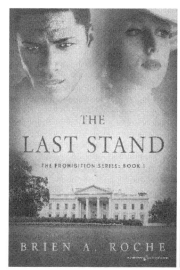 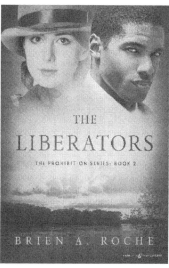

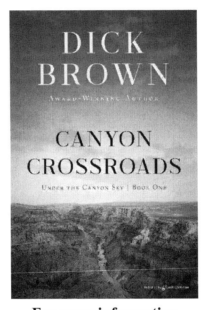

Made in the USA
Middletown, DE
11 October 2023

40592099R00179